M000214256

Hearts
OVERBOARD

Also by Becky Dean

Love & Other Great Expectations

Picture-Perfect Boyfriend

Hearts

OVERBOARD

Becky Dean

**Delacorte
Romance**

This is a work of fiction. Names, characters, places, and incidents either are the product of the author's imagination or are used fictitiously. Any resemblance to actual persons, living or dead, events, or locales is entirely coincidental.

Text copyright © 2024 by Becky Dean
Jacket art copyright © 2024 by Libby VanderPloeg
Map art copyright © 2024 by Michelle Cunningham

All rights reserved. Published in the United States by Delacorte Romance, an imprint of Random House Children's Books, a division of Penguin Random House LLC, New York.

Delacorte Romance and the colophon are trademarks of Penguin Random House LLC.

GetUnderlined.com

Educators and librarians, for a variety of teaching tools, visit us at RHTeachersLibrarians.com

Library of Congress Cataloging-in-Publication Data is available upon request.
ISBN 978-0-593-64784-4 (trade pbk.) — ISBN 978-0-593-64786-8 (lib. bdg.) — ISBN 978-0-593-64785-1 (ebook)

The text of this book is set in 11-point Warnock Pro Light.
Interior design by Cathy Bobak

Printed in the United States of America
10 9 8 7 6 5 4 3 2 1
First Edition

Random House Children's Books supports the First Amendment and celebrates the right to read.

Penguin Random House LLC supports copyright. Copyright fuels creativity, encourages diverse voices, promotes free speech, and creates a vibrant culture. Thank you for buying an authorized edition of this book and for complying with copyright laws by not reproducing, scanning, or distributing any part in any form without permission. You are supporting writers and allowing Penguin Random House to publish books for every reader.

For the Deans, who wouldn't be my family
if not for the Bears

SAVANNAH'S ALASKAN VOYAGE

DENALI NATIONAL PARK

ANCHORAGE

WHITTIER

SKAGWAY

JUNEAU

KETCHIKAN

VANCOUVER

chapter one

Los Angeles, California

~

Tanner Woods, the Geminid meteor shower, and the democratic process were conspiring against me.

"I'm sorry, Savannah," my physics teacher, Mr. Lin, was saying, "but I can't do anything."

I'd stopped by his room after my final class of the year for one last attempt to convince him that I should be president of the Astronomy Club next year, no matter the results of this week's club elections. He was our advisor, and I'd argued he should use his power of advisement to steer us away from the black hole Tanner would undoubtedly fly us into.

"You know how proud I am of you," he went on. "How you've grown the club, your ideas for it. The rocket you built was an excellent piece of work."

My chin lifted and my frown partially softened. It really had been.

1

"But Tanner won the election, and unless there's an ethical issue as to why he can't serve, or unless he steps down, the results are out of my hands. He might not have your technical science skills, but he's enthusiastic and the other members like him."

The scowl threatened to return. Tanner's election platform could be summed up as *space is cool* and *we should watch the meteor shower in the middle of a deadly wilderness,* never mind the fact that we lived near one of the greatest observatories in the world. With well-known speakers and indoor plumbing. And people had gone for it. Yeah. I was baffled, too.

"I'm confident your grade in my class will be the highest this year," Mr. Lin said. "And I couldn't have been more impressed with your bridge project, or your roller coaster."

The compliment should have cheered me up—I'd been proud of those accomplishments, and his physics class had been my favorite—but it didn't do much good as long as Tanner remained in charge of the club I cared about most. The one I'd joined first thing freshman year, dreaming of senior year and my chance to lead. It felt like something precious had been stolen, and I was still having trouble believing I had lost—to *him.*

"I have news that might help." Mr. Lin straightened a stack of papers on his desk. "I've submitted your name as our school's contender for the Physics and Engineering Consortium."

"What does that mean?" I asked.

"It's a program for high school seniors, with weekend visits to facilities around the country, a conference and competition in Boston next summer, plus online seminars and discussion groups. You would be perfect for it."

Interest spiked in me before my stomach turned over. In theory, that sounded incredible. Being picked was an honor. But it also sounded like lots of travel, which would mean missing events with Jordan and final-summer-before-college activities.

And as great an opportunity as the program was, Astronomy Club meant more to me.

Was this supposed to be a consolation prize, a boost to my future career, or a ploy to make me stop arguing so Mr. Lin could go home?

"I'll email you the details and a short application," he said.

"Okay. Thanks. And tell Mia I'm looking forward to coaching her after my vacation."

Mr. Lin's thirteen-year-old daughter was learning to pole-vault, and since that was my favorite of the track events I did—the physics behind it was fascinating—I'd offered to help her over the summer.

"She's very excited. Thanks again for being willing to meet with her. Now go enjoy your summer, Savannah. Watch for my email. And forget about Tanner. I'm sure you two will find a way to work together next year."

Um. Had he met us? Had he not been paying an ounce of attention for the last year? Or was he an eternal optimist who believed that in a few short months, Tanner Woods and I might miraculously overcome years of rivalry and somehow learn to get along?

"Thanks, Mr. Lin. See you soon."

I trudged out. My mind warred with itself. The program intrigued me, but I would need to see the specifics. How disappointed would Mr. Lin be if I decided not to apply? Surely not as disappointed as I was about the Astronomy Club.

I would have to come up with another plan for that. Make Tanner so miserable he resigned. Find an ethics violation that disqualified him. Or convince the club's other members to stage a coup. I wasn't above minor insurrection.

The last day of my junior year was already a disaster.

I should have known it wasn't going to stop there.

My boyfriend, Caleb, was waiting for me at the end of the corridor, and together we walked through emptying halls to the parking lot. Groups of people were talking and laughing and celebrating the upcoming three months of freedom.

"Ready for milkshakes?" I asked. "I need one today. At least ice cream never disappoints me. Ugh. Mr. Lin wouldn't do anything about the club. Can you believe Tanner? Why does he want to lead, anyway? He—" I stopped when I realized Caleb had paused in the middle of the parking lot.

"Savannah." Caleb's voice sounded pained.

I turned back to face him. "Yeah?"

Caleb shaded his eyes and stared at the car behind me. "I can't do this anymore."

I squinted at him in the bright summer sun on a smoggy LA June day. "You mean Shake It Up?"

Every Friday of our junior year, we'd made the drive from Beverly Hills to Westwood for milkshakes after school. I had issues with their name as a general life philosophy, but their ice cream was delicious. Mint chocolate for me, Snickers for Caleb. Sometimes with friends from Astronomy Club or Math Bowl or my track team or his newspaper group, and usually with my best friend, Jordan. This was the last Friday of the school year. Why would Caleb change the tradition now?

He ran a hand through his light brown curls. I'd always liked his hair, except he'd been letting it grow out lately so it fell over his ears. Now he looked a little like a Muppet who'd fallen on hard times, and even though I hated it, I hadn't said anything. Had he been secretly hating our Friday dates?

A flash of worry shot through me.

"I mean all of it," he said. "Shake It Up and homework sessions and volunteering at the Science Center and taco Tuesdays."

Wait, what? Everything I'd thought made our relationship nice? The routines, the traditions, the way we fit each other into our busy schedules and made time to do things together.

What kind of monster didn't like taco Tuesdays?

What, exactly, was he saying?

I clutched my backpack straps. Why was it so hard to breathe?

Caleb finally met my gaze. His honey-brown eyes were sympathetic, but his jaw had the stubborn set that it always got when he tackled a particularly challenging math problem. "I can't do *us*, Savannah."

His voice rang out, and he seemed to realize his volume a second too late. He winced as his words carried.

I was frozen. The words refused to sink in. They were bouncing off my brain, over and over, like tiny rocks pinging against the hull of a spaceship, unable to penetrate. Eventually one would crack the hull and my brain would be sucked out into the vacuum of space.

"But . . . what about our plans? For the summer? Next year's Math Bowl? Astronomy Club? The Science Center?"

Because he was not only my boyfriend. We would also be serving as co-captains of the Math Bowl for our senior year, with ambitions of winning first place in the state after being runners up this year. Caleb was supposed to help me handle Tanner's hostile takeover of the Astronomy Club. And we were going to prep for AP tests and start training to demonstrate the robotic spacecraft at the Science Center where we volunteered.

"We'll still do those," he said, his voice earnest. "Nothing has to change."

Heat flooded my chest. "Yeah, because spending senior year with your ex is absolutely no different than doing those things with your boyfriend."

"See? It won't be that bad."

I briefly closed my eyes and fought the urge to rub my temples. "That was sarcasm, Caleb."

"Right." He blinked. "I'm sorry, Savannah. I just can't take it anymore. Aren't you getting bored? You're—we're too stuck in our ways. I need excitement. Adventure. Something new."

"Are you saying I'm boring?" I leveled him with a look I hoped was neutral and calm. Unlike him, I kept my voice low.

I thought he liked our ways. We got along so well because we were determined, disciplined, and organized. We had common interests. Sure, neither of us had reached the *I love you* point, but that was because we were both cautious with our feelings.

But now he was shuffling his feet and avoiding my gaze.

The setting rushed back to me. Our classmates, hovering by cars or at the bike rack nearby, weren't even pretending not to listen. Cars idled, but none attempted to pass us, and the scent of exhaust assaulted my nose. Whispers carried on the breeze.

I needed a portal or a stargate or someone to beam me up. Maybe a previously undiscovered tar pit would open beneath me, like the one nearby in La Brea, and carry me away from this conversation and the audience.

If it was a worthy ending for the noble mammoths, it was good enough for me.

Caleb scuffed the toe of his sneaker on the pavement and stared at his shoe. "You can be . . . stuck in your ways."

A snicker came from a group nearby, followed by a girl's cackle.

"Moore the Bore. Good one," someone said. More laughter followed.

I whirled. Three girls from the soccer team and a few football guys huddled nearby, openly watching.

Of course Tanner was with them. I had no doubt the new nickname came from him. Real clever play on my last name, dude. Almost as good as Savannah Banana, the time he'd ruined my love for my favorite-ever yellow Easter dress in fourth grade. Rhyming was a specialty of his. That, and ruining my life.

I scowled and shifted back to Caleb. "So . . . that's it? We can't talk about it? Figure something out?"

He stepped closer and lowered his voice. "I didn't mean for it to happen like this."

"Well, it did."

"I didn't want to wait and ruin milkshake Fridays. You know, taint them by association."

A snort escaped my nose, and I didn't know if the burning sensation came from a desire to cry, scream, or laugh hysterically. "Oh, sure. This way was much better."

"Exactly."

Sarcasm detector: still malfunctioning.

He ducked his head and hair fell into his eyes. "It's just, some people from newspaper invited me to Manda's beach party."

Our part of LA wasn't super close to the beach, but I knew of the parties Manda Keller hosted. Although I wasn't sure how *hosting* worked, since the beach was public. Maybe she was the one to start the bonfire and provide the . . . what? Kegs? Marshmallows? Kegs full of marshmallows? I honestly had no idea, because I'd never been.

"You got invited to a party," I said slowly, "and that led you to break up with me?"

"No. Yes. I mean, I don't know. It's not just that. I knew you'd say no."

"To the party? I would not. Besides, isn't it tonight? We could have gone after milkshakes. Or you could have come to milkshakes then attended the party without me. You didn't even ask."

His face was earnest. "I've been asking. About lots of stuff. It's always the same—you don't want to try anything new."

I searched my memories for anything he'd suggested lately that I'd refused, but I came up empty.

"I want summer and senior year to be about getting ready for the new experiences we'll have in college," he went on. "Not repeating the same stuff we did this year."

But this year had been great. Why mess with a good thing? And what about what *I* wanted? I studied Caleb's familiar face, with his puppy dog eyes and arched brows, and waited to feel . . . something. Instead, I was numb.

Excuse me for knowing what I liked. For wanting to know what to expect and time to adjust to new ideas. If he'd mentioned the party in advance, given me time to mentally prepare, I might have agreed. Even if the beach at night freaked me out, the gaping blackness of the ocean after dark, when killer sea lions or a rogue wave or a kraken could sneak up on you undetected.

But Caleb hadn't given me that opportunity. Instead, he'd jumped to the most drastic possible outcome. One red warning light on the control panel? Forget trying to solve the problem. Just abort the whole mission.

"Heads up, S'more," called an all-too-familiar voice, with his favorite nickname for me—a shortened version of Savannah Moore that Tanner found hilarious and clever. He'd called me that ever since my mom remarried and my stepdad, Brian Moore, legally adopted me and I changed my name.

A figure rushed past us, followed by a football sailing through the air.

"Going long!" Tanner lunged for the ball.

He snagged it right before it collided with a trash can, but momentum carried him on. He took out the entire row of cans, like he'd bowled a strike, crashing to the ground and sending the contents flying. Food scraps, papers, compost, recycling. It was a thorough demolishment of every sort of carefully separated waste product.

He jumped to his feet, laughing loudly, and surveyed the mess. "That's a strike!"

Like he'd read my mind about the bowling metaphor. My scowl deepened.

Tanner flung a banana peel off himself dramatically, before holding the football aloft and doing the victory dance he did when he scored touchdowns, which, sadly, occurred often.

"Gross, dude," called another football player. "That was terrible."

"Your throw was terrible," Tanner yelled back.

"Whatever. Like you can do better?"

Tanner hurled an apple core at his friend, who ducked.

This was the guy who kept beating me on English quizzes and had stolen my presidency.

"There's something seriously wrong with him," Caleb said.

At least he and I still agreed on one thing.

Tanner waved to the watching crowd, tucked in the football, and brushed off his shirt. "Sorry, don't mind me. Happy last day of school, everyone," he called.

What was even happening?

"Hey, S'more." He strolled toward us. His dark brown hair, shorter on the sides and tousled on top, remained unruffled by his antics. His gray eyes glinted. "Did you know I was an expert bowler? Do they have bowling alleys on cruise ships? We should go next week. Bet I can beat you. I'm great at taking things out. Like trash." His pointed gaze lingered on Caleb.

Like I needed the reminder that I'd be stuck on a boat with him. In three days, my family was leaving for an Alaskan cruise with the company my parents worked for. Which also happened to be where Tanner's mom worked. Because our parents happened to be best friends.

Every episode of a show that began with people trapped on a ship ended with an alien creature eating everyone gruesomely.

Although, in this case, the gruesome eating was likely to occur on shore, thanks to Alaska's raging population of grizzly bears.

Tanner shifted his attention to me and grinned. "No hard feelings about the star club, right?"

Oh, there were hard feelings. Many of them. There was no way he cared about the club the way I did. He hadn't been the one, in the last three years, to suggest graduating from simple telescopes and Griffith Observatory field trips to telescope photography and building real rockets. He hadn't been dreaming of this opportunity for years.

"Can you please stop making it sound like we watch celebrities? There's far more to astronomy than stars."

"But when I call it the star club, you get that tic in your jaw, which is so satisfying."

He poked a finger toward my face, and I swatted his hand.

He smirked. "Don't worry. I promise to take your suggestions under advisement, like everyone else's."

"Or," I said, "and I'm just throwing this out there since you're so fond of catching things, you could step aside and let me lead."

"The members voted, S'more. I won fair and square. I must give the people what they want."

"*The people* meaning the ones with no real interest in astronomy who tagged along when you crashed the club?"

"Space is for everyone. Don't be so elitist."

I gritted my teeth. My dentist continually refused to accept *Tanner Woods* as a perfectly reasonable explanation for my grinding problem. "I'm not elitist. Didn't I win the Service Club's award for most volunteer hours this year?"

"Did you? I already forgot." His response sounded breezy, but a matching tic jumped in his jaw, which—wow, he was right—was very satisfying. He had wanted that award as badly as I'd wanted to win the Astronomy Club election.

"Well," he said. "Carry on. See you Monday."

"I can't wait. It's going to be the highlight of my summer," I deadpanned.

"Really?" Caleb asked. "Weren't you complaining about it?"

Tanner and I looked at him and somehow mutually decided not to bother responding.

Tanner strutted off toward his friends, tossing the ball in the air.

Leave it to him to play with trash, rub in the Astronomy Club, and give me a new nickname while I was getting dumped.

I met Caleb's gaze again, and the situation flooded back after the distraction and annoyance that was Tanner Woods. My stomach had hardened. Encounters with Tanner always readied me for battle.

"I'm sorry this year was so awful for you," I said, and this time my words had more bite. "I didn't realize I was boring you."

Caleb reached out a hand. "No, you weren't. It wasn't awful. I didn't mean it that way. Savannah."

"It's fine. Go have fun without me. Just next time, do this privately instead of . . ." I nodded toward the parking lot.

"We'll talk this summer. Make plans for Math Bowl. We can still work together, right? Be adult about everything?"

What was I supposed to say to that? That I wasn't the one not being an adult, by ending a nine-month relationship in front of half our school, beneath the mural of our noble knight mascot, who was certainly extremely disappointed in Caleb's lack of chivalry?

And then Caleb stuck out a hand.

Did he . . . expect me to shake it?

After too many awkward seconds of awaiting a response from me that wasn't going to come, Caleb realized his monumental stupidity and withdrew his hand.

Something like regret crossed his face, but he didn't move as I edged farther away. Didn't try to stop me.

Had he been unhappy all year? We'd had good times, right? Shouldn't he have raised his concerns earlier so we could have talked about them? That was what you did. You identified problems and found a way to fix them.

Aware of the attention on us, I kept my chin up. "Bye, Caleb."

I spun and strode away.

Not the brilliant parting shot I wanted, something that showed I was better off without him. Or better yet, something charming and funny that made him immediately change his mind, say he was wrong, and beg me to forget the last ten minutes.

My shoulders remained tense, my stomach tight, as I—

Oh frak.

Caleb was my ride.

I couldn't stop, though, not with everyone watching.

Had that even occurred to him? Had he known when he picked me up this morning that he'd be ending more than our junior year? Had he planned to drive me home after breaking up with me? Or had this breakup been a spur-of-the-moment decision, something I clearly wasn't capable of making?

Jordan was probably already at Shake It Up, since I'd told her to go ahead without me. If I texted her, she'd come, but that would take too long.

Steps shuffled behind me.

"I can give you a ride," Caleb said. "Drop you off . . . somewhere?" His voice sounded unsure. And *somewhere* implied he wasn't sorry enough to take me all the way to Shake It Up.

"I'm fine."

I kept walking and he didn't follow.

I tried to ignore my classmates' whispers that sounded suspiciously like *Moore the Bore*. As I passed the main group, my gaze leaped to Tanner's against my will. I stumbled. Rather than wearing the smirk I'd expected, a wrinkle had settled between his eyebrows, and his eyes were unusually solemn. He clutched the football, and a smear of something brown stained his LA Rams T-shirt.

My face heated up and I hurried past.

Nerves rattled inside me, but I shoved them down, because,

yet another problem? I had no idea where I was going. My only objective was to get as far away as possible. But I needed a plan, and quickly.

The parking lot bordered the gym. If someone had left a door open, I could sneak inside and hide under the bleachers. Too bad I didn't have my pole-vaulting pole. I could launch myself over the chain-link fence at the end of the lot. That would look dramatic.

I'd almost reached the end of the parking lot, the point where I was going to have to instantaneously invent a transporter or possibly learn how to pick the gym door lock when an SUV pulled up beside me. The passenger window rolled down.

"Get in," Tanner called.

"I'm fine." I kept walking. "You can go."

Unlike Caleb, Tanner didn't listen. His car continued to keep pace, inching along. If I didn't stop or he didn't, he was going to run into the fence.

"Come on, are you planning to walk home?" he asked. "It's three miles."

I could have run it in twenty minutes, if I weren't wearing sandals. "My ride's on the way."

"Everyone's watching, S'more. Just get in." His tone sounded weary.

I didn't want to check and confirm that statement, in case people were staring. Getting into a car with Tanner was slightly less objectionable than extending the public humiliation. Marginally.

"Fine." I yanked open the door and climbed inside.

"You're so stubborn," he said.

"It smells like garbage in here."

His rear window had been painted with SENIORS, BABY in bright red letters, and the passenger one by my face, which he rolled up, had #88, his football jersey number.

"Are you—" he started.

"I'm only staying in this car if you don't talk. Otherwise I'll jump out even if we're moving."

"That sounds fun. Wait until I speed up, though. Can we test how fast you'd be willing to attempt this? Twenty miles an hour? Thirty? The freeway?"

If it got me away from Caleb and the *Moore the Bore* whispers, I might consider it. "This is LA. You'd be lucky if the freeway *was* twenty miles an hour. No more talking."

I crossed my arms, faced the window, and imagined I was anywhere else.

chapter Two

Los Angeles, California

~

"I know you said no talking, but where am I taking you?" Tanner asked when we were down the block, the school thankfully behind me for three months. Which was sad, because I actually liked most aspects of school. "Home? No, wait, it's Friday. Milkshakes?"

How did he know that?

The route was familiar, with its palm trees and flowers, chain stores and boutiques. But I'd never taken it with Tanner. His SUV sat higher than Caleb's Corolla, and Tanner took corners too fast, and it smelled like deodorant, French fries, and faintly of whatever trash clung to Tanner, instead of Caleb's linen air freshener. I might never make this drive again in Caleb's car. That thought didn't help the churning in my stomach partially caused by Tanner's driving.

My muscles were tense as I waited for him to mock the

breakup and repeat the new nickname, but he adhered to my no-talking rule and cranked up his music. It was something screamy, the kind that usually gave me a headache, except today it suited my mood.

I was trying not to think about summer and next year and the plans I'd made that Caleb had imploded. My chest felt tight. I had a personal policy to avoid crying at all costs, but hyperventilation was a real threat.

Tanner pulled into the strip mall in a nice shopping center and parked outside Shake It Up.

As soon as the car stopped moving, I jumped out. "Thanks for the ride, I guess. See you. Unless you decide not to come to Alaska."

I slammed the door, not giving him a chance to reply.

He caught up with me on the sidewalk outside the shop.

"What are you doing?" I asked as he held the door open for me.

"I'm not driving all the way out here without getting a milkshake."

We stopped, blocking the door. The AC blasted from inside, competing with the warm air outside. Opposing forces, like us, as our eyes fought a battle. He towered over me, gazing down with gray eyes under dark brows, his lips tilted up at the corners like they always were, whether he was smiling or not.

Ugh. I stomped past him.

The interior was bright white with blue accents and cool light, the scent of sugar thick in the air. This had been my happy place. Once. Now it was defiled by an invading football player and the knowledge that everything about my life had changed.

Jordan sat in our usual booth, sipping a milkshake. Her eyebrows shot up when she saw me—and who I was with.

"What's up, Jordan? I like your hair," Tanner said. "What's good here? What are you having?"

"Peaches and cream with graham crackers. It sounded summer-like," she said, as if talking to him, here, was normal.

She'd made her way through the whole menu and had resorted to making up her own combinations, which the staff was always happy to attempt. It had even resulted in a new flavor being added to the official menu: Quadruple Chocolate—chocolate ice cream with chocolate chips, Oreos, and brownie bits.

I went to the counter and ordered my usual.

"Mint chocolate?" Tanner asked. "I'm very disappointed you're not getting s'mores."

"Disappointing you truly breaks my heart. Let me change that order right away."

Tanner read every single option aloud. "Hmm. I'll have to go with Milky Way. You know, in honor of my victory and because I love space so much."

"You should visit. I'll get you a one-way ticket."

"It wouldn't be the same without you, though. Who would I beat in the outer space competitions?"

I whipped out my card. "Put them both together," I told the cashier.

Tanner blinked at me.

I scowled. "You gave me a ride. It's fair."

He nodded once and grabbed his cup, raised it to Jordan in salute, and sauntered out.

I snatched mine and sank into the bench across from her.

"Why was Tanner Woods here?" Jordan craned to look out the window and watch him drive off. "Where's Caleb?"

The afternoon flooded back. I groaned. "I don't want to talk about it."

But I told her everything.

Her face maintained its usual calm, reassuring expression until I got to the end. Then her eyes widened and her lips pursed. "He tried to shake your hand? What is wrong with him? I'm sorry I wasn't there. Are you okay? Want to egg his house tonight while he's at the party?"

I huffed a semilaugh. "No, I wouldn't do that to his parents."

"What about his car? We could egg that."

"It's a long drive to the beach to throw a few eggs."

"A few? You severely underestimate my willingness to exact revenge."

I half laughed again and stared at my cup. I didn't want revenge. I wanted life to go back to how it had been an hour ago.

I pushed the straw up and down, making it squeal in a way that had always made Caleb cringe. As if the breakup wasn't bad enough, had he ruined milkshakes for me, too? I refused to give him that power. Even though I felt sick, I took a long sip that made my teeth hurt.

Jordan let me be silent. Along with the shop's sugary scent, I detected her customary faint vanilla lotion. That was the only part of her that stayed the same. Today, her nails were bright blue, and her natural hair formed two high puffs atop her head—Tanner was right; it looked great. We were complete opposites in that way. She was always experimenting with hair and makeup and clothes, while I kept things like my long, straight dark blond hair the same because, why take the risk on something new that I might not like?

"Forget him and the party," she said. "TV marathon tonight. You're about to leave for two weeks, and I'm going to miss you."

I stabbed my straw into the drink again. "Don't remind me."

"Oh, come on, you're excited, and you know it."

I wasn't *not* excited. I'd researched the ship and the places we'd see and planned our excursions. But it meant putting up with Tanner for two weeks.

My parents really needed new best friends.

Although . . . the ride today had been decent of him.

"Yeah, I can't wait to spend time with the guy who got me nicknamed Moore the Bore," I said. "You know that's sticking for all of senior year."

"I'm sure everyone will forget it by the fall."

Yeah, right. The name had accompanied an embarrassing moment in front of dozens of people. No one forgot that kind of thing. Plus, it rhymed. It was guaranteed to stick in everyone's mind until our fiftieth class reunion. Forget about whether I led the math team to a state championship, or set a record in the pole vault or two-mile run, or discovered a new comet that was named after me. Even if the Savannah Comet ended up on a collision course with Earth, *Moore the Bore* was going to be my high school legacy.

"Do you want to talk about it?" Jordan asked. "How are you feeling?"

The only thing worse than being dumped was discussing my feelings about it. "Please don't get out the chart."

Jordan wanted to be a counselor and was constantly trying the same tricks to make me talk that the family therapist had used on me when my mom and bio dad split. Including the stupid chart with cartoon faces for common emotions, since I had "trouble expressing my feelings," and apparently pointing to them was supposed to help kids process.

Thankfully, when I didn't want to talk, Jordan was far less pushy than the therapist had been.

"I love that you care, Jor, but I would rather make a plan."

She hummed. "A plan for what?"

"I don't know. How to show him he's wrong? So he changes his mind?"

She hummed again.

"What does that mean?"

"Nothing."

I waited. She was incapable of not sharing her opinions, as long as I was patient.

"I just think you should go have fun with Tanner Woods for two weeks," she said. "One day with those muscles and that smile, and you'll forget all about Caleb."

"'Those muscles and that smile,'" I quoted mockingly, "are the external package for a supervillain. He's Anakin to my Obi-Wan. Loki to my Thor."

"Yes, yes. Khan to your Kirk. But it sure is a nice external package. And that tight end."

"That's his position on the football field," I said. "Not a commentary on his backside."

She grinned. "Why can't it be both?"

"Because it's Tanner Woods. Can we please talk about something else now?"

"I'm just saying, he was nice enough to give you a ride."

So he could rub in all the ways today had gone wrong for me. Except he hadn't mentioned Caleb once. Why not? Him being . . . nice? . . . to me left me unbalanced.

"I know you would rather fix things than feel them," she said, "but I'm here if you need me."

"And I love you for it."

"Of course you do. How'd it go with Mr. Lin?"

"No luck on the Astronomy Club. But he wants me to join a special physics program next year."

"That's great. You love physics. For some odd reason. Are you going to do it?"

"I don't know yet." My instinct was to say no, but today had been stressful enough. I'd think about it later. "Enough about me. What happened with the job? Have you heard?"

She'd applied to help teach kids' singing lessons at a local music school.

Her eyes lit up. "I got it!"

I grabbed her hand. "I knew it. I'm so proud of you. They're lucky to have you. And the kids will love you."

She'd be busy this summer, and therefore not an available substitute for activities I'd planned with Caleb. But I was happy for her.

We tossed our cups and left the shop.

"I know what we need to watch tonight," she announced.

Our best friend last-day-of-school tradition was picking a

science fiction show we loved and binge-watching selected episodes. Last year had been *The Expanse* when I was into hard sci-fi and she was into broody guys like James Holden. Seventh grade had been our Ahsoka phase and *Clone Wars*. As kids, we'd devoted days to Captain Janeway and Peggy Carter and Starbuck.

"What's that?" I asked.

"Doctor Who," she said. "All the tearjerker episodes guaranteed to make us cry. Sad endings in honor of the last day of school. When Rose is stranded, and Amy and Rory and the Angels, and, oh, oh." She clasped her hands, and I swore she was already tearing up. "Vincent van Gogh."

That was a great episode, but . . . "Ugh. I don't want to cry. Especially today." If I started, I wouldn't stop, and crying made my nose a never-ending fountain and left me with a headache for twenty-four hours. "What about the River Song ones? I could use a brilliant, legendary lady."

"Fine. She does have fabulous hair."

I smiled and we climbed into her car. "You don't mind missing Manda's party?"

"Pshh. No. Not if *he's* going to be there."

If we showed up, it would prove Caleb wrong.

And give a giant crowd of people a chance to use my new nickname.

Never mind.

Her face sobered. "I really am sorry. I knew you guys were . . ."

"Were what?"

She shot me a sideways glance. "I don't know, you and Caleb

haven't seemed that close lately. Since spring break. You've barely mentioned him, and he hasn't been around as often."

Spring break. When I'd been trapped at a lakeside cabin with my parents and Tanner and his family, trying to read on the dock and ignore Tanner showing off on a wakeboard. While Caleb got to stay home and help with kids' camp at the Science Center.

Jordan wasn't wrong. Afterward, Caleb had been more distant, busier, canceled plans more often. Which wasn't like him—I'd always appreciated his consistency. I'd assumed it was the stress of finals. But had we been on a real date since then? How had I missed that?

I sighed. "Why didn't he talk to me about it?"

"Um. Because he's a guy."

"That means he's incapable of a discussion?"

"About relationships? Yeah."

"That's what I liked about him, though. He was low drama, serious about school. I thought we were similar." I chewed my lip. "Do you think I'm boring?"

"Do *you* think you're boring?"

I leveled a finger at her. "No Jedi mind tricks. I'm onto your ways."

She laughed. "Sorry. I think you're perfect."

"You're my best friend. You have to say that. It's in the contract."

"You know what you like and you stick to it. That's not a bad thing. You find something good—like a best friend—and you don't change it. I have obviously benefited from your loyalty."

"Oh, please." I waved a hand toward her. "You're way cooler than I am. If anyone was going to look for a new best friend in the last eight or nine years, it would have been you."

"Pshh. Whatever. No more talk of new best friends. You're stuck with me forever. Besides, your behavior is understandable, after everything."

There she went, analyzing me again. She meant the first six years of my life, when my bio dad was in the picture. A messy, drawn-out divorce. Custody fights. Never knowing if he would show up for our scheduled times or cancel last minute or take me to a monster truck rally or a casino instead of for burgers or to the zoo. Culminating in the cops being called when we went camping and he refused to accompany me to the bathroom in the middle of the night. I'd ended up thinking I saw a bear, sobbing, and stumbling into a stranger's tent, incoherent.

Those years might have given me an obsession with sticking to schedules, liking routine, and wanting to know what to expect at all times. According to my therapist. And Jordan.

But she was right—there was nothing wrong with that. I was fine. It was possible to have routines and also enjoy life and be a fun girlfriend. So how did I make Caleb see that?

Maybe after a few weeks of summer, he'd realize what he was missing.

"Now," Jordan said. "River Song awaits. Are you ready?"

Our history, this tradition, and my best friend made the darkness inside me a little brighter.

"Let's do it."

Caleb could have his beach party. I hoped he spent the whole time thinking about me. He'd regret what he'd said, come to Shake It Up, and be shocked not to find me there waiting. Then he'd see he'd been wrong about us and call to apologize. We'd walk his dog in the park tomorrow, like we always did on Saturdays, before my parents and I left on Monday, and life would go back to normal.

Just how I liked it.

chapter Three

Los Angeles, California

~

By Monday morning, the first official day of summer vacation,
I hadn't heard from Caleb. My plan of him seeking me out and
wanting me back wasn't off to a great start. It *had* been a weak
plan. Definitely needed work.

I'd only spent five minutes . . . Okay, ten . . . Okay, half an
hour, looking at Instagram reels and pictures from Manda's
party. His face wore a bigger smile than any I'd seen in the last
couple months. Did he like volleyball and boogie boards? Were
those things he'd supposedly asked about and I had said no to?
Or was he doing this to prove a point?

My insides were hollow. If he'd given me a chance, maybe
I would've been there, too, and we would have been laughing
together.

I shoved my phone into the thigh pocket of my leggings
and took a final glance at my room, with its space posters and

the row of LEGO spaceships on the bookshelf and the picture of Jordan and me in Star Wars costumes on Halloween at age eight, the day we met. It was dumb, but I'd miss the room the next two weeks, having space to myself. Even though I loved my parents, sharing a tiny cruise ship cabin with two other people was not ideal.

When I lugged my suitcase down the stairs, my mom was double-checking her bag by the door while my dad looked at his fitness watch.

"It's not too late to let me stay home," I said.

Mom shook her head. "Savannah. This is a family vacation."

"No, it's a company cruise that families are invited on. Won't you be busy with work? And wouldn't you have more fun if you didn't have to worry about me?"

Mom raised an eyebrow, smiling. "Are you saying I should worry about you? Planning to cause trouble?"

"Loads and loads of it."

She laughed. Which was fair, because the only time I'd ever gotten detention or been in any trouble whatsoever was in eighth grade when Tanner had tossed his potato light bulb at me and told me to lighten up, and for some reason I'd ducked and it had hit our science teacher in the face. Not my proudest moment, and I still didn't see why I'd gotten in trouble when he'd been the one throwing vegetables.

I shouldn't have been so hesitant about the trip. An Alaskan cruise was an amazing opportunity, and I was grateful we had the chance to go. Upper management from my parents' company, plus their families, were invited, with the basic cruise fare paid for.

Travel was just so much work. Packing and flying and being away from home.

I'd probably enjoy it. And once we got home, I knew I'd be glad I'd gone. But I would miss my bed and my telescope and my fuzzy blanket. Plus, Alaska was so full of nature. Ever since that camping incident that Jordan called a *formative moment*, I'd felt safer knowing nature had limits.

"What if there isn't anyone my age?" I asked. "What if I get seasick?"

"We have medicine for that. And you know Tanner will be there."

He didn't count as *my age* since most of the time, he acted like a six-year-old. Evidence: yesterday's garbage incident.

"Now you're really making me want to stay home."

She laughed again. Our parents didn't grasp the full depth of Tanner's and my dislike. Despite our complaints, frequent arguments, and attempts to avoid each other, our parents made us participate in family dinners, joint vacations, holidays.

"It will be good for you," Mom said. "Try to get along with him this trip, okay? I know asking you two to be best friends is pointless, but I need you to behave."

I wasn't the one who misbehaved. "I'll be nice if he is."

She gave me a patented parent look that I was pretty sure a person was only capable of mastering after they had teenagers. "Mr. Ramirez will be there, and you know how important this is to me."

I sighed. "I know."

Mrs. Woods, who was my mom's best friend in college, had

helped Mom get a job at the marketing company when we relocated to LA after we were free of my bio dad. This cruise was to reward staff but also to court new clients, and someone—most likely my mom or her best friend—was coming out of it with a promotion.

She and Mrs. Woods competed much more cordially than Tanner and I did.

My mom zipped her bag shut and straightened. "Besides, it might be good for you to spend time with Tanner. Have some fun."

Now she sounded like Caleb.

"I'm capable of having fun. I just have more fun without Tanner."

Dad winked at me as he opened the front door. Though we weren't biologically related, and he'd only entered my life ten years ago, I was more like him than my mom. Mom was a nice, more mature Tanner—in the good ways, not the ways that made me want to run away screaming. Outgoing, creative, a people person, but without the constant showing off. She often encouraged me to branch out, to go places, to be more social. Every time she tried to convince me, I wanted to join even less.

Outside, the Uber was waiting—and so was Jordan. Today, she'd replicated River Song's crown of curls, minus the blond, and it looked gorgeous.

"I couldn't let you leave without saying goodbye." She wrapped me in a comforting, vanilla-scented hug. "How are you?" she asked quietly.

"Fine," I said automatically.

She waited.

"Okay, not fine. But fine. You know?"

She rolled her eyes.

She did not need to know I'd been cyber-stalking Caleb for two days.

"Have fun," she said.

"You mean that thing I don't know how to do?"

"Stop letting Caleb live in your head. Go see all the cool things. And don't kill Tanner. Or maybe you'll find you don't want to kill him." She wagged her eyebrows.

"If you make another tight end joke, I'm not bringing you any presents."

She laughed.

"Good luck with your job. I'll miss you."

"Of course you will."

I'd asked if she could come with us. It was an only child problem. Usually I enjoyed not having siblings, because no one stole my things or broke into my room or ate the last cup of yogurt. Vacations were the one time I wished for company. My mom was usually a more-the-merrier type of person, which meant Jordan often tagged along. But Mom had thought it was unprofessional to bring a friend on this trip, because it would have meant needing two rooms instead of one, and the company was paying.

Jordan waved from our driveway as we loaded into the car. I cast a final, longing look at our house and my best friend and palm trees and civilization.

Tanner and his parents were waiting at the check-in area. His older sisters weren't coming home from college for the trip. One more year, and we would be in college, too. I planned to stay here, but hopefully he'd go far away. I should subscribe him to mailers from East Coast schools.

Mrs. Woods hugged me. Other than Jordan and my family, she was the only one I let get away with it. It was hard to believe someone so nice and who made the world's best lasagna had spawned Tanner.

"I bet you're glad the school year is over, aren't you?" she asked.

Wait, why? Had she heard about the breakup? Had Tanner regaled them with the story and his clever new name for me over burgers last night? I narrowed my eyes at him, but he didn't acknowledge me. I was probably reading too much into this.

"I am definitely glad it's over," I said.

Meaning, the last day of school, if nothing else. I preferred the routine of classes and practice and clubs to the wide-open days of summer. I'd planned to partially fix that—coaching Mia Lin and volunteering and dog walks and preparing for next year's Math Bowl—except now it would be without Caleb, and the gaping black hole of not having a plan was tugging me toward panic.

"I heard there was a big party on Friday?" my mom asked Tanner.

How did she know these things?

"Yep, Savannah missed out."

"I tried to convince her to go," Mom said.

"I had fun with Jordan." And River Song.

"You always see Jordan." Mom faced Tanner. "What did you do?"

As he showed off his superior social skills, I turned to Mrs. Woods. "I found a new app you'll like."

"Ooh, another one? I love that workout tracker you told me about."

"This one lets you type your to-do list for the week, and then you give it ten-minute slots of time when you're free. It randomly assigns you tasks to get done in those times, and when you do them, it gives you a word game to play."

"Oh, great. I'm always looking for ways to be more productive. And I love word games."

Tanner coughed something that sounded suspiciously like *nerd* before continuing to tell my mom about the nighttime bodysurfing contest, which sounded like an emergency room visit waiting to happen, as we made our way through the winding security line. My cough in return sounded a lot like *suck-up*.

When it was his turn to present his passport, he was describing his winning run and waving his hands.

I cleared my throat.

He didn't move.

"Were you planning to hold up the line forever?" I asked.

"Yes, because I know it bothers you." He moved forward and continued chatting with Mom as we took off our shoes and slung our carry-ons onto the belt.

Tanner was right in front of me heading for the scanner but stopped so suddenly I bumped into him. He removed his fitness watch and hurried to toss it into the tray on the belt before it went through, then got back into line. Where he set off the alarm.

"Whoops, sorry." He emptied his pockets of keys and phone.

"Have you never flown before?" I asked. "Emptying your pockets is the first rule."

My mom laughed, and his mom sighed his name.

I went through quietly with no problems, retrieved my items efficiently, and was standing waiting for the others, bag repacked and shoes on, while Tanner was still getting an overly friendly pat-down from a burly TSA agent.

In the waiting area at our gate, my mom took a seat next to Mrs. Woods. They immediately started reliving the recent conference they'd gone to in Phoenix. My dad sat across from Mr. Woods, and they were discussing a report about the future of self-driving cars, and I wished I could hear more because I'd read that, too. Mr. Woods worked in a chemistry lab and was always up for talking about the latest scientific discoveries.

Tanner sprawled at the end of the row, his long legs extended into the aisle. He wore giant headphones and was tapping his foot along with whatever music played, drumming his fingers on the arm of the chair.

I sat as far away as possible, put in my earbuds, and loaded a podcast where two funny guys debated the most realistic fictional spaceships until it was time to board the flight to Vancouver.

As we passed the exit row, I eyed the people sitting there, trying to figure out if I could trust them with my survival in the event of a crisis situation.

I waited for my mom to slide into the middle seat, where I was supposed to have the aisle. But she and Mrs. Woods compared boarding passes and shuffled us around.

"I don't think that's allowed," I said. "Aren't you supposed to sit in your assigned seat?"

"Are you going to report us to the airplane authorities?" Tanner glanced around with a fake worried expression. "Should I be scared?"

"It will be fine," Mom said. "We're not taking strangers' seats. They're assigned to us."

I swallowed a growl. I didn't want to argue and give Tanner additional reasons to mock me, so instead of my nice aisle seat, I ended up crammed into the middle with Tanner next to me on the aisle *because he was tall and needed space.*

I was tall, too, thank you. Five eight and a half was well above average for a girl, and I had long runner's legs. But I wasn't star-tight-end tall, with broad shoulders that took up more than his fair share of room. I shifted to avoid touching Tanner. Jordan was right. He did have impressive muscles.

No. I was not noticing that. Why couldn't he wear a hoodie over that T-shirt to hide those things? Music leaked from his fancy headphones, and his bare elbow kept brushing mine.

I read the stuff in the seatback pocket, from the airplane chart to the travel magazine.

Tanner shifted again, further crushing me between him and the turbaned Sikh man in the window seat. I nudged Tanner's elbow hard enough to knock it off our shared armrest. He raised his eyebrows at me and inched the headphones off his ears.

"You get the aisle one." I pointed. "This one's mine."

"Is that another airplane rule? Planning to submit a complaint?"

"It's a common courtesy rule. I don't know why I expected you to know any of those."

"Are you sure? You don't want to tell on me like you did with the fireworks? Or the Christmas when I opened the presents early. Or the picnic where I accidentally knocked over the drink table. Wow, there really are a lot of examples of times you got me in trouble."

I refused to feel guilty for any of those. He could have burned the house down with those fireworks. "Maybe you should reconsider the life choices that lead you to situations where you could get in trouble in the first place."

He nudged the armrest. "I'll arm wrestle you for it."

"Seriously? What are you, twelve?"

He shrugged. "It seems like something that should be earned. Wouldn't it be more satisfying to win it?"

"And that's why you suggested arm wrestling? Because I stand a chance of winning?" I tried and failed not to look at the muscles straining the sleeves of his T-shirt.

"Not with that attitude, you don't."

To my surprise, he tucked his arm in awkwardly, shifting so his feet extended farther into the aisle. Was it too much to hope that a flight attendant would roll over them with the drink cart?

"How do you think you did on finals?" he asked.

The annoying thing was, for all that Tanner acted like a dumb jock, he competed with me for near-top grades. Despite having no ability whatsoever to pay attention in class, to take actual notes, or to do homework more than a day—or a class period—before it was due.

"Great," I said. "What about you?"

"Also great. Better than great."

"I guess we'll see."

Final grades would be uploaded to the online portal later this week, and I was glad they would arrive on a port day since we wouldn't have internet when the ship was at sea.

He shifted. "Sorry about, you know."

His voice was serious now, and a rare solemn expression flickered across his face.

Did he mean Friday? My public humiliation? The new nickname? My neck grew hot, and I couldn't decide if I wanted to snap at him or pretend I had no idea what he was talking about.

"You're better off, anyway," he went on. "Caleb is boring."

"Doesn't that mean we're perfect for each other?"

He shifted again. "You're not boring."

"That's not what you said on Friday."

"What?"

I snorted. "Like you don't know."

He frowned and opened his mouth. Then his face morphed—he crossed his eyes and stuck out his tongue.

Seriously?

Oh. A baby in front of us was staring at him over the top of the seat.

Fine. It was better if Tanner and I ignored each other. I smiled at the baby, who barely noticed me, sucked in by Tanner's goofy faces. A tiny hand came through the seats, and he let the kid grab his finger.

It was not cute. At all. Nope. And I definitely wasn't watching.

The seat in front of me reclined violently, trapping me in a tight prison.

"Will you stop?" came a woman's voice from directly behind me, sharp and loud. I jumped.

I couldn't make out a guy's mumbled reply.

"This was supposed to be a fun vacation," the woman went on, and like, come on, lady, the whole plane doesn't need to hear your business. "You didn't want to see the beach, the Dodgers game was too crowded, the Walk of Fame was dumb. Why did you even want to come?"

"But . . . I had a great time, babe. Because I was with you."

Hearing a couple fighting was near the top of my *things I don't want to do* list. I tried to reach down, hoping to find earbuds, but I couldn't get to my backpack on the floor with the seat in front of me reclined so far.

"You know what? I can't." Her voice rang out. "They say traveling together is a good test, and we failed. It's over."

Heat spread up my neck as my stomach sank. Every second of last Friday washed over me. The eyes on me. The whispers. The need to escape. This guy had fewer options than I'd had, unless he could get a flight attendant to bring him a parachute.

Silence surrounded us, heavy with awkwardness. The hush of people who very much wanted not to have witnessed such a private moment.

"But," the guy said, "I love you. I don't understand."

39

I hoped I hadn't sounded so desperate in the parking lot. My heart twisted for him.

"That's the problem. You don't." Her voice lacked sympathy. "This week, we were on totally different pages."

Of course they were seated two feet from me and not thirty rows away. Because that was my life lately.

"But—"

An elbow bumped mine, and the man's reply was smothered as Tanner settled his noise-canceling headphones over my ears. They were playing a loud rock song, but he tapped his phone and handed it over, loaded to his Spotify account, which included a wider variety than I would have expected.

The music completely drowned out the couple.

My heart stuttered. I tried to peer at him without moving my head.

But Tanner returned to playing with the baby in front of him and didn't acknowledge me once.

Chapter Four

Port of Embarkation: Vancouver, British Columbia

~

Halfway through the three-hour flight, Tanner had taken his headphones back. I was able to twist a couple degrees to see that the aisle seat behind us was empty. Hopefully a flight attendant had had pity on the guy and found him an empty spot elsewhere. Or that parachute.

Tanner didn't seem inclined to acknowledge the awkward kindness of blocking that conversation for me. Since I had no idea what to do with the gesture, I was going to pretend nothing had happened. Two nice acts from him in the last few days was messing with my mind.

The rest of the flight was uneventful, and, with no time difference, we arrived around dinnertime. After customs, we'd taken a car to our hotel on Vancouver's waterfront and spent the night. My parents had planned a day to see the city before the cruise ship left.

Now, I stood studying the breakfast options. Every morning, I ate a banana, wheat toast, and a strawberry Greek yogurt. The hotel buffet had toast and bananas, but the yogurt was a strange brand. Would it be sweet enough? And if it wasn't Greek, I wouldn't get protein and then I'd be hungry before lunch.

Tanner stopped beside me. "Are you going to eat it, or did you develop X-ray vision and you're scanning it with your robot brain?"

"If I were a robot, I'd be threatening to assimilate you or exterminate you or upgrade you."

"You know a frightening amount about killer robots. It's good for the safety of the world that you aren't on the school robotics team."

I'd considered it. Not because I wanted to build an evil robot. Just a regular one. But I was already too busy.

I started to grab a yogurt cup then changed my mind. Better to go without than risk it. I took a carton of milk instead and grabbed an extra banana, thinking longingly of my perfectly stocked refrigerator at home.

"Savannah Banana." Tanner grinned and added two yogurts to his plate, which contained a mountain of eggs, toast, fruit, pastries, and some sort of ham/bacon that probably failed to live up to Canadian-style meat promised by American pizzas.

"Planning to feed a small country?" I asked.

"Yes. The one in my stomach." He patted it, which unfortunately drew my gaze. If he always ate this much, how in the world was it so flat?

And why was I looking?

I plopped down next to my dad and focused on my bananas.

Our parents were discussing the plans for the day, and Tanner gulped one yogurt cup and waved the other in my face. "Sure you don't want one?"

"I'm fine."

"It did taste a little . . ."

"Off? Spoiled? Unsweetened?"

"Canadian," he said.

I rolled my eyes as he laughed and opened the top.

When we finished—Tanner ate his three meals' worth of food faster than I ate my toast—we walked a couple blocks to a stop where we'd catch a bus to the nearby Capilano Suspension Bridge Park. I'd researched its famous wooden simple suspension bridge and was excited to see it.

Actually, Caleb and I had researched it together. I would not, as I had originally planned, be sending him pictures, and that made me twitchy. I didn't like plans changing, and after one day, this trip wasn't going as I had imagined.

It was fine. I would be fine. Just because I liked things a certain way didn't mean I was *too* set in my ways, like Caleb had said. I could adapt.

Maybe I would send him a picture, after all. If we were going to be friends or whatever, then friends texted. It didn't have to be weird.

It would be weird.

The morning air was cool and crisp, and not many people were out yet. The city was beautiful, with the water, shiny skyscrapers, and mountains in the distance. To get to the park, the bus crossed the bay on an elegant suspension bridge that reminded me of the Golden Gate Bridge before arriving in a parking lot ringed by enormous trees. The sky was bluer here than at home, the trees greener, the edges sharper. Not dulled by smog.

"I bet the stars are amazing out here."

I'd meant to say it to my dad, but Tanner was the one behind me.

"I wonder if they have night tours," he said. "See, imagine how cool the campout this fall will be."

I crossed my arms. "Or, we could do the observatory, like we planned."

"Like *you* planned. A majority obviously agreed with my idea."

Because they clearly didn't see the possibilities of getting attacked by wild animals, or how equally impressive the meteors would be from Griffith Park with scientists giving talks.

If he ruined the meteor shower for me, I would totally attempt that coup.

A trading post and a large wooden deck overlooked a river gorge, with the simple suspension bridge stretching across it. It would have been unnerving if I didn't know the science was solid. And impressive—no towers or piers, just a hanging structure of rope and wood in an elegant hyperbolic curve.

A sign warned visitors not to run, jump, or shake the bridge. We really needed to pause, read it aloud, and let it sink in, since every one of those sounded like something Tanner would do.

As we crossed it, the bridge swayed slightly. All I saw was the narrow ribbon of it stretching through treetops. The scent of pine, multiple shades of deep green, and the mark of human ingenuity were stunning.

Halfway out, I stopped and peered at the river below, mountains in the distance, pointy fir trees stretching to the sky. The rope railing was smooth from years of hands. The wind whispered through the gorge.

I had the same feeling I got when staring at the night sky, as the hugeness of the world enveloped me, welcomed me into it, promised infinite possibility.

"See, you're not dull," Tanner murmured as he brushed past me. "If only Caleb could see you now."

I twitched, coming back to the present. Was he mocking me? He'd stopped nearby, but he wasn't smirking, was just looking at the view.

What was Caleb doing this week? Our volunteer slots at the museum? Walking his dog? The idea of him participating in our typical activities hurt more than him attending parties without me.

Did he miss me? Was he regretting the breakup?

"Is this safe? It's shaky." Tanner put his arms out and pretended to wobble.

Instead of Caleb, I was stuck with Tanner.

"It's shaky because they used the handrails as the primary supports instead of the deck. It makes the deck swing more. Simple suspension bridges are quite safe."

"School's over," he said. "No science during the summer."

"Science is awesome. Especially because I'm better at it than you."

"Imagine doing that egg drop experiment over the side of this." He peered over the edge.

"I'd like to never think about that again."

We'd been assigned as partners, and let's just say we wouldn't have gone through enough eggs to make a hundred omelets if Tanner hadn't argued with all my ideas.

But now he had me contemplating. It was an intriguing problem. Were we high enough for a parachute? Was that the kind of project I might attempt if I agreed to Mr. Lin's program? He hadn't emailed me yet, and though I was curious, I was also relieved, because that prolonged my having to make a decision.

"Aw, come on," Tanner said. "We had fun."

"You had fun because we made a huge mess. The janitor is probably still cleaning egg off that sidewalk."

"You enjoyed explaining why my attempts failed, and don't try to deny it."

Okay, he had a point. That had been enjoyable.

I continued on. Wait. We were missing a person. Mrs. Woods had stopped halfway across. Rather than appreciating the view, she stood frozen with her head down and clutched the rope.

Tanner immediately backtracked to join her.

"Afraid of heights," Mr. Woods said. "I should have thought of that."

Mom tsked. "Husband fail. Tanner's handling it."

And he was—within minutes, his mom was laughing, and Tanner had her arm and was leading her toward us. Mr. Woods took over, gripping her hand.

When we reached the other side, Mr. Woods asked, "Why

did the bear cross the road?" Without waiting for us to guess, he said, "To eat the chicken."

He laughed, a low chuckle that didn't resemble Tanner's loud one, and Tanner pretended not to hear him.

I shuddered. Like I needed the reminder that we might see bears on this trip, and that they were fully capable of eating not only chickens, but me.

"I'm just glad to be off that bridge," Mrs. Woods said.

A trail led into an old-growth forest, where a series of platforms and walkways had been built into the trees and canopy, around the trunks. I felt like I had stepped into the Ewok village.

"It's like in that old movie," Tanner said. "With the short, furry teddy bears who fight stormtroopers."

I squinted at him.

"You know, before Rey and the emo dude?"

"I know Star Wars, Tanner."

"Those little guys are awesome."

I'd loved them as a kid, all clever with how they used homemade hang gliders, catapults, and rocks to fight the Empire. Even if it was wildly unlikely that their crude arrows would pierce stormtrooper armor.

He turned to walk backward on a bridge. "We should watch the movies in star club next year. Oh! Or we should try to replicate their weapons."

That had nothing to do with astronomy . . . but it sounded pretty fun. Not that I'd tell him that, the usurper. Thanks for the reminder that he'd be the one making those decisions, not me.

He faced forward again and peered over his shoulder at me

as we circled a platform around a massive tree trunk. "Want to race?"

"Sure. I'm right behind you."

"Really?" He took a couple steps toward the next bridge. "Oh. You're messing with me."

"No, racing across narrow bridges high in the trees, filled with tourists and little kids, is a great idea. It definitely won't get us kicked out of the park."

"Or you're afraid you'd lose."

"More like afraid you'd sprain my ankle again."

"Excuse me, *I* didn't sprain your ankle," he said. "The mountain did."

"Because you told me I could ride the chairlift down, and then they wouldn't let me, and I had to ski down the mountain even though I didn't know how."

"I tried to coach you, but you wouldn't listen to me."

"Excuse *me* if I wasn't feeling especially trusting at that point."

Whatever. Debating was useless. He never saw himself as wrong, no matter what wild things he was attempting—and attempting to drag me into, like that winter break at Big Bear our freshman year. Right before my first high school track season.

The same arguments, over and over, never produced different outcomes. Since I was fairly certain someone had said that was the definition of insanity, I didn't know why I bothered engaging with him.

We walked in silence, until Tanner's dad stopped beside a fish pond and stared at the platform above us.

"It's fascinating, isn't it, the way they're built without nails or bolts so they don't harm the trees?" he asked.

"I read that they can be loosened and moved to expand as the tree grows," I said.

Tanner jumped to stand on a log that bordered the shallow pond. "Look at all the fish. I wonder if they'd let us spearfish in there."

This was going to be a long vacation.

Chapter Five

Port of Embarkation: Vancouver, British Columbia

~

After exploring part of Vancouver on foot after lunch—old Victorian buildings and a fascinating steam clock in Gastown—I laced up my running shoes. If I wanted to break that two-mile record in the fall in any attempt at undoing *Moore the Bore*, I needed to stay in shape.

My parents were resting, Mom reviewing info on the potential new clients and Dad reading an ebook.

When I got to the hotel's small gym, I saw through the glass wall that the room was occupied—by Tanner. He was lying on the bench press machine, wearing a loose T-shirt with the sleeves ripped out, which gave me a view of his muscles as he heaved the weights. Shirts like that should be outlawed when they made your nemesis look hot.

Not that I found Tanner attractive. Just that, objectively, he wasn't bad-looking. Why was my face warm?

I shook my head. My run would not be deterred. By his muscles, or by the fact that he was dedicated enough to also be working out on the first day of vacation. He was a star player, with the school's coach specifically designing plays that had allowed him to break tight end receiving records. His discipline shouldn't have surprised me. But it did.

As I entered, he sat up. "Hey, S'more. Want me to spot you?"

"I'm going to run." I motioned to the treadmill.

"No, you're not."

"Excuse me?"

"It's broken."

Sure enough, a paper taped to the screen said *Out of Order.*

Well, that was unfair.

"We could run outside," Tanner said. "The weather's great."

We? "And we could get lost in a strange city."

"That's what maps are for. Come on," he said. "It will be fun. I'll text my mom."

I eyed the nice, safe, and broken treadmill.

Tanner wiggled his phone. "She says okay, and your mom agreed. Don't worry. I'll keep you from getting mugged."

He flexed, and I tried not to stare at his biceps. How did I always forget that Tanner had gotten buff? Probably because as soon as he opened his mouth, that was the only thing I noticed. He stood and wiped off the bench, chugged a cup of water from the dispenser, and motioned to the door.

"Are you sure about this?" I asked as we crossed the lobby.

"It will be fine."

"I meant, do you think you can keep up?"

He grinned. "The better question is, can you keep up with me?"

"There are no balls involved here. No catching. No fans. Just running. And that's my domain."

"We'll see, S'more."

We left the hotel and jogged along the waterfront, with skyscrapers on one side and the harbor on the other. Seaplanes puttered on the water, and mountains framed the bay. It was pretty and far greener than I was used to, even on the clearest days in LA.

It was kind of nice, that I wasn't the only one who wanted to work out. My parents stayed in shape, but neither was so into fitness that they found it necessary on vacation. Maybe Tanner wasn't 100 percent an alien. Or we both were. That was a disturbing thought.

"Hey, check it out." Tanner was veering off the sidewalk onto a platform that extended over the bay.

"Need a break already?" I asked.

"You wish. Look."

A large sculpture of a leaping orca stretched into the sky, blocky like it was made out of big LEGOs. We slowed to circle it. It was pretty cool, especially against the backdrop of mountains, clouds, and water.

"Stand next to it," Tanner said.

"Are we running or sightseeing?"

"Both. Come on, I want a picture, but I want to show the scale."

"So why don't I take your picture?"

"Just smile, S'more. Or don't smile. Turn around and pretend you're enjoying the view and you don't see me."

"I wish I could pretend that every day." I paused next to the statue.

He snapped a picture and I rejoined him, jogging in place.

"You used to love LEGOs," Tanner said.

I narrowed my eyes. I still enjoyed them, carefully following instructions in complicated kits, sometimes creating my own designs. When I needed to clear my mind, it helped to focus on a project. Given that my plans with Caleb this summer had exploded like a supernova, I saw many breakup LEGOs in my future.

I scowled at Tanner as I left the statue and returned to the sidewalk. "You only know that because you broke into my room."

"I thought it was the bathroom," he said. "And it wasn't breaking. The door was cracked."

"You knew it wasn't the bathroom. You'd been to our house a hundred times. Once you opened the door, you didn't have to go in."

"Of course I did. You had a three-foot-tall replica of the *Enterprise*. It was impressive."

Another argument we'd had many times. He consistently failed to understand why a twelve-year-old girl might not have wanted a boy going into her room behind her back. Especially when she had a giant spaceship in there.

"What happened to it?" he asked, pocketing his phone and joining me as I resumed a jog.

"It's off exploring strange new worlds and fighting LEGO Klingons."

"Cool. I hope it's winning."

"I took it apart," I said.

"Aw, how come?"

"That's what LEGOs are for. You build something, then you use the blocks to build something new. I didn't exactly have room to leave it forever."

I did keep a few smaller builds that didn't make it impossible to cross my bedroom floor, but if I told him that, he might break and enter again.

"How long did it take to build?" he asked.

"Couple weeks."

"Wow."

"What?"

"Seems a shame to take apart something so cool. What else have you built?"

"All kinds of stuff."

Why this sudden interest in my hobbies?

"Are you stalling because you're afraid you can't keep up?" I asked, and increased the pace, to see if he could.

Sadly for me, he stayed at my side with no panting for breath or begging for mercy.

We crossed a bridge and entered a green park along the water with huge trees, a rose garden, a display of totem poles. Lots of people were biking and walking. None of them looked like hardened criminals, and many had kids. I doubted Tanner's bodyguard skills would be needed. But I was slightly glad not to be alone.

We circled a few trails then turned around. According to my watch, the run here had been two miles, and I pushed the pace on the return trip. Running with Tanner regularly might help me improve, given our constant desire to beat each other.

Tanner's red face was the only indication I might have pushed him harder than he was used to. I refused to be mildly impressed.

We stopped outside the hotel to stretch, and my phone dinged as it reconnected to the Wi-Fi. I went inside, grabbed water from the fancy dispenser with sliced cucumbers, and sat on a bench.

Tanner joined me.

"Tired?" I asked.

"Tired of you doubting my athletic prowess."

I snorted and took my phone from the pocket of my running pants. Texts from Jordan waited. She wanted to know how Canada was, if I'd seen a bear yet, and how many times I'd checked Caleb's social media today.

I replied: *Canadian, thankfully no, and I'm not answering that.* Then I decided to blow her mind by telling her that I'd gone running with Tanner and I deserved a brownie because I'd burned lots of calories and because I'd refrained from tripping him into the harbor.

Her other text was a selfie of her hair, different from yesterday, this time with complicated braids. I gave her a fire emoji.

Since my phone was out, it wouldn't hurt to see if Caleb had posted today.

"Please tell me you aren't stalking that guy," Tanner said, and I quickly placed my phone screen-down on my thigh. "He dumped you in public on the last day of school. You do not need him."

"Thank you for the unsolicited opinion on my personal life. Would you also like to advise me on the experiences of women in STEM, my wardrobe, and my dental hygiene?"

"If you need advice, sure. Do you drink coffee? You should try whitening toothpaste."

I glared at him.

"I'm just saying. He's, what?" Tanner leaned over so his shoulder pressed mine and grabbed my phone to flip it over. He scoffed. "He's playing video games the week after school let out, which is the biggest cliché ever."

"You'd be playing video games if we weren't here."

"Meanwhile," he said, "you're in another country about to go on an adventure."

"I don't know if Canada counts. Even if they do have weird yogurt."

He slapped a hand to his chest. "I'm going to pretend you didn't insult our fine northern neighbors or their dairy foods, because that's not the point. The point is, you're about to have way more fun than he is."

I supposed he was right.

A comment on Caleb's post from a guy from newspaper said, *Let's hang out.* Caleb's reply: *Yeah, man. I have lots of free time.*

Because he didn't have to spend any of it with me.

Numbness threatened to freeze my chest again.

Their consensus was to see the new superhero movie, which was something Caleb and I had planned to do. *Thanks for making those plans publicly, for me to see, dude.* Technically, that made him the boring one this week. Except it didn't sound boring, and the idea of him at the movies without me made my lungs seize up.

"Did you take any pictures today?" Tanner's question cut into my thoughts. "At the bridge?"

"Yeah. Why?"

"You should post one. Or, wait. Here."

He pulled his phone from his shorts pocket and scrolled. A second later, my phone buzzed. He'd sent me a photo of the view from the bridge. I was in the edge of the shot, in profile as I stared at the canyon stretching beneath me. It looked like I stood among the trees. Or was about to jump, which, considering I'd been with him, was a possibility.

Above the photo, in our text thread, I saw the last messages from Tanner—from the end-of-year sports banquet planning committee, when I had booked a classic bar and grill to cater tri-tip for the meal, and he'd changed it to a build-your-own tacos bar without telling me, a reminder I should be hesitant to trust him.

"I didn't realize you were in the shot when I took it," he said. "But that one's perfect. It shows you doing something new. And it's impressive."

It was a good picture.

"Can I post it?" he asked.

"I guess so."

He clicked, and my phone told me I'd been tagged in a post. He'd used hashtags like *adventure* and *travel* and *wanderlust,*

which didn't sound like me, but did sound exciting and glamor-
ous. Likes from our classmates appeared immediately.

Huh.

"You're not embarrassed to admit you're hanging out with
me?" I asked.

"Why? Are you embarrassed to be with me?"

"Not embarrassed. Maybe annoyed. Disappointed? Aggra-
vated?"

"Thanks for the SAT list. I was just trying to help."

"Why? I mean, why help me?"

"What he did sucked. No one deserves that."

So he felt sorry for me. Wonderful. That was worse than him
teasing me about it.

"Plus," he said, "it's an awesome picture. Shows I'm doing
something more exciting than PlayStation. Something new."

There was that word again. That had been Caleb's comment—
that I never wanted to do anything new.

Just because I preferred not to didn't mean I couldn't. It was
an unfair accusation. Most people were creatures of habit. Besides, I didn't think I was boring. Sure, I liked routine. But I ran
track and did pole vault, and volunteered at the Science Center,
and led the Math Bowl team. Maybe it wasn't as unique as Jordan's style and her singing ability, or the guy in our class who
had developed three apps, or the senior girl who was a semipro
skateboarder, but I had a life and I liked it. I'd never cared before.
Why did I feel this need to prove myself?

Moore the Bore. The whispers in my mind refused to go
away.

I studied the picture again. The bridge and park had been

new. And I had liked it. Despite Tanner and bear jokes and a lack of suitable pre-excursion yogurt, the engineering, scenery, and fresh air had been nice. This vacation, I would literally be doing all kinds of new things.

Freshman year, Jordan had gone through a phase where she tried a different hairstyle every day for a month. She'd watched YouTube tutorials to learn and taken pictures of each one and posted polls so people could vote on their favorites.

"What?" Tanner asked.

"What?"

He waved a hand in a circle in front of me. "You have a look on your face."

"That's what faces do."

"But what are you thinking?"

"Again, why do you care?"

He shrugged.

The photo called to me. I could be fun. "I was thinking about trying new things on this trip. Like, intentionally finding stuff I've never done before."

As soon as the words were out, the idea sounded stupid. Or terrifying. Or both. And I'd said it to Tanner, which meant he'd never let it go and I couldn't take it back.

His face lit up. "Oh, yeah! That's great. There will be so many things to try."

"I can only handle one per day." Or none.

"Okay, then." He rubbed his hands together. "One new thing per day. That's excellent. You should post pictures of them. Document it."

That had worked for Jordan and her hair. It would show

Caleb that he'd been wrong about me. Hopefully our classmates, too. They couldn't keep calling me Moore the Bore if there was photographic proof of me having amazing, wanderlusting adventures. And Caleb would remember the fun times we'd had and realize he'd made a mistake. See that we could have a great senior year as planned, like our junior one.

"I'll be your photographer, if you want," Tanner said. "And I can suggest ideas."

He was watching me with his head angled, his gray eyes bright. The idea sank in, spreading through my brain. What would his suggestions be?

Was I certain that I wanted to commit to unknown activities I couldn't properly prepare for?

"You're looking at me weird again," he said. "You want to do it alone? Where's the fun in that?"

That wasn't what I'd been thinking. I'd been thinking, *Why couldn't I have kept my mouth shut?*

He had a point, though. If I did this, I would need accountability.

But . . . Tanner.

He leaned forward. "We're on this cruise together, and in the same situation—let's be honest, with parents who are going to let us fend for ourselves. Let me help."

"What, be, like, my Fun Coach?"

"Exactly."

There was no getting out of it now, not without appearing weak.

It was fine. This could work. I might not have fun, exactly—it would be too stressful for that—but if it made Caleb take me back, made people forget the nickname, and set senior year on course, I could do it.

I narrowed my eyes at him. "I would get veto power, if you propose ideas I don't like."

"Isn't the point to stretch yourself, S'more? If you play it too safe, it won't work. *New* doesn't mean running in a new city." He waved a hand toward the door.

"I know. But I'm not doing anything illegal or that might get me in trouble or risk severe injury."

A shadow flickered in his eyes, and his voice was flat. "That's exactly what I was going to suggest. High diving off the cruise ship and hand-feeding a wild bear and robbing a convenience store in ski masks."

"I'm not getting near a bear."

"Fine," he said, his voice light again. "Veto power. I'll help you come up with ideas, but the final decision is yours."

I twisted to face him, suspicion creeping in. We didn't willingly spend time together. Certainly didn't actively help each other. He'd been far too nice lately. It worried me.

"What do you get out of this? Besides seeing me uncomfortable, embarrassed, and out of my comfort zone? What's in it for you?"

"The joy of your presence, S'more," he drawled. "And what else is there to do, listen to our moms suck up to their boss all week?"

"So you're desperate, and I'm your entertainment?"

He studied me, his eyes serious for once. He opened his

mouth. Closed it. Then his usual smirk reappeared. "Of course not. I expect repayment. You can help me with something in return. A summer project."

"Oh, yeah?"

"Help me pick a college major."

I sniffed.

He continued to look at me.

"What? For real?"

"For real," he said.

"Didn't you talk to the guidance counselor about that?"

He waved a hand. "We mostly talked about football. Can you believe he's a Niners fan? Besides, it's hard being so talented that I have too many options." He ignored my groan and continued. "My parents think I should have an idea of what I want to study. I need something that will make them happy. And they love you and everything you do. It's all I ever hear about, how great Savannah is. If I tell them it was your idea, they'll say it's brilliant."

A slight note of bitterness laced his words, and I knew the feeling, since my parents frequently talked about how much they loved Tanner.

"Plus," he said, "you're organized and into research. Isn't this the kind of thing you love?"

"I suppose I could do that . . ."

It did sound fun. Not helping Tanner, specifically. But narrowing down fields and subjects. The brochures our guidance counselor had about finding your passion had looked interesting, but I knew I was going to study math and teach one day, so there hadn't been much work involved. And he and I hadn't talked about football during my appointment.

"Excellent." Tanner rubbed his hands together. "We have a deal. I coach you in trying new things, and in exchange, you'll figure out what I should do with my considerable talents. This is going to be fun."

This was going to have a worse ending than the TV show *Lost*.

And possibly the same number of casualties.

"We should probably make an additional agreement to get along," I said. "Call a two-week truce. No fighting."

His eyes glinted. "Now you're asking too much. No reporting me to the cruise ship cops or Alaskan dogsled police or anything?"

"If you do something worthy of being reported to the dogsled police, I make no promises."

He snorted.

We studied each other. His features were familiar, his expressive brows and ready smile, but I tried to see him through new eyes, as an ally. I was agreeing not only to spend time with him willingly, but to let him participate in something that could end badly for me.

The clean Canadian air clearly contained mind-altering substances. The oxygen was too pure after the LA smog.

Tanner offered his hand, and I wanted to laugh wildly as I thought of Caleb. Apparently shaking hands had been ruined for me forever. This would come back and bite me when I applied for jobs one day.

What had I gotten into? Sure, this was a good idea in theory. Accomplishing the plan with Jordan might have been fun, because she'd allow me to play it safe. But Tanner wouldn't let me off easy. What was I going to have to do? And how mercilessly would he mock me when I got nervous or wanted to change my mind?

I reluctantly slid my hand into his. His was big and warm, completely enveloping mine. No wonder he was so good at catching footballs. He had a scar at the base of his thumb that I'd never noticed. A shiver went through me and I tried to hide it.

He squeezed and let go.

"This vacation just got more interesting." He stood. "Race you up the stairs." He took off.

Ignoring the sudden flood of worry and regret, I flexed my hand and followed.

chapter six

Port of Embarkation: Vancouver, British Columbia

~

The episodes of *Epic Cruise Ships* I'd watched had not prepared me for the real-life epicness. This might not have been the fanciest vessel sailing the seas, but I was impressed.

What did the engine room look like? I was really hoping for a chance to see the machinery and high-tech controls. I imagined the bridge resembled a spaceship.

After checking in, we walked up a gangway and into the main atrium lobby. It stretched up three stories from a polished tile floor, with grand curving staircases, scattered gleaming metal sculptures, and huge flower arrangements. Golden light pooled from an intricate glass chandelier high overhead, and darker areas off the center of the room held clusters of chairs.

Crewmembers in crisp shirts and vests welcomed us and handed champagne flutes to our parents. We roamed around, taking in the huge space. It was hard to believe this was a boat; it felt more like a small city. I snapped pictures to send to Jordan. We went up several floors to the lunch buffet.

In the main casual dining room, seating areas lined both sides next to giant windows, while the center was a maze of food options. There were too many choices. Where did I even start? Colorful salad bars and fruit displays, more types of cheese than I knew existed, approximately eighty-seven styles of cuisines, and a dozen desserts.

Tanner ended up with a bowl of pasta, a small mountain of pizza, fried rice, and three tacos, like his taste buds were taking a world tour in a single meal. I inspected several dishes before making myself a salad and a turkey sandwich.

After we ate, Mom and Mrs. Woods wanted to check out the company's welcome-aboard reception. It was on the deck we'd entered on, through doors that opened into a bar. My parents' co-workers, most of whom I recognized from company events over the years, were standing around drinking more champagne and eating appetizers like there wasn't an enormous buffet upstairs.

My mom and Mrs. Woods made a beeline for their boss, Mr. Ramirez, a jovial older man with a thick mustache who was always smiling.

"Are we going to see them this week?" Mr. Woods asked.

"I doubt it," my dad said. "Not unless Luis is there, too."

"They do know only one of them can get the promotion, right?"

"Amy said if she doesn't get the job, if it goes to Stephanie, she'll be happy. As long as Michael from client services doesn't get it."

Mr. Woods laughed. "Steph said the same. Should we keep

an eye on them to make sure they don't put Michael in a lifeboat and set him loose?"

"Probably a good idea. This is why I stick with crunching numbers." Dad winked at me. "It's far less cutthroat."

I loved that Mom and Mrs. Woods supported each other. My dad worked in the company's accounting division, which meant he and Mom didn't compete for positions. It was where they'd met, after Mrs. Woods helped Mom get the job. I half suspected Mom had met him, realized he was dependable, kind, and stable—the exact opposite of my bio dad—and asked him out on the spot, though it had taken her months of dating before she introduced him to me.

He'd won me over in less than three minutes. Bringing me a toy lightsaber, kneeling to my level, and listening like I was an adult when he asked about my interests had done it. He cemented my approval in the following weeks when he did everything my bio dad didn't—remembered special occasions and what I liked, kept his promises, willingly adapted to our traditions and eased me into his by explaining them in advance, then asked my permission before proposing to Mom.

I shuffled after him as he joined my mom. I had no interest in making small talk with their coworkers, who always commented on how big I'd gotten and how old I was, then shook their heads and murmured about how old *they* were, like that was somehow my fault.

I took more pictures to send Jordan later. After Tanner's post yesterday, she had texted to ask why Tanner Woods was sharing pictures of me, and I'd told her about my plan to try new things. Our exchange had gone as follows:

Jordan: *I thought you hated him. Is he blackmailing you? No, wait, are you blackmailing him?*

Me: *No blackmail involved. Not yet, anyway. I wouldn't put it past him.*

Jordan: *I think the plan sounds brilliant. I wish I was there.*

Me: *Me too. I hope Caleb agrees it's brilliant. Maybe he'll see that he was wrong.*

Jordan: *Of course he was wrong.*

Then those dreaded three dots lingered forever, but whatever else she'd been typing, she must have changed her mind, because after two minutes, she didn't send anything except *have fun, miss you.* It had led me to check Caleb's account again. He'd had tacos last night without me—apparently the taco Tuesday tradition itself wasn't boring, and he wasn't a complete monster.

I'd posted pictures of the park and the city with the caption *great place to run,* as well as one of Mom's fancy dinner from the night before even though I'd eaten a salad.

Yes, it was ridiculous. And it felt like trying too hard, considering I was a private person and rarely posted on social media. But desperate times and all that. Also ridiculous? The fact that part of me wished I were at home, eating those familiar tacos at the truck Caleb and I always went to. They had fantastic carne asada.

I edged away from the mingling, left the bar, and wandered toward the elevators, where a map of the ship listed the name of each deck and what could be found there. If I was going to spend a week onboard, I wanted to learn where everything was.

"Setting foot on a ship does not count as something new," Tanner said.

I whirled. He was strolling toward me. Did he think our agreement meant I wanted to spend every minute of the week with him?

"I didn't say it did. But there isn't much to do while we're in port."

"It's already afternoon," he said. "We have to get on this."

"Thanks, Fun Coach."

"Not in the mood to talk marketing?"

"I'm surprised you aren't there letting their coworkers fawn over you," I said. "Or that your mom isn't using you to win over Mr. Ramirez."

"Don't be jealous. And I won't help with the promotion. It wouldn't be fair to give my mom such an advantage."

Barf. I waited while people passed us to board the elevator before asking, "Did you want something?"

"I found the place to book shore excursions."

"You didn't plan yours?"

He waved a hand. "My parents did. And I'm sure you scheduled yours. Let me guess. Walking tours and car rides and other old-person things?"

"Those aren't just for old people," I said. "They're for people with limited mobility or health issues or who can't—"

"Okay, fair, but you don't have limited mobility," he said. "You said you wanted to be fun."

I glared at him. How many people got to see Alaska? That totally counted.

He shrugged. "You're the one who wants to impress Caveman. That's why you're doing this, right? If you think taking pictures next to a tree will do it, then go right ahead."

"Caveman?"

"Yeah, because it sounds like *Caleb* and because he has no manners and is obviously not very bright."

"Cavemen might have been very polite and intelligent. You don't know."

"If I ever meet one, I'll be happy to be proved wrong. Now. Excursions."

"Fine." It didn't hurt to consider options. I *had* gravitated toward the less adventurous ones. "But remember, I get veto power."

"Great." He bounded down the corridor and I followed more slowly. When he rejoined me, he held a paper booklet with lots of small print. He made a show of presenting it to me.

I took it. "You don't want to look?"

"Too much reading. I'm on summer break."

"This was your idea. Forget it. Fine." I opened the booklet, which was divided by each of our three ports days, with multiple options for each.

Tanner moved to read over my shoulder, his breath brushing my neck. "Dogsledding for sure."

I moved away. "I thought you didn't want to read."

"It occurred to me that you might cheat and not tell me about the most exciting ones."

"Yes, because *I'm* the cheater."

"That fifth grade fundraiser does not count."

"You faked signatures on your pledge card so you'd have the most and then raided the mall fountain for coins," I said. "Totally cheating."

"Fine, but one fountain dive doesn't make me a chronic cheater. You never returned my book about submarines, and I don't go around calling you a thief."

"It was a library book, genius. And you have plenty of other terrible nicknames for me."

"I do not! Like what?"

"Moore the Bore, for one. Savannah Banana. Or what about Savannahsaurus Rex when we studied dinosaurs in third grade?"

"That was a great nickname. Made you sound like an apex predator."

"You went around for a week pretending to have tiny dino arms and trying to swat me."

"Why are we talking about dinosaurs? Are you trying to distract me from this mission of finding awesome things to do?" He jabbed the papers.

I sighed and reopened the booklet to read as we ambled toward the reception. Our parents surrounded Mr. Ramirez in a huddle.

"What is that?" Mom asked, looking over at us as we approached.

"Shore excursions," Tanner said. "We were discussing how we might want to change some of them. Try new things." He emphasized the last two words.

My mom's face brightened. "That's great. Don't forget the train ride with Luis on Sunday, though."

Mr. Ramirez beamed his huge smile. "Diana and I are looking forward to it. It's supposed to have amazing views."

"Some of these are expensive," I said.

Surely I could use that as an excuse not to hike with bears or ride a seaplane of death or fall into an ice cave on a glacier.

Mr. Ramirez laughed loudly. "Let the kids have fun. It's great that they want to experience everything they can. Such a wonderful opportunity at their age."

Which of course meant our moms instantly told us to do anything we wanted.

Tanner and Mr. Ramirez started talking about the upcoming NFL training camp, and as Tanner made Mr. Ramirez chuckle, Mom turned to me.

"It will be good for you two to spend time together this week," she said for my ears alone, probably assuming if I was busy with Tanner, she could focus on work. "I'm glad you want to branch out. And that you and Tanner are getting along."

"What happened to family time?" I raised my eyebrows.

"We'll do that, too. But I want you to enjoy yourself."

I would enjoy myself plenty on my own or with my dad. "I'll try. I'm going to explore the ship."

"Okay, sweetie. Have fun."

I headed for the door. Tanner jogged over and fell into step beside me.

"Where are you going? Can I come?"

Seriously? "Just looking around."

"Cool."

Okay then. We were doing this.

We took the elevator to the lowest deck, which contained closed, official-looking doors and a medical office. As long as Tanner didn't sprain my ankle again, I wouldn't need that.

I lingered outside a hatch that was emitting whirring noises. Were the engines in there? I hoped the engineers wore red uniforms like Scotty's.

Tanner poked my arm. "You're the one who said nothing illegal. No sneaking into off-limits areas on the first day."

"Good advice. Always save crime for at least day three."

"Because it takes that long to case the joint?"

"Exactly," I said.

"Like you've ever contemplated crime in your life."

"Like you'd ever have the patience to case a joint."

He let out a startled laugh that made a smile spread across my face, which I quickly smothered. He laughed often, but somehow earning a genuine, surprised one felt like an accomplishment.

Next was a floor of nothing but cabins, with narrow hallways and door after uniform door. Wood-paneled walls and sconces with golden light weren't enough to overcome the dizzying effect that I was stuck in a time loop. Many had luggage outside, and we had to dodge the bags.

"This tour is truly fascinating, S'more. Hey, a suitcase. Oh look, another suitcase."

"I want to make sure you're familiar with the vast multitude of luggage options. Also, I didn't actually invite you, so . . ."

The next deck was the one we'd boarded on. We walked from back to front—stern to bow—and found a cavernous theater taking up three floors, with movie theater seats and multiple levels facing a stage and giant screen.

We went up one more level and retraced from front to back,

finding more lounges with a variety of couches and tables nestled near windows. There was an art gallery and a casino that was closed since we were in port, though screens glowed in the bank of slot machines.

"Have you ever gambled?" Tanner leaned against a table with bright green felt.

"Pretty sure it's illegal for minors."

"I wasn't suggesting we do it this week. I was asking. You should listen more carefully." He rummaged in his backpack and removed a deck of cards. "I challenge you."

"Why do you have playing cards in your backpack?"

"You never know when you'll need entertainment." He set them on the table. "I'll teach you blackjack."

"Is this allowed?" No workers were present. "Are you trying to get me in trouble already? We haven't even cased the joint first."

"We're not exchanging money. It's fine. Now, the point is to get twenty-one without going over."

"I know what blackjack is."

He gave us each two cards, and we played a few rounds, trading wins, until I had a four and a ten.

"Hit me," I said.

"Are you sure?"

"Yeah, you've been through eight of the face cards, so the odds are better than usual of getting something smaller."

He clucked. "That would get you kicked out of Vegas."

"What would? Knowing how to do basic math? Do they think everyone there is incapable of counting?"

He flipped a card over for me. It was a seven. He stared at it, then me. Then laughed loudly. "Oh, S'more. You kill me. Okay, we're done here."

"Conceding defeat? Does that mean I win?"

"Fine. You and your card counting can have this one."

"Thank you. How do you know so much about gambling, anyway?"

"Poker nights with the football team. Roddy has a big table and fancy poker chips, and losers have to do extra speed ladders and squats and stuff. You should come sometime. With that math brain, you'd clean up. But I'm guessing you'd hate it."

"Why?"

"Because gambling is the very definition of risk."

"Hey. I can take risks."

He raised an eyebrow and moved away, and I scowled at his back. Just because I didn't *like* risks and didn't see the fun in gambling anything of value in a game of chance where you couldn't control the outcome didn't mean I was Moore the Bore.

"For example," I said, following him, "it's a risk that I'm spending time with you this week when it could easily lead to me accidentally pushing you into the ocean."

"Good thing I like risk, then. And that the ship has high railings." His smile shifted to a mock glare, and he poked my arm. "We agreed not to fight. No more threats. You're already breaking the rules."

On the rest of this deck were two bars, more meeting spaces, and the lower level of the main dining room. Then came a deck with a coffee shop, gelato bar, and fancy stores with items ranging from expensive watches to cigars to lingerie.

The sound of a bike horn blared through the hall.

I whirled.

An older lady with a walker was approaching. The horn sounded again. She had it attached to the handle of her walker, along with pink and purple streamers.

Tanner laughed. "I love your horn, ma'am."

"Why, thank you, young man. It never hurts to let people know you're coming."

"And the streamers?" he asked.

"So no one gets my walker mixed up with theirs and tries to steal it. People my age can have trouble seeing, you know."

Tanner laughed again. "Very wise."

"Aren't you two precious," she said. "Are you on your honeymoon?"

I snorted so hard I choked on my own spit.

Tanner smiled. "Not sure that's legal, ma'am. We're seventeen."

"Well, you're adorable. And how fun that you get to take this trip together."

"Yes, we're very lucky," he said. "What about you? What brings you here?"

They continued to chat, and if he was appalled by the idea that someone might believe we were together, he didn't show it. He learned that her name was Dottie, she and her husband were on their twenty-seventh cruise, and they lived in Las Vegas. Tanner was ready to adopt her as his grandmother.

"Got any advice for first-time cruisers?" he asked.

"Oh, yes," she said. "If you tell them it's your anniversary, you might get free drinks. In the main dining room, don't pay attention to those menus. You can order as many dishes as you want, and the food doesn't even have to be on the menu. And don't sunbathe nude on the balcony. They aren't as private as you'd think—workers on scaffolds clean the windows all the time."

That image was going to live rent-free in my brain for eternity.

"Good to know," Tanner said, his eyes sparkling.

He escorted Dottie to the elevator. "Can I honk the horn?"

"Of course."

He did, but I was impressed that he restrained himself and only did it twice. Dottie was laughing as the elevator doors closed.

"You meet so many great people when you travel," he said. "Are we continuing this tour?"

"I'm going to tell your grandma you're cheating on her."

"Gigi will understand. I can't help it if old ladies love me."

Babies. Old ladies. Bosses. They all clearly saw something I didn't.

Our self-tour continued. Four levels contained more rooms, including ours. We were both sharing with our parents in side-by-side balcony rooms. A bed filled most of our room, and a couch pulled out into another, which was where I'd be sleeping. I would have appreciated the efficient use of space if the next week wasn't going to be so cramped.

Then we reached the open-air deck, with an outdoor bar and grill next to the pool, the dining room where we'd eaten lunch, and a spa.

Tanner entered the spa, which was all white walls and ferns and soothing music, with a menu of options like haircuts, seaweed wraps, and scrubs.

He picked up a paper outlining the services. "You could get a massage or a manicure this week."

"I'm not letting you take a picture of me getting a massage, and I've had manicures. Jordan loves them." She always got a different bright or sparkly color, while I went for a classic light pink.

"Seaweed wrap? No, hot stone massage? That sounds hardcore."

"I'll keep it in mind."

I would not, in fact. Having strangers touch me while I was in any state of undress held no appeal, not even if it relaxed your muscles or helped your pores. Although it was good to know there were options to decrease anxiety if I needed them after a week with Tanner. Besides, I doubted spa rocks were going to convince Caleb I wasn't stuck in my ways.

An open level looking down on the pool had a track that I'd definitely be using and then a cool lounge with windows facing the front of the boat, complete with a library. We peeked in on an arcade and a kids club, and finally, on the top level, found an outdoor movie theater, a basketball court, and a sun deck with lounge chairs.

Tanner plopped into a chair. "Okay, you've walked every inch of the ship. That was more tiring than two-a-days in August with stadium stair runs and pushing Roddy on the sled. I'm starting to suspect you're avoiding the shore excursions." He waved the guide in my face.

"Excuse me for not wanting to get lost. Plus, the use of space is fascinating. Not to mention the buoyancy and the way the ship maneuvers."

"Nerd."

"I'm guessing engineering isn't on your list of possible college majors?"

"Veto. Why, is that what you want to do?"

Images flashed through my mind—me building cool inventions or visiting engineering labs in Mr. Lin's program, me learning to build real rockets, me at NASA—before I shoved them away. "We're not talking about me."

"Fine. Then we're talking adventures. Glacier treks. Canoeing or kayaking. Dogsledding, which is totally happening. Whale watching."

"Panning for gold?"

"Please stop."

"Duck boat?"

"Veto," he said.

"I thought I was the one with veto power."

"As your Fun Coach in charge of making sure you enjoy yourself, I've granted myself that power as well."

"Salmon bake?" I asked, to annoy him. "I've never eaten salmon before."

"Seriously?"

"I'm not an adventurous eater."

"Then we're definitely trying seafood this week. But not for a shore excursion when you could be riding a helicopter over a glacier."

I waited for him to joke about my boring diet or it being no wonder Caleb broke up with me, but he didn't. That put me more on edge, like he was saving up all his mocking to spring on me at once.

"In Ketchikan, you can take a floatplane and see bears," he said.

I shuddered, the spike of fear shooting through me like it always did when I imagined meeting one of those giant creatures in the wild. "We don't have to decide today."

He sighed dramatically and handed me the guide. "Take this. Study it. There will be a test, which I know you enjoy. But you won't ace this test by memorizing options. I'll be grading you on whether you try something fun and different."

I grabbed it from him. "I'll have more fun if you go away."

"Then who would help you prove yourself to Caveman?"

Right. I squeezed the guide. I *would* prove myself.

We retraced our steps to our rooms.

He stopped outside his door. "I'll come collect you for the sail-away party."

"If you must."

"Oh, I must."

At least I'd have time to mentally prepare myself, the way I would have if Caleb had just asked about Manda's party instead of dumping me.

Caleb. I hadn't really done anything new yet today. I needed to find something at the party or after dinner. Everything was fine. I had a plan and a partner, even if he was a dubious one. Things would be back on track soon.

chapter seven

Port of Embarkation: Vancouver, British Columbia

~

Music was playing on the pool deck when the six of us left our rooms to join the fun. I used the term *fun* loosely. The bass vibrated my bones before we even left the interior hall and went outside. Waiters circulated with drinks and appetizers. Dancers in matching polo shirts were leading enthusiastic guests in a dance as a band played.

The horn bellowed, and the ship inched away from the dock. Everyone cheered.

I pushed through the dense crowd so I could watch over the railing. It was impressive how they moved an enormous vessel with such precision. Too bad I couldn't go underwater and see the Azipods. I'd read about the cool underwater thrusters, pods with propellers that could rotate and made it possible to steer the giant ship so accurately. Way more interesting than dancing with strangers.

People on the dock waved at us, and many fellow cruisers waved back.

And okay, I was glad I was there.

The cruise director, a guy with a Scottish accent, was urging everyone to clap along. My parents were enthusiastically joining in. Well, Mom looked enthusiastic. Dad looked reluctant, but he was doing it, if not completely on beat. Apparently they had no problem letting loose in front of coworkers. I would have had to immediately resign, move, and change my name.

Tanner approached, his hands overflowing with appetizers. "Want to try anything?"

When I declined, he ate them all himself.

A conga line was aiming for us, and it suddenly seemed like an excellent time for the TARDIS to appear and carry me away. To the end of the universe, Pompeii five minutes pre-eruption. Anywhere that got me away from conga dancers.

Tanner raised his eyebrows.

"Right behind you," I said.

When he slipped into the line, I melted away.

You'd think he would stop falling for that.

The ship aimed for the suspension bridge we'd driven across the day before. I caught my dad's eye and pointed up, then moved to the highest deck. The music reached from below, and lots of people stood here as well, but it was calmer, and many, like me, were watching the scenery as the city skyline became small blocks behind us.

We sailed toward the point of land where one end of the bridge was anchored. It didn't look like the massive ship would fit underneath. People were staring up at it, taking pictures, so I snapped a few. We went under with plenty of room to spare, but the beam of the bridge so close overhead was cool.

"This is not what I had in mind." Tanner's voice came from behind me.

I didn't bother turning. "No one said you had to keep me company every second."

"Your mom did. She asked where you were and suggested I find you."

"I told my dad I was leaving the party." I was still watching the bridge, only partly paying attention to the conversation.

"What are you doing up here? Oh. You wanted to see the bridge."

How did he know me so well?

We had passed under it, and it was fading behind us, with the city skyline on the horizon. Nothing but ocean waited ahead.

A small tremor shuddered through me at the idea of leaving civilization behind. Vancouver was the largest city we'd see before we flew home to LA in two weeks, and I wasn't ready to contemplate the massive emptiness of what was to come.

I faced Tanner, in need of a distraction so I didn't consider stealing a lifeboat and sailing back to shore. "You gave me homework, so now it's your turn."

He blinked at me.

"Picking a major? The thing you asked me for help with literally yesterday?"

"Oh. Right. I didn't mean it had to be immediate."

"When do you want it to be? After two years of college as an undecided? Which is perfectly acceptable."

"Tell that to my parents," he muttered. Before I had time to process the rare glimpse of anything less than carefree from him, he blinked and shook his head, twinkling eyes in place once more. "Summer homework. Hit me." He spread his arms as if awaiting a physical tackle.

"It's easy, don't worry. I want you to think about which classes you enjoy the most."

"Football?"

I shot him a look. "And what your hobbies are."

"Football?"

I ignored him. "And what interests you."

"Watching f—"

"If you say football one more time, I'm shoving you overboard. Think about it. And maybe stretch first so you don't hurt yourself. I know thinking isn't something you do often."

"It's really not. But for you I'll make the effort."

Why did he need this, anyway? He got disgustingly good grades. Somehow. He had plenty of options. But we weren't friends enough for me to ask. He was helping me, so I'd help him. This arrangement didn't need to get more personal than that.

We ate dinner in the casual dining room, another buffet that offered more dishes than I could count. Tanner once again overloaded his plate with a random assortment of everything. It wasn't Tuesday, but I was happy to find tacos, even if they weren't as good as the ones from the truck at home.

I'd found a paper schedule in our room with the next day's

activities. The list of shore excursions had slightly terrified me, so I'd been looking for activities I could do on the ship that would be new and different. Maybe if I spent a day easing into the challenge, excursions would be less scary. I read the schedule while I ate.

Tanner grabbed it, because asking was apparently too difficult. "What are you thinking about?"

"Pottery painting? Bingo?"

"If we're just intentionally suggesting ridiculous ideas, how about this informational talk? How to Look Ten Years Younger." He flicked my cheek. "You could use that."

"If it was How to Act Ten Years Younger, you could teach it."

"Thanks. Ooh. How to Improve Your Posture." He studied me. "You are rather hunched."

"It's because I'm trying not to be seen with you."

"How to Relieve Back Pain," he said. "I don't need to go to that talk. I know how to do that. I just have to avoid you. Because you're the biggest pain in my back. Side. Get it?"

"No, I need you to explain it to me. What happened to a truce? No fighting?"

"We're not fighting. We're discussing options."

"Insulting me counts as fighting."

"I deserved a free one after you threatened to push me overboard. Now we're even."

Our parents joined us, and we fell silent.

"Did I see you checking out the suspension bridge?" Mr. Woods asked me.

My heart surged. "Yes! It reminded me of the Golden Gate

Bridge, though it's not as long or tall. Suspension bridges are so elegant."

Mrs. Woods smiled. "I love your passion. I wish Tanner would find something like that."

"Oh, but he has football," my mom said. "He's so fun to watch on the field. And all that community service."

I did community service. We were in the same club, and I had beaten him for the club's award. But I helped organize exhibits at the Science Center while Tanner had a Little Bro in a mentoring program, which my mom found sweet. Jordan did the same program, and Mom wished I had joined her.

"Savannah does Math Bowl," Mr. Woods said. "That's impressive. Maybe she can help Tanner with calculus next year. He struggles in math."

I snuck a glance at Tanner, who was stuffing his face. His eyes were blank. Usually I would take this opportunity to talk about my hopes for next year's Math Bowl. Then Tanner would bring up football or discuss the latest social event with my mom. Whether because it now seemed like the over-the-top sucking up that our moms were doing with Mr. Ramirez, or for some mysterious unknown reason, I remained silent.

"How are the girls?" my mom asked.

Mrs. Woods's face brightened. "Charlotte placed second in her last mock trial competition. She's ready for her final year of law school and has her eye on a trial law firm in San Francisco. And Livvy switched her major from marketing to sales and got an internship at a tech company this summer. They're both so driven and determined."

"That's wonderful."

"I can't believe neither of them has been to a football game," Tanner said. "Michigan and U-Dub, and they haven't been once."

"There's more to life than sports, Tanner," his dad said.

"Sure, but everything else is boring."

I tried not to roll my eyes. I had actually wanted to know how his sisters were doing. They'd always been nice to me. Too bad one of them couldn't have been my age. Then our parents being friends might have made us friends, too, and I wouldn't have minded being forced together.

After dessert—a chocolate chip cookie for me while Tanner devoured a cupcake, a dish of chocolate mousse, and three cookies—my mom said, "We thought we'd go to the show tonight."

The big theater we'd seen earlier was now illuminated with flashing spotlights, and Top 40 music was playing. We sat near the back of the lowest level.

The Scottish cruise director, who had changed into a suit since the sail-away party, gave a welcome-aboard message and introduced the entertainers—dancers, singers, a band. Tonight's performance was show tunes from famous musicals.

It was . . . fine. The sets and lighting were professional. The dancers were in sync and had an impressive number of costume changes between songs. I couldn't get out of a sports bra that quickly, and they were donning entirely new outfits. The singers were good—though selfishly I thought Jordan was better. But it wasn't my thing. I'd never understood musicals, despite Jordan's best efforts.

Next to me, Tanner was shifting in his seat.

His elbow nudged mine. After it happened two more times, I looked at him. He was watching me like he'd been waiting. He angled his head toward the back of the theater.

"Let's go," he mouthed, and jerked his head twice, insistent.

Why was he involving me in his delinquency? It couldn't be because he enjoyed my company. Probably because he had to have an audience for everything and was incapable of being alone, and I was the only option.

I eyed my parents and the stage.

Why was I considering this?

Because boring people stayed in theaters when they didn't want to, trapped by the belief that it was the polite thing to do. Caleb would never believe me capable of ditching my family and sneaking out.

I met Tanner's gaze and nodded.

His eyes lit up and he stood, crouching, and edged between knees and seats to exit the row. I tapped my dad's arm and pointed, not waiting for permission, then followed Tanner, hunching and trying to hurry.

People mumbled as we bumped their legs.

"Sorry, sorry," I whispered.

Tanner almost took out a waiter carrying a tray of drinks, spinning around the guy like he would have on the football field. The server didn't say anything—they were probably trained to be polite—but I wouldn't have blamed him for a few choice swear words.

What had I been thinking?

Once we left the dark theater and stood in the brightly lit hall outside, Tanner laughed.

"You did it," he said.

I narrowed my eyes. "Was that some kind of trick? Or a test or something?"

"I was bored. You looked like you were, too. Don't keep doing something you aren't enjoying if there's a way out. There are so many things to do on this ship. A cruise is too short to do anything you don't want to."

"You mean like talk to you?" I asked, but couldn't stop a smile.

"Exactly." He grinned. "Let's find something else."

"Not a fan of musicals?" I asked.

"I don't mind them if there's a whole story, but I don't need to see the songs randomly. Let me guess, you don't like them? Too much spontaneous joy for you?"

I knew he was teasing, but I said vehemently, "It makes no sense. Why are people constantly breaking into song and dance? With perfect choreography and harmonies? And no one around them ever finds it strange? I mean, sure, Jordan sings all the time. But lines here and there, and no one has ever busted into a dance to back her up."

Tanner let out the laugh again, the one that implied he truly found me funny, and my lips curved in response.

We wandered the deck then climbed a level. In the atrium, live piano music floated in the air, and we passed it, heading into a darker area.

It was weird to stroll around with Tanner, not arguing, not even talking. We had a relationship routine—him pestering me to do dumb things, me trying to ignore him, sucking up to each other's parents, comparing our latest accomplishments. But we'd done very little of that today. This trip was disrupting the routine, and it left me flailing, unsure how to act around him outside the security of our familiar interactions.

Also, I couldn't stop eying him. Solely because the polo shirt accentuated his biceps. It would happen with anyone. It didn't mean I found him at all attractive.

Tanner stopped at a set of closed doors, bronze and heavy. Jazz music leaked out, the rise and fall of a trumpet seeping through.

He raised his eyebrows. I shrugged.

He opened a door, motioning me inside. "Ladies first."

"I've always hated that policy. What if the lady doesn't want to go first?"

What if she wanted the guy to enter ahead of her to make sure a bear wasn't waiting? What if she wanted more time to mentally prepare herself or a chance to peek around him to see what was inside, instead of being the first one thrust into a new situation?

His lips quirked. "Fair enough."

He stepped through the doors, leaving a hand on one to hold it for me to follow. I did, entering a dark room. Smoke and lights made a stage glow blue, while shadows blurred the rest of the room. Rounded booths with high backs formed intimate nooks perfect for romantic trysts or Mafia deals. It felt like we'd stepped back in time to a secret Prohibition-era club.

We slipped into an empty booth.

"I feel like a mobster," Tanner whispered.

It was seriously disturbing how often his thoughts echoed mine.

A full band played—trumpet, sax, trombone, piano, drums—and a Black woman in a shimmery dress was singing with a smooth voice. I wished Jordan were here.

The blue glow of the stage was the brightest part of the room. Our booth had one small light that left Tanner's face mostly in shadows.

When a server approached to take our orders, Tanner said, "May I?"

I was so surprised that I nodded without realizing what he meant until he was ordering for both of us.

"We'll have virgin versions of whatever your most popular cocktail is."

After the server left, I stared at him.

"What? I asked if it was okay. If you don't like the drink, I'll have both and you can order a Coke."

"It's fine." The drink hadn't worried me. It was more the whole situation.

He leaned back. "This is cool. I bet Caleb is drinking Mountain Dew and watching the Dodgers. Isn't this more sophisticated?"

"I like the Dodgers."

But I knew what he meant. Which was weird. *Mysterious, grown-up*, and *sophisticated* were not words I'd ever expected to feel while hanging out with Tanner Woods. He was tapping the table with his fingers and bobbing his head in time with the beat. It reminded me of sixth grade, when he'd tried to learn the drums and carried drumsticks around to beat on everything— the dinner table, the car dashboard, my head. This wasn't the usual type of music I heard from him, but he seemed to be enjoying it.

When the server brought our drinks, Tanner took out his phone. "Raise your glass."

I lifted the tall, clear glass filled with ice and pale pink liquid.

We held them up like we were toasting, with the stage in the background, and he snapped a photo.

I sniffed the liquid, curious. Sipped. I didn't know what it was, but it was fizzy and sort of sweet and acceptable. I took another swallow and settled in with my fancy drink to listen to the fancy music. Which was way better than show tunes. Chill and mellow and yet oddly thrilling.

More words I'd never thought I'd associate with Tanner Woods. Life was weird.

But maybe I could handle this *trying new things* goal after all.

chapter Eight

Cruising the Inside Passage

~

Tanner was going to injure a child or an old man, and it was going to be my fault.

It was our first full day at sea, and he'd entered us in a Ping-Pong tournament. The tables were located on the top deck, protected from the wind by a clear barrier but offering expansive views of the sea. It had seemed like a decent way to spend the morning.

Only, I'd had no idea he was a vicious table tennis enthusiast. His serves had fancy spins, he moved so fast I could barely see the ball, and he had no hesitation about hitting it so hard it bounced off the forehead of an old man to win us a point.

"Does the football team play this, too?" I asked.

"Yep. Table in Brady's garage."

The school quarterback. How did Tanner have time for such an active social life?

"Maybe relax a little?" I suggested. "So we don't send anyone to the cruise ship hospital with Ping-Pong ball bruises?"

"It's hard to hide true talent, S'more. And if you're going to play, you should try to win."

"Too bad Ping-Pong isn't a college major."

"It should be. It really should be. Now, you'll improve your serve if you angle the paddle like this." He demonstrated the grip and waited until I mimicked him properly.

Our opponents couldn't return my next serve, and he offered me a paddle high five.

"Nice," he said. "You're not a bad partner."

It was weird being on the same team, rather than competing against him. Like the planet had tilted on its axis or gravity had shifted or the Federation had allied with the Borg.

"Next time, try hitting it harder," he said.

I tried to beam a mental apology to the preteen girl and her dad who were our current victims.

After we beat them, he gave the girl pointers, too.

An hour later, Tanner took a selfie of us holding a small plastic trophy with a gold cruise ship on top.

"I'm not kissing that," I said.

"Hashtag champs."

"I feel myself getting less boring every second."

"Yeah, you do. We should play each other, you know, to determine the champion of champions."

After that display? No chance. I'd learned years ago not to compete against him unless I stood a solid chance of winning. "I'll just let you keep the trophy."

We couldn't post the picture yet, the same way we hadn't been able to post last night, since our parents had colluded to decide they weren't springing for the ship's expensive Wi-Fi. Being so unconnected was weird. What was Jordan doing today? Had she texted? And what about Caleb? Had he seen the pictures from before we'd left? Was he impressed?

"So. Have you decided about tomorrow?" Tanner asked.

I dragged my thoughts away from home and pulled the list from my small backpack. "Maybe zip-lining?"

He leaned in and pretended to inspect my face.

How had I never noticed rings of gold in the middle of his gray eyes? Like sunbursts. I wanted to study them. Wait. I shook myself. This was Tanner.

"Who are you, and what did you do with the real Savannah?" He poked my arm.

I swatted him. Zip-lining had been one of the more manageable options, and it relied on physics. "It sounds fun, right?"

Ugh, it sounded like I needed validation. From *him.*

"Definitely. But I didn't expect you to dive right in on the first day. What about zip-lining plus off-road vehicles?" He pointed to the guide.

That seemed excessive. But the shock on his face had been nice, proving I was capable of surprising him, being more fun than he thought I could be. "Okay."

He blinked at me. "Are you messing with me? You aren't going to back out, like you always do?"

"You're finally learning." I smirked. "I said I'd do new things this week. Go book it before I change my mind, Coach."

He saluted, grinned, and scampered off.

Finally alone, I took a few pictures of the scenery then went to the forward lounge with the large windows. Today the ship was cruising through the Inside Passage, a narrow, protected waterway along the coast of British Columbia, dotted with islands. Our route wound through sounds and twisting channels. Sometimes the passage was narrow, the mountains close on either side.

The water was deep, vivid blue, and bright green trees swathed the hills. Many mountains were capped with snow.

The vast emptiness of it all hit me like a wave. Ocean and mountains stretched as far as I could see, and our ship was the lone beacon of civilization. No cities on the shores, no cell towers in the hills, hardly any other boats.

I was glad for the genius of engineering that offered a sturdy mode of transportation, a way of venturing into beautiful places. But it was unnerving. The sheer scope of nature threatened to overwhelm me. If anything happened here, we were hours from help and had only the ship to rely on.

I loved looking into the expanse of the night sky, the endless stars and galaxies. But I did that from the safety of Earth, knowing those were distant, unreachable. No chance of me getting lost in them.

My dad came up and took a seat next to me. "There you are."

"Where's Mom? Wait, don't answer that."

"Client meetings," he said.

"I hope there are windows so they don't miss the views."

"Yeah," he said. "Have you decided what you want to do this week?"

"Tanner's booking ATVs and zip-lining for tomorrow. I hope that's okay." Most of the excursions required adult supervision for minors, but thankfully our dads had said they were game for whatever.

"Sounds fun." He studied the view. "What prompted this desire to branch out?"

"Thought it was time for something new."

"Does it have anything to do with what happened with Caleb?"

I spun toward him. "What—how?"

I hadn't told my parents the gory details because I hadn't wanted constant questions about how I was feeling, but they'd known something was up when I didn't meet him for our regular Saturday dog-walking.

"I'm your dad," he said. "I know things."

Because he knew me, he didn't ask if I was okay. He understood that I'd tell him if I wanted to talk.

What was Caleb doing today? It was Thursday, which was Science Center day. If I were there, we'd be making sure the exhibits were in order, greeting guests. Not that I wasn't glad to be here, but a small part of me longed for the familiarity of home.

All I had to do was glance at those endless mountains and that drowning feeling threatened to return, everything uncertain and overwhelming.

"How'd Ping-Pong go?" Dad asked.

"We won. Tanner was a little scary."

Dad laughed. "Tanner's a nice kid. I know you don't like him, but I'm glad he's here so you have someone. You might find some things in common."

I snorted. But . . . bowling for trash cans. Ewoks. Mafia deals.

Ridiculous. Those were common thoughts people would have. It didn't mean Tanner and I were on the same wavelength or anything like that.

A guide came in for a nature talk, so we listened as the woman described the Inside Passage, its one-thousand-plus islands, the wildlife we might see. Whales, orcas, sea lions, seals, eagles, caribou . . . those sounded cool. We even saw a couple humpback whales out the window while she was talking. But then of course she had to mention the bears. They were replacing Tanner as my number one nemesis. Temporarily, of course.

When she finished, Dad said, "We're a long way from LA, aren't we?"

"Yeah." My answer came out like a sigh.

"Don't see this view from my desk, that's for sure."

"That's because your office has no windows."

"Harsh, kid."

"You should be with Mom trying to convince Mr. Ramirez to give you a better office."

"Nah, I'm happy. I've been there for twelve years. It would be too much work to move. Plus, that exact cubicle is where I met your mom."

I couldn't argue with liking what you knew.

I watched the mountains. "How'd you pick accounting, anyway?"

"After I started business school, I found I was more into details than networking and the social aspect, the way your mom is. I'd always liked numbers and organizing. It fit. Why? Do you need help figuring out options? You haven't talked much about your plans."

"Just curious," I said.

I hadn't talked about it because I was trying to forget that in one year, life would be changing drastically. I'd decided I liked math, and I liked school, and teaching math seemed like a good career. Helping kids make sense of the universe through the simplicity and steadiness of numbers. I'd made a list of colleges in LA and their application deadlines, and with that done, I could put off thinking about it for now.

But . . . thoughts of Mr. Lin's program intruded. Physics. Engineering. Projects.

No. I wouldn't worry about it now. I hadn't been able to check my email for the details. I had time to decide. And doing the program didn't have to mean altering my plans for the future.

My dad's situation was interesting, though. Even if I came up with a great idea for Tanner that satisfied his parents, he could always change his mind later. It wasn't like he had to know what his whole life would look like, just because I did.

My dad left to check on my mom, and a while later, Tanner found me listening to a podcast and watching the views.

"You can't sit here all day," he said. "Let's do something."

"I am doing something. I'm enjoying nature."

"Enjoying nature doesn't count as something new."

"In Alaska it does. We saw whales."

"You've seen whales. Whale watching is a standard field trip in Southern California."

He had a point. I remembered him spending two straight hours making whale song noises while I tried to help Jordan through seasickness.

"We won a Ping-Pong trophy today," I said.

"You mean *I* won. Pretty much singlehandedly."

Yet another good point.

"There are lots of options," he said. "Come on. I'm bored."

"I'm not your personal entertainment." But I found myself standing and pocketing my earbuds.

"Excellent." He handed me a rumpled daily schedule from his back pocket.

I scanned it. "Afternoon tea?"

"Yawn."

"Pictionary?"

"Are you messing me with me again?"

I totally was. "Dance lessons?"

"Are you sure you can handle this on a dance floor?" He did an exaggerated hip swivel.

"Oh, yeah, good point. It might make me sick."

He snatched the paper. "Nope, too late. You can't take it back. What kind of dance?"

"I don't know. You stole the paper."

"Line dancing? No, that was this morning. Ballroom is starting soon. That sounds . . ." He grimaced.

"New and challenging?" I suggested. If he was stretching my comfort zone this week, it was only fair to return the favor.

I had little desire to learn to ballroom dance. Describing my rhythm as *nonexistent* would've been generous. In the short amount of time we'd spent at junior prom, Caleb and I had watched from the sidelines, and we'd both been fine with it. Or, I had been. I'd thought he was. Now I was trying to remember if he had wanted to dance and I had declined, or if he'd wanted to ask but hadn't bothered because he'd assumed I'd say no.

"Are you going to veto this, Fun Coach? Are you afraid?"

Tanner set his jaw. "No veto needed. I will wow you with my moves."

"I'm sure I will be saying *wow*. Just not the way you think."

We took the stairs—the elevators on this ship took forever—and I asked, "Did you do your homework?"

"You sound like my mom."

"I promised I'd help you, and I keep my word."

He sighed. "Fine. Remind me what it was?"

I inhaled slowly and counted to five. "Subjects you like, hobbies, anything at all that interests you outside of football and tormenting me?"

"Can I major in that? I would ace tormenting you."

"I have no doubt."

"Where do you want to go to college? I'll just apply there."

What game was he playing? Surely he was as eager to escape me as I was him. "I told you this isn't about me. Stop avoiding the question. Favorite class? *Academic* class."

He shrugged.

"What do you do outside of football and tormenting me?"

"Does working out count? Ping-Pong, obviously. Poker. Parties."

He would not make me give up. No matter how hopeless

this seemed, he couldn't be a completely lost cause. "Okay, what class do you hate the least?"

"I liked lit last year. We watched a lot of movies, which meant I didn't have to read the books. Did Jane Austen really have that proud guy climb out of a pond in a wet shirt? Oh, I also liked art. As long as you said you were *feeling the muse*, Ms. Reynolds didn't care if your painting looked like a drunk cat did it or if your ceramic mug leaked coffee all over your shirt."

"We'll come back to this later."

"Good idea. I need to focus now."

"On what?"

"Learning to dance, obviously. So I can be better than you."

I shook my head. The quality of his art didn't surprise me. Neither of us had ever been big on art, music, theater. I'd won honorable mention in an art fair once, and he'd had a single line of dialogue as a spoon in *Beauty and the Beast* while I played a nontalking chair. But mostly it hadn't been worth competing. Sometimes I wondered if he'd given up everything I didn't care about, other than football, because he didn't find it worth the effort if it wasn't something he could beat me at. Sometimes I wondered if I'd done the same thing.

He swept into the main promenade with its gleaming floors and high ceilings. Whose brilliant idea had it been to hold dance lessons in such a public place? This seemed better suited to hidden corners or dark rooms or places with guards outside to keep spectators at bay.

Two people from last night's show were teaching, and the students were all older, including one of Mom's coworkers, who beamed at us.

Tanner, of course, kept going, front and center. I stopped midway back to the side and refused to move, and he looked around until he spotted me. He shook his head and joined me.

"I said I'd try something new, not that I'd do it on center stage," I said.

"Oh, S'more," he sighed my name.

The instructors demonstrated the basic hold and steps of the foxtrot, "a gliding, graceful dance perfect for elegant occasions." Elegant occasions weren't exactly my thing.

I was going to have to partner with Tanner. Everyone was here in couples. Why hadn't this occurred to me before I suggested the lesson?

Around us, hands clasped or slid to their partners' shoulders.

Tanner and I eyed each other. I'd never realized how tall he was. He made me feel short in a way Caleb never had. When he stepped in front of me, his broad shoulders blocked my view of everyone else.

My face got hot. Tanner shuffled his feet. Was he nervous, too? Or hesitant to touch me?

Why did that bother me?

This didn't mean anything. It would be fine.

I tentatively placed a hand on his shoulder. He was wearing a T-shirt and jeans, same as me—not exactly ballroom attire. Through the thin cotton, he was warm, and his muscles were solid. His hand slid to my middle back, and I jumped slightly when his fingers pressed my spine.

Our other hands lifted and started toward each other, but we both hesitated before his fingers closed around mine. He clutched my hand gently, as if it were fragile. I swallowed hard.

The teachers were calling out instructions, reminding us of the steps. I moved back, back, side, as the woman had demonstrated.

I'd half expected Tanner's complaining to be a front to hide secret skills. But he . . . was not that great. He managed the footwork fine, but he wasn't as graceful as I'd feared, with none of the rhythmic hip action our teachers had. It was nice to see him not be awesome at something, but since he didn't care, and since I wasn't any better, there was no point in teasing him.

"Aren't you two precious?" asked Mom's coworker as she and her husband glided past us, far more graceful than we were.

I was going to go hide now. Forever.

We settled into trying for real. *Gliding* and *elegant* were not words to accurately describe either of us, but Tanner's face was set with concentration as he repeated the steps. It was incredibly inconvenient that I found determination an attractive trait.

His arms were strong and secure, like he would hold me up if I needed it. I couldn't meet his eye, instead focusing on his collar when I wasn't watching my feet.

"Chin up," he said.

"I'm trying not to step on your feet."

"They can take it."

I glanced up and found him gazing into my eyes. No. Not gazing. Tanner didn't *gaze* at me. Just watching me.

"Try taking bigger steps."

"Now you're an expert? Says the guy whose hip swivel looks like you're having a chiropractic adjustment?"

His lips quirked. "Excuse me. Not having natural rhythm doesn't mean I can't grasp the steps."

He had a point. I complied, and we moved easier.

Every millimeter of where his fingers pressed my back tingled. His hand was warm and solid on mine.

We bumped into each other, thighs and knees knocking. A few steps later, we ran into another couple.

"You're supposed to let me lead," Tanner murmured after we apologized.

"Why, because you're the guy?"

"Well, yeah."

"Why can't I lead?"

"You can if you want."

I tried to reverse what we'd been doing, go forward instead of backward and steer him at the same time. I ended up planting my nose into his firm chest.

"Ow." I took my hand from his long enough to rub my nose.

He snorted. "May I?"

"Fine."

The male instructor came up beside us. "This isn't a competition. You're a team. You need to work together, not fight each other."

Fighting was our natural state.

But Ping-Pong had worked out. Surely we could manage to be partners for a bit longer.

"Now, feel the music." The instructor placed his hands on our shoulders to guide us.

I listened for the beat, and we began again. This time, I tried to relax my arms and shoulders and let Tanner steer.

He might not have had a dancer's grace, but he remembered instructions, mimicked the steps, and soon we were, if not gliding, at least not bumbling across the room.

"We won't be winning any trophies for this," he said once we'd gotten into rhythm. His voice was light.

"That doesn't bother you?"

"Why would it?"

"I thought you always had to be the best."

"I like to be good at the things I care about, but I also like to have fun. There's no reason you can't do something you enjoy, for fun, without having to win."

Huh.

"Does it bother you?" he asked. "I mean, I know it bothers you that I'm better than you, but in general?" The words were teasing, and I shook my head and smiled.

Nah," I said. "I want to set a record at the two-mile or the pole vault, or win the Math Bowl, but I'm also fine doing something just because it's fun."

"Like what? What's fun?"

He seemed to genuinely want to know, and it wasn't like he hadn't heard most of this through our moms, anyway. Still, it felt weird having a normal conversation with him while we were inches apart and moving across the dance floor.

"I like watching sci-fi shows. Building stuff. Podcasts. Looking at the stars." *Astronomy Club.* But I wouldn't say it and give him the chance to gloat. Our temporary partnership hadn't erased his theft of my presidency.

"Ha," he said. "I knew you still did LEGOs."

I twitched a shoulder. "It helps relax me. Gives me something to focus on."

We attempted the spin they'd shown us, and I managed not to break my nose again.

"You didn't ask me what I find fun," he said.

"You already told me."

"It's called being friendly, S'more. Is it so hard to make pleasant conversation?"

"Let me guess, football?"

"Obviously. But also watching with people. I like cheering in a group."

"And Ping-Pong and poker," I added. "No matter what you just said, I'm sensing a theme of games you can win."

His hand shifted on mine, fingers readjusting until he held it more securely. My hand felt tiny, enveloped by his, and the contact was sending waves of not-unpleasant shivers up my arm. "I guess so. I do like games. But I like them *with* people, when you're talking and teasing each other and laughing and there's food. Oh, food, for sure. And stars, obviously. I love outer space."

"Uh-huh. Right."

He meant taking over the club, but we'd had a decent conversation, and it helped me understand him a little more, so I didn't argue. He did like games, and he was competitive, but mostly he liked to have fun with people. Somehow, it was something I'd known but never really understood before this moment.

He paused and took out his phone. "Can you take a picture of us?" he asked a lady nearby.

She raised the phone, and he resumed our pose, but right as

she said, "Smile," Tanner dipped me backward. His arms were so secure, I never even considered he might drop me.

When he pulled me up, I was out of breath. I took a second to straighten my shirt to hide it.

He showed me the photo. My long ponytail brushed the floor, and I was mid-laugh because he'd surprised me. The muscles in his arms were obvious as he held me tightly.

It made a strange warmth pool in my chest, and I didn't want to dwell on what it might mean.

I also wasn't sure I wanted him to post that one.

Chapter Nine

Cruising the Inside Passage

~

We returned to our rooms to change for the ship's first formal night. Dad wore the same suit he'd worn to every event for the last five years—he claimed if you bought something classic, you only needed one. Mom wore a nice dress, and I put on a short, floaty green dress, one of the new outfits Jordan had helped me pick out after declaring my wardrobe not spectacular enough for a cruise. I added low heels and makeup.

When we stepped into the hall, Tanner and his parents were waiting.

His attention leaped to me, and he blinked twice. "You don't look half bad, S'more."

"Touching, really. You know how to make a girl feel special." I switched to my sweetest voice. "Tanner, you look very handsome tonight."

"I know."

The annoying thing was, he did. His gray button-down shirt, undone at the top with no tie, brought out his eyes, and the blue suit jacket accentuated his broad shoulders. My fingers flexed subconsciously, as if they remembered touching him. No. I would not let the dance change anything between us. It meant nothing that we'd worked together today more than once, that by the end we'd been moving in sync and had conversed like normal people, or something like friends.

Our parents headed down the hall, and we trailed more slowly.

"Is that outfit from the banquet?" I asked.

"Yep. The one where you insisted on cutting the worst plays of the year from the commemorative video."

"We were there to celebrate, not laugh at each other. And I think you mean the one where half the crowd spilled salsa on their outfits because you changed the caterer, and the new one brought *paper plates*."

He waved a hand. "Agree to disagree."

At our school, individual teams had end-of-season dinners to give out awards, but we also had one large banquet for all the sports. Tanner and I had represented football and track on the planning committee. Within an hour at the first meeting, the rest of the committee had been desperately wishing our teams had chosen other representatives.

"What award did you win?" he asked. "Most extra miles run? Most time practicing?"

"Most Consistent," I admitted.

He grinned. "I knew it."

Because it implied I was also the most boring? The one who worked hard every single day, never took a break?

"You got the leadership award, right?" I asked.

"Much to my parents' surprise." His voice was light, but when I glanced at him, a muscle was twitching in his jaw.

It was less satisfying when I wasn't the one who'd made it happen.

When his name had been called for that award, my surprise had lasted only seconds. I didn't even like him, and I saw the way others followed him. How had his parents missed that? And this was yet another hint that his parent situation was awkward. It almost made me feel bad for my attempts to make them like me over the years. Almost.

On the way to the dining room, Tanner stopped at a door to the outside deck and opened it. The ship was still in the Inside Passage, and the sun was up but getting lower. Gentle evening light bathed the nearby mountains in shadows.

"You need a picture," he said. "Stand at the rail."

I posed and let him take a photo.

"Caleb will regret that breakup as soon as he sees this." Tanner shook his phone. "I'm going to have lots to post once we escape this internet desert. Our parents don't realize how cruel it is. I've probably missed hundreds of texts in the football group."

"It must be hard, being so popular."

"It's a curse, S'more, but one I must endure." He opened the door for me, and I went inside. "You could be, too."

"What, popular? Yeah, right."

"Why not?"

"Because I lead the math club and like science fiction shows and LEGOs."

"You're saying science isn't cool?"

"I think it is."

He stopped, so I did, too, and we faced each other in the hall. "That's what matters. Owning what you love is cool, no matter what it is."

Easy for the football player to say. "It's fine. If I were popular, I'd have to go to parties. Although that would make my mom happy."

"You can join me anytime you want."

"My mom would also like that. She was a social butterfly when she was in school and believes I'm missing out."

"Do *you* think you're missing out?"

"Nope."

"Will you think you missed out when you're, like, old and reflecting on life?"

His direct attention was making the temperature rise. "No, I don't think so."

"Then who cares?"

His concentrated gaze lingered another few heartbeats before he moved on, leaving that simple statement in his wake.

I was happy with my life—other than the uncertainty of next year, with the possibility that Caleb wouldn't be in it. I didn't bother considering how things could be different, not even when my mom urged me to be more of a joiner. But I wouldn't have expected someone like Tanner, who was the actual definition of joiner, to believe a science nerd was capable of being cool.

The main dining room was huge, packed with two levels of tables covered in white linens, with gleaming wood and golden light. A chandelier glimmered overhead, and servers dressed in black carried huge trays of dishes or bottles of wine. Windows offered views of the ocean and mountains. The clinking of glasses and silverware, the hum of conversation, and faint music drifted in the air.

We were escorted to a table by the window. My parents sat on one side, Tanner's on the other across from them, leaving the two end seats for Tanner and me.

It felt like a double date and we were interlopers, tacked on like an afterthought.

Or like a triple date, which was even worse.

When the server handed me a menu, I lost my appetite.

Duck. Lamb. Pasta with mussels. Escargot.

Were these foods that people actually ate, or was this a list of animals I could see at the cruise ship zoo? I half expected to find giraffe or penguin on the menu.

"What's polenta?" I asked.

"Ooh," Tanner said. "No idea, but this is perfect. You can try a bunch of new things. Want to start with snails?"

My stomach jolted. I sipped my water and eyed the path to the door, estimating how many tables I'd have to dodge if I made a run for it. There was a pizza place on the pool deck.

"How about capers?" Tanner asked. "I have no idea what they are, either, but they sound fun. Or calamari? It's fried, and everything is good when it's fried. I'll happily sample everything first, if you want. Like a poison tester."

"I'll just get chicken."

"What? No. You can get that anywhere." Tanner sounded personally injured, as if my food choice was physically wounding him. "Where else can you try fancy foods so easily? Dottie said if you don't like it, you can order something else. I'm getting, like, three different dishes."

"Good for you. You do that. While I enjoy my chicken."

"You're honestly using a veto on dinner?"

"I told you, I'm not an adventurous eater. And I'm not wasting a bunch of food."

"One thing?"

"Why do you care so much? Just leave it, okay?"

I spoke louder than I meant to, my voice ringing out. Our parents fell silent and turned our way. Heat rushed to my face, and I focused on buttering my roll, mumbling, "Sorry."

"She gets mad when you try to take her bread," Tanner said lightly.

When the waiter brought Tanner's escargot appetizer, the sight made me ill. It came in a round dish with little indentations full of brown globs in yellow liquid.

I focused on my salad instead.

Tanner waved a miniature spoon under my nose, giving me a glimpse of a round blob that resembled an eyeball. "Want to try one?"

"Do you want me to puke in your lap?"

"Yes, that's always been my greatest dream. Come on, they mostly taste like slimy balls of butter."

I swallowed a gag. "That really sells it. It's disgusting."

He made a slurping noise as he ate it. When he finished, he tried to scoop up another, but it escaped his spoon and rolled across the table, leaving a greasy trail on the white table-cloth. Tanner reached for it, trying to grab it with his bare hand.

"We got a runaway," he said. "These guys move faster dead than they do alive."

He made one final grab before the snail plummeted to its doom on the carpet. A second later, there was a squelching noise as a waiter stepped on it. He slipped and barely righted a tray full of plates.

Tanner laughed loudly.

"Grow up, Tanner." I sounded mean, but I didn't care.

"You grow up. Want me to order chicken nuggets for you? Applesauce? Maybe chocolate milk and Goldfish? Excuse me for trying to help."

"Will you two please behave yourselves?" My mom hissed the words.

"Sorry, Mrs. Moore." Tanner leaned away from me, and I tried to ignore the buttery trail the escaped snail had left across the white tablecloth. "Savannah and I were debating the origins of escargot. And one got away."

He carefully scooped the last one from the dish and held it toward me, as if daring me now that everyone was watching.

He could dare me in front of Caleb, and even if it would prevent me from getting dumped all over again, I was not letting that thing near my mouth.

I pressed my lips together and glared at him. We were like

Old West gunfighters in a standoff. My weapon was laser eyes, and his was a greasy, dead snail in a spoon.

He shrugged and popped it into his mouth, but somehow, I didn't feel like I'd won.

Once the waiter arrived with the main course and settled the plates, Tanner ducked his head slightly. "I'm sorry, S'more."

"What?"

He didn't pick up his fork. "I told you that you had veto power and I wouldn't make you do anything. I shouldn't have pushed."

I blinked at him. His apology had broken my brain so the words that came out were "I'm sorry if I insulted your snail."

His lips twitched. So did mine.

"He was very offended," Tanner said, "but I won't make you apologize. This time."

Soon we were both cracking up. His laugh was loud and free and joyful, making his eyes crinkle at the corners. Our gazes met, and his joy was contagious, filling me with light like a star being birthed inside my chest.

When he finally stopped laughing, he said, "If you want Goldfish and applesauce, that's fine."

"Thank you. See, I do eat seafood."

He grinned and shook his head.

"I might have brought some for a snack this week . . . ," I admitted.

"You brought food to a ship with literally thousands of pounds of it?"

"In case all they had here was snails."

"I know where to come if the midnight buffet runs out of food."

"I'll have nice fish-shaped orange crackers waiting for you."

I ate my chicken breast and tried not to glance at Tanner's meal, which was also some kind of bird, except one with bones sticking out of it in a way that looked more artistic than anatomically correct.

Tanner was wrestling with it. "I possibly overestimated how meaty this guy would be. But quail sounded fun."

He waved down the waiter, gave the man a charming smile, and requested a steak. The waiter was happy to comply, but Mr. and Mrs. Woods sighed.

"What?" he asked. "The bird was tiny. I need lots of calories, and that did not have enough protein."

"The steak is excellent," my dad said. "Let the boy eat. We're in no rush."

Even if we had been, it wouldn't have been a problem, with how quickly Tanner devoured the meat. Plus the dish on the side, which they called polenta but resembled gritty mashed potatoes.

He waved a fork in my face. "Want to try it? It's the least threatening new food on the menu."

"I'll pass."

"Ping-Pong and chicken. You're rocking this goal to try new things."

"I learned to dance."

"I don't know if what either of us did could truly be considered dancing."

Fair point. "It's the first day. I'm easing into it."

"Fine. But I hope you're ready for tomorrow."

"I am."

Surely the shore excursion would be an easier step forward than eating those snails. As long as I didn't get eaten by a bear.

After dessert, we went to the theater for tonight's show, which was a magician. I ended up seated next to Tanner again, three rows from the stage.

A man came onstage to an introduction of smoke, dramatic music, and flashing laser lights, like how eighties movies imagined futuristic nightclubs would be. He wore all black, including a leather jacket and a shirt unbuttoned at the top, and carried a bowling ball. Without speaking, he did a trick and made the ball vanish under a thin scarf, and okay, it was impressive.

After the audience had finished applauding, he moved to the front of the stage and introduced himself as Giovanni, an illusionist and enchanter, not a magician, while images of flames and smoke played on the screen behind him.

He did tricks with metal hoops and scarves before saying, "Now, I need two volunteers from the audience."

Tanner leaned into me. "Are you afraid of public speaking?"

"No. Why?"

"You, sir." Giovanni pointed to a middle-aged Asian man.

Tanner grabbed my hand and lifted my arm. I started to pull free.

"New things, S'more."

Oh fine. I wouldn't get picked, anyway. And if I fought him, Tanner might think I was afraid. I let him keep my hand up. But then Tanner made it wave overhead and used his free hand to point to me dramatically.

"What are you doing?" I hissed.

He grinned. "Helping."

"And this young lady up front."

Before I knew it, I was standing on the massive stage in front of hundreds of people with Giovanni the Illusionist-Not-Magician.

chapter ten

Cruising the Inside Passage

~

I was going to kill Tanner.

Assuming I didn't die of embarrassment first.

I was standing in front of hundreds of people, wishing I'd worn a longer dress. The outfit had seemed fine until I knew everyone was looking at my long legs, and now I was certain this garment had been designed for someone three inches shorter and why did fashion designers hate tall girls?

The other volunteer was waving to his family, who waved back enthusiastically.

My parents, and Tanner's, were grinning like mad, looking as proud as if I'd discovered a new planet or set a world track record.

Special effects smoke drifted across the stage. It felt like every set of eyes in the room had laser vision. It was so hot. Were those normal stage lights or broilers? They were roasting me like those snails, in sweat instead of butter.

Why had I let Tanner volunteer me? I could have refused.

I didn't fear public speaking when it was something like a class presentation, a factual one that I'd studied for. But I had a recurring nightmare of being in front of an audience and I was supposed to talk, except my note cards were blank, I didn't remember my topic, and I was wearing my Baby Yoda pajamas.

Despite the earlier suggestion to Tanner, I hated Pictionary. And charades and any game where I was in front of people unprepared. As a kid, if someone even mentioned those at a party, I'd hidden in the bathroom. Here, I was unprepared, with no idea what this magician guy was going to ask me to do. I definitely wasn't letting him lock me in anything tight and dark. Or come near me with a saw. Did magicians still do that?

Tanner had his phone camera aimed at me. He shot me a thumbs-up. I fought the urge to flash him a different finger and set my jaw instead. This was marginally better than escargot, so I would prove to him that I was fine with it. Plus, if he filmed me, Caleb could see me being confident and cool onstage.

Well, as cool as you could be with a magician on a cruise ship.

Come to think of it, I didn't know how much this would actually help.

"Go, Savannah," Tanner yelled, and a few people—I was assuming my parents and their coworkers, but given the amount of alcohol being distributed, it could have been anyone—whooped.

Giovanni moved to my side. "I was going to ask our volunteers to introduce themselves, but I'm guessing you're Savannah."

"That's me."

"Where are you from, Savannah? Georgia?"

I forced a smile. I'd heard that one from Tanner, too. Along with Havana. And Montana. Did I mention he was fond of rhyming? "Los Angeles."

"City of Angels! Excellent. And what about you, sir?"

While the magician learned Gary was from Portland, I glared at Tanner, who mouthed "Smile," because a guy telling a girl to do that was guaranteed to end well.

"Are you ready?" Giovanni asked.

The lights dimmed. Dramatic music swelled again, accompanied by flashing lights.

That was a dumb question. Ready for what? How could a person possibly be ready when they had no idea what was about to happen? This guy needed a contract, laying out what was expected of us. Surely this wasn't legal. I was a minor.

Giovanni picked up a top hat from the table, put it on his head, then let Gary examine it. He waved it around, then suddenly he was holding a fluffy white rabbit. Everyone clapped, and he gave the animal to Gary.

Okay, fine, I could handle bunnies.

Giovanni peered inside the hat, let me look. Then waved his hand, and this time he was holding a dove. He handed the bird to me. I cradled it between my palms. Its body was warm, the feathers soft and gray. It studied me with a beady eye.

The crowd cheered again.

Even being this close and knowing there was a logical explanation for his illusion, I had no idea where these creatures had come from. The dimensions of that hat did not allow for concealed animals.

"Shall I make them vanish?" Giovanni asked the audience, who yelled, "Yes!"

The dove squirmed. I tried to hold it tight enough that it couldn't escape but not so tight that I hurt it and it ended up on someone's dinner plate. Something was freaking it out, though. Wings fluttered against the cage of my hands. A pointy beak bit into my finger. I flinched.

Before I knew it, the dove was shooting out of my hands and fluttering across the stage.

Now I knew where the bird came from. Clearly it had emerged from a portal to an alternate dimension full of demons that Giovanni the Enchanter-Illusionist had sold his soul to access.

My heart was racing, but I couldn't move. Should I move? Chase it?

The bird's wings must have been partially clipped, because it wasn't fully flying, but it managed to get semi-airborne. The creature was a gray blur, aiming for the edge of the stage. Then it flapped into the audience. I stared after it. My gaze found Tanner's, wide-eyed and stunned. He jumped out of his seat.

With another flutter of wings, the bird aimed for Mr. Ramirez in the row in front of my parents. The demon bird landed on his head.

Tanner clambered past our moms, leaped over the row of seats between two people, to the row where Mr. Ramirez sat. He lunged for the bird, nearly tackling Mr. Ramirez like he was an opposing linebacker.

As the bird fluttered up again, it left a bright white trail on the shoulder of Mr. Ramirez's black suit, and its wings mussed his dark hair. Tanner's hands closed around the bird as surely as they caught footballs. He was practically in Mr. Ramirez's lap.

Mom and Mrs. Woods could kiss that promotion goodbye.

I was still on the stage, under the bright, hot lights, unmoving. Were people staring at me or watching Tanner? He clutched the bird against him. It was perfectly calm now. Traitor.

Tanner climbed on stage and lifted his hands, which held the bird. The audience cheered.

"I guess this guy didn't want to go back into the hat," he said. "I can't blame him. It's dark in there."

The people in the first few rows who could hear him laughed.

"Should I stay?" he asked me, quieter. "To help?"

"As long as that bird goes away, stay as long as you want," I muttered.

The magician approached to take the bird from Tanner. "Thank you, young hero. This little lady has had enough excitement."

Based on the tender look he gave the dove, he meant it, not me. He shot *me* an evil glare, like it was my fault his demon bird had bit me. Dude, try pet training classes, or exorcisms, instead of inflicting underfed, feathered monsters on innocent teenage girls.

Tanner bowed, took my hand, and stepped out as if to display me.

My face was on fire.

"Bow," Tanner murmured.

I bent over partway, to more cheering, and let Tanner lead me off the stage. He kept my hand until we reached our seats.

My stomach churned as if I had eaten those snails. Or Tanner's bird, which had been about the size of that dove. And now I really wanted to puke.

His hand brushed my arm, so lightly I might have imagined it. "Breathe, S'more. It's over."

I focused on inhaling and exhaling slowly. My face went from surface of the sun to, like, Mercury, and eventually cooled to Sahara Desert. I barely paid attention to the rest of the show or the magician, who kept giving me dirty looks, which I returned.

"I don't think he's all that enchanting," Tanner muttered. "And his jacket is ugly."

I snorted.

After a few minutes of watching in silence, an imaginary bird fluttering around inside my chest, I murmured, "Thank you."

A brief bob of his head was the only indication he'd heard me.

I woke the next morning to my face. On the room's television. The Cruise News morning show was playing, with updates from around the ship and information on today's port, Ketchikan. And the current clip was from the magic show the night before, of me onstage in all my short-skirt glory, as frozen and grotesque as Han in carbonite. The camera followed the escaped bird, showed Tanner chasing it. Captured it pooping on Mr. Ramirez, and Tanner triumphantly catching it and marching to the stage, us taking bows, and him freeing me like he was my Leia.

It was horrifying, and yet I watched until the end.

"Make it stop," I said, and buried my face under my pillow.

"Oh good, you're awake," Mom said. "Breakfast is here."

"I'm too sick to eat when my face is on there." My voice came out muffled by the pillow. "Please tell me this is a special channel just for our room, and that two thousand guests are not currently watching a replay of last night."

"I'm sure all two thousand passengers don't use their televisions," Mom said.

"And some are still sleeping," Dad added.

"Ugh. Please make it go away."

The room went silent and I removed the pillow from over my face. This was all Tanner's fault.

Room service breakfast awaited so we could get off the ship nice and early for the day's tour. Mom and Dad had ordered my usual toast, yogurt, and banana. Bless the cruise ship for having normal yogurt brands.

The open curtains revealed the view. It was early morning, and dark green hills were visible. Too bad I'd missed the captain navigating this massive ship into port without crashing. It would have been interesting to see. I needed to check the schedule for the next day and make sure to wake up in time.

I folded up my couch bed so we had more room to eat, and we removed silver domes from plates of eggs, bacon, and my toast and banana.

I spun my phone on the table next to my plate.

My mom eyed it.

"Grades are being posted later today," I said.

I was glad we'd be on shore to have internet. I wasn't nervous. I'd done well on finals, after studying with Caleb. I was mostly looking forward to comparing my grades to Tanner's and hopefully beating him.

"You know they'll be good," Mom said. "You should wait until we get home to check. Don't worry about it on vacation."

Like that was going to happen.

I loved her. She was seriously a great mom, and she'd been my rock through the madness that was my bio dad. She'd always done her best to stick to schedules I liked and make me feel safe and give me alone time. And I hadn't known until I was older how hard she'd fought to get full custody.

But some days I wondered how it was possible that we were related.

I exchanged an understanding look with my dad. He would also want to know as soon as possible and would have helped me sneak Wi-Fi access if today had been a sea day.

After eating and dressing, Dad and I assembled in the theater to await our tour. Mom and Mrs. Woods were planning to walk around town.

As we found seats, someone called out, "Hey, it's Pigeon Girl."

"Yeah, I saw you on TV," said another person.

"You were hilarious," said the first.

"I think it was a dove."

"What?"

"Not a pigeon. A dove."

"Fine, Bird Girl."

"Where's Bird Boy?"

"Do you know him? Are you dating?"

"That was so funny."

I slumped into a seat. Returning to the scene of the crime bright and early the next day hadn't been the best idea. Was Mr. Ramirez here? He'd been incredibly chill about the incident, waving off my many apologies after the show. But should I have offered to dry-clean that suit? Did cruise laundry cover magic show mishaps?

And why did strangers keep assuming Tanner and I were together?

Someone settled into the seat beside me.

"We're famous" was how Tanner greeted me.

I could pretend he didn't exist. That usually made him try harder to get my attention, but today, that might be good. If he was doing something ridiculous, people could talk about him instead of me. He probably loved videos of him playing on every screen in the entire ship.

He waved at the people who pointed at him, accepted fist bumps from some who passed our row.

"Come on, S'more. This is fun. We made people laugh. Isn't that a good feeling?"

"Yeah, laugh at my misfortune."

"Nah, at the situation. It was funny. They're not mocking you. No one blames you."

"The magician did."

"Then he shouldn't have given you a bird that was going to

fly away. Forget him and focus on the fact that we brought people joy on their vacation."

It was an interesting perspective. I'd always thought he did stunts because he liked the attention, but what if there was more to it than that?

"Aw, is that your boyfriend?" asked a woman passing by. "He saved you. It's so sweet."

"I did save you," Tanner said, pretending to prop his chin on his fist as he smiled at me.

"You were also the one who volunteered me in the first place, so . . ."

The lady beamed, and Tanner chuckled.

A woman down front was calling groups one at a time. I simultaneously wanted to get to our number so we could leave and for her never to get there. No. That was wrong. I was maybe a teeny-tiny bit excited about our excursion. The excitement was just mixed with nerves, a churning soup inside me.

Why couldn't I be happy about a day on shore, like everyone else?

Oh. Right. Because I had decided to announce a not-fully-formed plan to my nemesis, which had led to me signing up for something I hadn't had a chance to research. Without proper research, you ended up believing the Earth was the center of the universe or yetis lived on Mars or Twinkies remained edible for decades.

When our number was called, we joined a line of people waiting to get off the ship, scanned our cards, and followed signs to our bus.

A cute town nestled at the base of the incredibly green

mountains. An arching sign welcomed us to Ketchikan, Alaska's first city. Other than the paved road and cars, it didn't appear to have changed much since it was founded. Colorful wooden buildings made it feel like a frontier outpost, barely holding their own against the tree-covered hills.

Even though the ship was so large, it was nice to be on land again and to see real buildings and civilization, no matter how small.

Our bus held about twenty people. I took a window seat and pulled my dad into the one beside me, hoping he'd hide me from anyone else who might view my aviary misfortune as worthy of celebrating.

I buried myself in my phone. It was too early for grades, so I read Jordan's messages and updates on her first day at work, during which she had met one boy who wouldn't stop singing *Frozen* songs and a girl who knew way too many rap lyrics and had been dropped off by a cute older brother. Then I posted my photos from the last few days. I shared the drink picture without tagging Tanner. Let people wonder who I was hanging out with in fancy music clubs. Maybe Caleb would see and wish it was him.

My phone chimed. Tanner had posted the Ping-Pong photo, tagging me. Hashtag champs.

Why was he so chill about letting everyone know he was hanging out with Moore the Bore?

I selected a few more to make the week look amazing—views from the Inside Passage, me in the fancy dress. If Tanner posted anything from the magician show, I would set a flock of rabid doves loose on him. They could be trained to attack, right? Pigeons delivered messages. Surely attack doves were possible.

He did tag me again, but it was the dancing picture. The first time I'd seen it, I hadn't noticed Tanner's face, but it drew my attention now. He was smiling down at me, a genuine grin with no hint of the slyness he usually wore when teasing me. The smile was like a shot of pure light and seared through my chest.

I hurried to click away.

To find an email from Mr. Lin, which sent a different tremor through me. He'd given me a link and an attachment with details about the physics and engineering program. I wasn't sure I wanted to read it. I had enough new things to worry about today. But curiosity won.

The brochure included a list of facilities the group would tour. The names sent my heart skyrocketing. Top physics labs, engineering companies, NASA. A list of potential speakers for online seminars further increased my pulse. Bridge- and rocket-building competitions. Online discussion groups.

Despite the thrill stirring inside me, my hands shook. Multiple weekend trips in states I'd never considered visiting, a week in Boston, extra assignments that sounded intriguing but time-consuming. What would I miss or have to give up?

Eyes lingering on a spring visit to Houston, I closed the email. I'd think about it later.

Chapter Eleven

Port of Call: Ketchikan, Alaska

~

The math was not in my favor. Pictures posted, I'd done a search to prepare for today's excursion. Apparently the off-road vehicles traveled at twenty-five or thirty miles per hour.

Bears could top out at thirty-five.

It was like a problem at a beginner Math Bowl competition. If the ATV leaves Point A at noon, and the bear who hasn't eaten in weeks leaves Point B at 12:15, how long until the ATV driver becomes lunch?

Nothing like jumping into the deep end of new things.

The sky was gray and drizzly as the bus took us through town. Mountains and trees quickly replaced buildings, and the guide talked about Ketchikan's history. It had the world's largest collection of totem poles and was considered one of the rainiest cities in America, which explained why everything was so green.

The bus took us to a base camp in the woods, with a single

wooden building that resembled a place a prepper might live. I knew where to come in the event of alien invasion or zombie apocalypse. Unless they were zombie bears.

Great. *Thanks for that mental image, brain.*

Rows of off-road vehicles waited, like a cross between old-fashioned buggies and golf carts, but with heavy-duty tires. Or like something you'd drive on the moon. We exited the bus to a misty sky.

Tanner rubbed his hands together. "I can't wait to drive one of those."

We'd picked this excursion because as long as you were sixteen with a valid license, you were allowed to drive.

I raised my eyebrows.

"What?" he asked. "I'm a good driver."

"I know a trash can that disagrees."

"That was in a golf cart. And I was twelve."

"Not helping your case. Have you ever had a ticket? Or an accident?"

"Does the time I hit a preschool bus count?" he asked.

My head whipped toward him.

He was laughing. "Kidding. Other than the golf cart, I've never caused an accident."

"Caused? Oh, that's right. Last year with the guy at the stop sign." I remembered he'd been worried he would miss the first football game.

"Aw, S'more. I didn't know you cared."

Caring had nothing to do with it. I couldn't escape learning every detail of his life. "My mom was worried for you."

"You can admit you were, too. It was very motivating to make me want to drive safely. The attention was nice, though. I had freshmen guys carrying my stuff and bringing me lunch for two weeks."

"Of course you did. I notice you avoided the question of a ticket."

"Nope. Almost got one for parking in a loading zone, but I came out in time to talk the cop into giving me a warning instead. Good thing you weren't there to report me." He poked my arm. "I don't need to ask about your driving record. I'm sure it's spotless."

We went inside the prepper structure and found benches, rain gear, and a gift shop rather than shelves of ammo, canned beans, and SPAM. After a safety briefing, the staff handed out bright yellow rain suits, gloves, and helmets with clear face plates. I tugged the pants on over my jeans. They were big, with suspenders, and I fumbled with the straps before turning to my dad.

"Can you help?"

But it wasn't my dad standing behind me. It was Tanner.

He stepped right in front of me, reminding me again how tall he was. His hands closed around the straps, wiggling the buckles to shorten my suspenders. His fingers brushed my collarbone, and his breath whispered against my forehead.

I froze. Why wasn't he saying anything? And why was he being so nice?

He wiggled the suspenders gently. "Good?"

I nodded.

He stepped back and watched as I put the jacket on over the

pants, struggling with the stiff fabric. His eyes were charcoal, his face solemn, and his attention was making me forget how to use my fingers.

"What?" I asked.

"I'm debating."

My stomach squirmed. "Debating what?"

"Whether the outfits are unsexy enough that I shouldn't take your picture, or whether they show we're about to do something hard-core enough that the rain suit is needed, and therefore the sheer awesomeness makes up for the ugliness. Of the outfits. Not you."

Why had he added that? So casually, like complimenting me came naturally. Well, not complimenting, exactly. But not insulting, either.

"It's the second," he announced as he lifted his phone. "Smile."

I posed, hands on my hips to show off the rain outfit, and he took a picture, and then we went outside, where he took another, this time of the two of us next to a car. We weren't standing particularly close, no touching shoulders or anything, but weird energy bounded around in my stomach.

Each vehicle seated two people. I had planned to go with my dad but for some reason, Tanner stayed by my side. My dad raised his eyebrows. I shrugged, and he flashed me a thumbs-up and joined Mr. Woods.

"Why don't bears eat fast food?" Mr. Woods asked. "Because they can't catch it."

"I have one," my dad said. "What does a bear call a driver who runs out of gas? ATV dinner."

That one made Tanner snort, but most of my attention was on the vehicles, not the bad jokes.

"I want to drive first," I said.

Tanner spun toward me. "Really? What about not liking *ladies first*?"

"Only applies when the lady isn't volunteering. Or you could, you know, go with your dad."

It sounded better to be the one in control than to be at Tanner's mercy, no matter what claims he made about his driving history.

"Not getting rid of me that easily, S'more. I'll take a video while we're cruising through the backwoods of Alaska."

"I'm pretty sure there's a path."

"Nope, I'm certain we're making our own trail where no one has ever been before."

"Oh, you know what, you're right. I did see that in the description. In two hours, with cars full of small children, we're going to become true pioneers. Hope you brought a machete."

"Sadly, Canada wouldn't let me bring it through customs."

"Stupid Canada."

It was nice to have someone who caught my sarcasm. Caleb would have taken me seriously and double-checked the tour description.

We climbed into a vehicle near the back of the line, and I fiddled with the fancy seatbelt harness that made me imagine I was traveling to space. One by one the buggies pulled away, falling into line. I started the engine.

When it was our turn, I pushed the gas pedal. We didn't move.

"Are you caressing it?" Tanner asked. "Stomp that sucker."

I pressed harder, and we lurched forward. My stomach remained behind. I immediately removed my foot, and we jolted to a stop.

It happened two more times.

I hoped Alaska had good health care, because I was going to give us whiplash.

"Savannah." Tanner turned my name into a sigh, and hearing him say my full name was odd. "I would like to see more of Alaska than this parking lot. And the people behind us are about to get road rage."

"All right, all right."

I pressed the gas again, and when we hurtled forward, I kept my foot down despite my brain screaming at me to stop.

The buggy bumped across the dirt lot. Ahead of us, the other vehicles were nearly out of sight. My heart was racing, but I made myself keep up. The ride was rough, the giant tires carrying us over every dip and rock. The trail led through a treed area, nothing but forest on either side.

When we reached the first curve, I slowed again. The other carts were still way ahead.

"I'm trying to restrain myself from getting out to run beside you to show you just how slow we're going," Tanner said.

"Please do. This would be better without you stressing me out."

"I'm stressing you out?"

"The entire situation is stressing me out."

He shifted. "Look, S'more, they let kids in these. They use this path every single day. The cars are built for this. I know it's bumpy, but think of that as part of the fun."

His words—in a calm, reasonable, sympathetic tone—were surprisingly comforting.

"And then imagine Caveman standing in front of us, breaking up with you in public, and hit that gas pedal like you mean it." His playful voice had returned.

A laugh erupted before I could stop it.

I didn't want to run over Caleb. I wanted to go back to a time when we were together and comfortable and happy. But Tanner's support made me push the pedal harder. We zoomed forward on a straightaway.

A giant puddle appeared before I could swerve around it. We splashed through it, splattering our faceplates with mud.

"Woohoo!" Tanner yelled.

A small thrill raced through me.

I kept up our speed until we caught the other buggies, in time to slow for a series of sharp curves. Not slow enough, but I kept pace with the car in front of us, anyway, even though I felt like we were seconds away from tipping over or dislocating every bone in my backside.

When the cars pulled into a clearing, I stopped. My hands were clenched so tightly around the steering wheel, I didn't know if I could pry them off.

"See, we survived. Was that so bad?" Tanner reached over and peeled my fingers up one by one. "You even looked like you were having fun."

He showed me his phone. The image of my face, just visible inside the helmet, looked more like I was having a panic attack than the time of my life.

But . . . I supposed it had been enjoyable. Despite the worry that I would lose control and send us careening down a hillside or face-first into a tree. Adrenaline surged through me, and I felt powerful, like a shot of super-soldier serum was coursing through my veins.

Tanner jumped out, removed his helmet, and fluffed his hair. I followed, my legs shaking when I stood, arms trembling as I set my helmet on the seat.

We joined the group standing at the edge of a clearing. The overlook offered a sprawling view—a rainforest-covered hillside, leading down to a deep blue lake dotted with hilly green islands. Peeks of blue sky were visible in the clouds. Scattered sprinkles hit my face.

The high of a thrill was seeping out of me, replaced by a sense of awe and peace.

Dad came up beside me. "Okay?"

"Yeah." I actually was.

The guide gave us more history, describing how the town first grew around gold, silver, and copper mines before that waned and fishing took over. It sounded so Wild West, and the lack of people out here made the past feel much closer.

Tanner stood unnaturally still, his gaze on the view, but his head cocked. He didn't meet my eye or smirk or make a joke. Interesting.

As soon as the guide said it was time to move on and we could switch drivers, Tanner's mischievous smile emerged.

"My turn." He bounded toward the buggy.

I was doomed.

Tanner had no love-hate relationship with the gas pedal, like I did. With him, it was nothing but love. He was as close to the bumper in front of us as he was to me. If there had been room on the trail, I had no doubt he would have raced past everyone.

Whether it was the trail or Tanner's driving, the car felt bumpier in the passenger seat. Likely because he intentionally steered us into every hole. I gripped the handle above me on the roll bar. Which, why did they name it that? How often did these roll over?

With driving like this, fairly often, probably.

I refused to give Tanner the satisfaction of asking him to slow down.

When he did, I was surprised. He let a gap form between us and the cars ahead. I was about to ask why when a lurch shoved the words back down my throat.

That was why—because he'd needed room to see if he could break the speedometer. With him driving, we might outrun a bear.

Trees whooshed past, and glimpses of rolling hills were a blur of green. I was bouncing in the seat, and I was surprised that with his height, his head wasn't hitting the ceiling.

"The last time we rode together, you threatened to jump out of a moving vehicle," he said. "Are we trying that here?"

"I do have a helmet this time. I'll think about it."

He laughed.

The guide made another stop, this time at a towering water-fall that formed a bright splash of white against brilliant green trees. He talked about the species found in the rainforest, and

Tanner wandered around inspecting plants. Apparently he'd learned enough for today.

The same uncanny sensation hit me that I'd had in the Inside Passage, of being surrounded by so much nature. The little cars weren't as reassuring as the ship, but at least we were with a group.

"Want to race on the way back?" Tanner asked me.

"No," said Mr. Woods.

"Guess we'll never know who would have won," I said.

"Oh, we know."

"Do we, though?"

I surprised us both by letting him drive again. He was enjoying it more it than I was, so it seemed fair.

I didn't hate it once I got used to the rattling and the dirt and mud spraying my face and the way my stomach kept jumping into my throat. I accepted we were unlikely to tip, and Tanner's speed was restrained by the rest of the group. I even took a few pictures.

Once I got over the out-of-control feeling, the open air, without a car surrounding me, was sort of thrilling.

"Come on, yell," Tanner said.

"What?"

"Whoooo! Like that."

"Woo," I said half-heartedly.

"Let it out, S'more. On three. One. Two. Three. Whoooo! Hey, you didn't say it."

I laughed and he did, too.

When we reached the prepper hut, Tanner gave me a high

five. "Wasn't that better than walking around town and eating salmon?"

"Well, the salmon part, anyway."

He reached out and wiped mud off my chin where it had splattered beneath the faceplate. My suit was covered, too.

His eyes glinted, and he hesitated with his muddy fingers over my cheek like he intended to smear them.

"Don't you dare." I meant to sound tough, but my smile ruined any threat.

His lips quirked up, and our laughing eyes locked. We were frozen, his muddy fingers hovering inches from my face, and my insides felt like gravity had vanished and I might float away.

chapter Twelve

Port of Call: Ketchikan, Alaska

~

I stood on another platform in the treetops, except unlike in Vancouver, this time I was preparing to jump off it. The harness I wore was giving me a wedgie, and my helmet resembled a plastic cereal bowl far more suited to holding Cinnamon Toast Crunch than protecting my head if I plummeted to the forest floor.

Our tour group had shucked the dirty rain suits and taken the bus to an older area of the rainforest, with taller, denser trees. The air was thick with the scent of wet leaves, and other than a cool breeze rustling the trees, it was overwhelmingly quiet. The sun had emerged after the morning gloom, with spotty white clouds puffy against a brilliant blue sky, a shade I was certain had never been achieved in Los Angeles since the invention of cars.

The science behind zip lines was solid. As long as they were well constructed, you could count on them to do exactly what they were supposed to. Unlike wild animals, which were unpredictable and deadly.

Tanner was more like a wild animal than a zip line.

I had survived riding with him in an off-road vehicle, so surely this couldn't be worse.

That moment at the end was another story. That had been nothing more than our usual teasing, surely. Definitely not flirting. But when I recalled his closeness and the sparkle in his eyes, my insides bounced around again.

We'd graduated from ground school, where we'd learned how the harness attached to the line, how to grip the handle, how to press the line above us to slow ourselves with our thick gloves. Then we'd hiked to the first platform and climbed to the treetops.

Our guide was finishing his talk with "And there's lots of wildlife out here, so watch for eagles, and if we're lucky, we might see a bear."

Say what now? Good thing I was off the ground. Bears couldn't climb this high, surely. Wait. Could they climb?

Tanner slid up next to me. "We should race here since we couldn't in the cars."

I tried to shift my thoughts from images of giant monsters scaling trees like squirrels. "Do you even know how these work? You weigh more than I do. Mathematically, I can't beat you."

"That sounds like you're giving up."

"That sounds like science. So we've obviously eliminated one entire branch of study from your possible college majors."

"Don't be hasty. Maybe I want to study why I'm destined to beat you."

"Then you're going to need remedial math classes first. You might not want to look at your physics grade today."

He elbowed me. "I think you're using science as an excuse. If you really wanted to win, you'd find a way. You just don't want to admit that I'm superior."

A half snort, half laugh escaped from my throat. He was impossible. And not at all cute, eyes glinting, lips smirking, expression teasing under the ridiculous bowl helmet.

"What if I got you a backpack full of rocks?" he asked. "To even out our weight? Take that, science."

I stepped away from him and raised my hand. "Can I go now? I'm ready to jump off anything to get away from him."

Tanner smothered a smile.

Wait. Had that taunting been intentional, to distract me from my nerves?

Sneaky jerk. Also, that was sweet.

My stomach was already swooping as the guide clipped my harness to the line. The line stretched through the treetops to another platform that was barely visible, where I hoped someone was waiting to catch me before I face-planted into a tree trunk.

Given the science of zip lines, that was more likely to happen to Tanner and his greater mass, which cheered me up greatly.

I took a deep breath, grasped the handle by my head, and stepped off the platform.

Gravity took over. My lungs stayed behind temporarily

before air whooshed back into them, and then I was weightless, or as close as I would ever come to zero-gravity without going to space. I picked up speed down the line.

Once I was breathing again, I looked around.

The trees surrounded me, enormous, a cocoon of green. They were so dense, I thought they might smack my face as I sailed through them. Fresh pine scented the cool air, and the sky stretched endless above me. I felt like a bird soaring, and oddly secure, with the harness forming a chair. Everything was so quiet.

All too soon, the second platform grew larger in front of me. The slack in the line meant I slowed as I approached it. My feet hit the wood, and the guide grabbed my harness to keep me from stumbling as I came to a stop.

That had been fun. Like sprinting into the wind on the track, but with gravity doing the work. And nicer views.

The guide unhooked me, and I moved to the side of the platform, shaky, but maybe in a good way?

Tanner went next. Immediately after leaving the platform, he began twisting into nontraditional positions—on his stomach with his arms out like he was an airplane, twirling from side to side, slumping backward as if unconscious. Was he even noticing the view?

He straightened in time to come in for the landing. The others on the platform laughed and applauded, and he took a bow, glowing under their attention. As soon as the guide unhooked him, he winked at me.

I shook my head. No. He was not funny or entertaining. He

was a show-off. What was wrong with my brain? The ATV must have jostled neural connections out of place.

"I videoed you jumping," he said. "Next time I'll go first so I can get you coming in for the landing. Make sure to wave for the camera. And if you want to return the favor, I'll be extra daring."

"Does it count as daring when you're attached to a line? Isn't it the same amount of daring no matter what position you're in?"

"You're the science person. You tell me." He glanced at me sideways. "What did you think?"

That it was really fun, but I didn't want to admit it.

He poked my arm. "You liked it. I can see it in your face. Wait, can you not pronounce *fun*?"

"F-f-f. Nope, can't do it."

"Repeat after me. I."

I suppressed a smile. "I."

"Had."

"Had."

"Fun."

"A not completely horrible time."

He threw his head back and laughed, then rested his hand on my shoulder and gave me a serious look, though his lips still curved upward slightly, their natural state. "I'm glad."

He seemed to mean it, holding eye contact. A shiver went through me. As another person arrived, we moved aside, and his hand fell away. I almost missed its weight.

We waited for our dads, and after mine reached us, he

hugged me. "I hadn't done that since our honeymoon," my dad said. "This was a great idea."

When Mr. Woods landed, he said, "How do bears travel? A bear-o-plane!"

People around us chuckled, showing that a desire to make people laugh ran in the family, but I wished he'd stop. I didn't mind dad jokes in general—when they came from someone else's dad—but why did his all have to do with bears? Was that like an entire genre of comedy? I should learn his fear and make jokes about it.

The platform was connected to another line, and another. We sailed down several more of varying lengths. Some offered views of a silver river winding through the trees or a distant bay glinting in the sun. To reach some, we walked across narrow bridges with treetops swaying around us. An eagle glided overhead.

"I'm glad Steph didn't come," said Mr. Woods. "This is not an excursion for anyone afraid of heights."

I didn't mind heights, and was fairly relaxed until I spotted a large, dark shape below and stumbled. Tanner gripped my arm.

When we reached the platform, I saw it again.

Tanner pressed against me as he stared in the direction I was looking. "I think that's a bush."

"It's the same shape as before," I said. "I think it's stalking us."

"Or, there are lots of bushes in, you know, a forest."

The others huddled at the edge of the platform to watch as, far below, a bear-shaped form ambled to the river.

"Your bush is moving," I said.

"Someone call National Geographic. I've discovered a new species."

I hung back as the others watched the animal splash into the river. I couldn't stop a tremor from shaking my body.

After the group moved on, Tanner asked, "What's up with you and bears, anyway?"

"What do you mean?"

"Come on. You were the only one not excited to see that. Anytime someone mentions them, even my dad's dumb jokes, your shoulders get tense and your face gets pale."

He'd noticed? "Maybe I just don't like your dad's jokes."

He waited, watching me.

I huffed. "I have a healthy respect for animals that can eat me, that's all."

"I do, too. Like with opposing players. Don't underestimate them. But also don't *over*estimate them. If you know your limits and theirs, and if you understand them, you don't need to be afraid."

When did he get so wise?

"Plus," he said, "I don't think that many people actually get eaten by bears. I feel like that would be in the news."

"It might be, up here. You don't watch Alaskan news."

"I could. There's this thing called the internet. Since you like math, I'm guessing that statistically, seeing a bear is way safer than driving in LA."

Why did he have to be so logical? That was my job, but somehow bears gobbled up my common sense. My brain knew I was safe, but that didn't stop my heart from racing or some primal instinct inside me from screaming, bypassing my brain and sending signals to my body that I should be afraid. I wasn't sure how to stop it.

"Especially the way you drive," I managed to lob at him.

The course ended with an extra-long, steep line, and I couldn't see the platform at the end. I was supposed to trust it was out there, with people waiting for me, not a bear lying in ambush to maul me.

Maybe I'd let Tanner go first. It would take a while for a bear to eat him because he was so big, and I'd have time to get away.

This line carried me faster than the rest—thanks, gravity—and when I landed, I was sad it was over. When everyone finished, we climbed down to the forest floor.

Tanner grinned at me, and I returned it without thinking.

I'd always enjoyed the simplicity of doing things I liked with people I liked. Today that had oddly included zip-lining and Tanner. I felt like I had accomplished something, overcome a mental block. I'd done something new, and it hadn't turned out too badly.

While our group waited for the bus back to town and our ship, I sat on a log bench beneath the trees and posted pictures and videos. Tanner did the same.

Once we were driving, I received a message from Jordan.

Jordan: *Are you with Tanner again???*

Me: *Yeah.*

Jordan: *Huh.*

It was breaking my brain, too.

Jordan: *Your pics are amazing.*

She'd already loved or given a fire emoji to the ones from the jazz club, dance lessons, and formal night.

Jordan: *I told you you'd have fun.*

Me: *Yeah, yeah, you're always right and I will never question you again.*

Me: *What's everyone up to at home?*

Jordan: *I'm going to pretend you mean me and not that you're digging for info on Caleb.*

Caleb had liked my post of the suspension bridge, the only one he'd acknowledged. What did it mean that it was engineering-related, and not me in a dress? Was it enough to make him regret the breakup? Was he planning a post in which he said I wasn't boring, and he didn't know what he'd been thinking? He'd publicly declare that he couldn't wait until I got home so we could talk and he could undo what he'd said.

I clicked over to his account. Nothing new. Ha. Who was boring now? Except it wasn't his fault I was on vacation and he wasn't.

Me: *Of course I mean you.*

Jordan sent me a rundown of her last two days of work and informed me that her little sister, who was going to be a freshman, had decided she wanted to try out for volleyball, even though she was five-three and had never played.

Then my phone chimed with a new email—from the school. Grades were in.

I peeked over my shoulder at Tanner before opening it and accessing the school portal.

Tanner slid into the seat next to me, holding his phone. "Want to do it together?"

I sure hoped this ended well for me. I might have preferred privacy in case he somehow outscored me.

We opened our files. I'd gotten an A in precalculus, physics, and US history, an A minus in Spanish, and a B in American lit, plus I'd had track this semester. Tanner held his screen next to mine. He had the exact same grades, except his A minus was in precalc and his B was in physics. He'd taken art this semester as an elective, and since football was in the fall, when I'd taken a film elective, our GPAs for the year were identical.

My teeth were doing the Tanner Woods grind again.

Seriously, how did he do it? I'd been convinced he would do worse than that in physics and precalc, especially given the recent ignorance of the basics of gravity.

"Did you even study?" I asked. "Pretty sure I never saw you open a book this year."

"Oh, it's been far longer than that. I can't help being a natural genius," he said.

Life was so unfair.

"Looks like it will come down to senior year, S'more."

Neither of us was going to be valedictorian. We weren't taking enough advanced electives like some classmates, and liberal arts weren't my strength. But getting a higher GPA than him would be enough to prove once and for all that discipline and planning were superior to . . . whatever you could call his particular brand of chaos.

He stayed next to me, showing me videos he'd taken of the

day, before I showed him mine. I was proud to be able to say I'd done it. Despite my nerves, I'd pushed through, and I'd enjoyed it.

When the bus returned to town, we were just in time for the deadline to board the ship. We joined the line on the dock, and they had us scan our cards again, I assumed so they could ensure everyone was here.

"Do people ever get left behind?" Tanner asked the guy manning the scanner.

"Sometimes. We have to keep to the schedule for the ports. It disrupts everyone if we leave late. If someone isn't on an official cruise excursion and they don't make it back in time, we don't wait. It's up to them to get themselves to the next port to meet us."

Yikes. This was why I found punctuality attractive—great protection against marooning.

After I showered, I went to our balcony for the sail-away views, clutching a blanket. The room had two personal-sized plaid ones in a tiny cabinet, I assumed for this purpose. I wrapped it around me and settled onto a chair, watching floatplanes come and go against a quaint backdrop of small buildings along the water. The way the planes could both fly and float was cool, with pontoons for landing gear.

The ship eased away and slowly cruised along the coast. It didn't take long for the town to fall behind us until once again it was just water and sky and mountains.

"You're not sunbathing nude, are you?"

I leaped off my chair. The voice had been Tanner's.

Oh. Right. The balcony next to ours.

"Like I'd tell you if I were?" I called. "How long have you been there?"

"How long have *you* been there?"

"I'm enjoying the view. Isn't that why you get a balcony room?"

"I thought it was so you could feed the birds and go fishing over the side."

"No, it's definitely so you can spit at people below you."

"Nice," he said.

I retrieved the blanket from where I'd dropped it and leaned my forearms on the rail, peering around the divider that separated our balconies. He was in the same position. The wind ruffled his hair, and his eyes were bluer than their usual gray.

I didn't know what to say. We'd been . . . friendly today? Ish? He'd been less annoying than usual, or I'd had enough to distract me that I hadn't noticed. There had been moments when he'd helped with my outfit or encouraged me or we'd laughed together that I hadn't wanted to kill him. Thinking about those sent a swoop through my stomach like I was soaring through the air.

"What did you like best today?" he asked.

"Zip-lining."

"Me, too, because I'll always beat you."

"The way you beat me at physics?"

"No, the way I beat you at English."

"You realize we could go on like this forever?"

"Nah, eventually you'd run out of things to beat me at."

"I think you have that backward." I was grinning, but it faded. "Hey, Fun Coach? I enjoyed today."

"Yes! I knew it."

"Don't let it go to your head."

"No matter what you might think, I want you to enjoy all this," he said, and his voice was serious. "I'm not trying to change you. You don't have to prove yourself to me. I just want to make sure you don't miss out."

I leaned back. It was easier to talk when I couldn't see his face. "I guess I would have missed out. I mean, I wouldn't have known I did. But I know now."

If I'd walked around town with my mom, it would have been nice, pleasant, relaxing. I never would have imagined I'd enjoy the adventure of the excursion.

"Does that make you more willing to try other things? See what else is out there? This week?" he added quickly. "Like, make the most of your vacation."

What else had he possibly meant? "Maybe."

I was contemplating thanking him, sincerely. He'd been encouraging, supportive, and patient. He'd made the day easier, shockingly, and also possibly more fun.

Before I could find words, the door behind me cracked, and my mom stuck her head out.

"There you are."

"There *you* are," I said. She waved me inside, so I called, "Later, Tanner," and followed her in.

"Your dad said you had fun today." She leaned toward the mirror and smoothed her hair.

"We did. What did you do?"

"Explored the town, took a short tour, did some shopping. Did you check your grades?"

"They're fine." She didn't approve of my need to beat Tanner, since it meant exactly nothing in the grand scheme of the universe, getting into college, or finding a job, so I kept those thoughts to myself.

"I never doubted," she said. "We'll have our usual report card cupcakes when we get home. We're going to dinner now."

"In the fancy room?"

"Yes, but it's not formal night. You can just wear a nice sweater."

"No, thanks," I said. "You guys go ahead. I'll get something in the casual place."

I was not revisiting runaway snails and creepy birds. My stomach didn't need more adventure today.

"Are you sure?" she asked.

"Yeah, I'll be fine. I'll get a burger by the pool."

After they left, I made my way to the pool deck and watched the scenery from the rail. The ship was cutting through silvery blue water, hugging the rugged shoreline. It was peaceful up here. Quiet. A strong wind blew off the water, whipping my hair and making me glad for the hoodie I'd thrown on.

As I got in line for a burger at the bar next to the pool, someone stepped behind me.

"Hey," said Tanner. He was wearing jeans and a sweater that

hugged his muscles, and he looked nicer than I did. Too nice. That sweater, with his chest and shoulders, was criminal.

"What are you doing here?"

Tanner smirked like he'd caught me admiring his arms. "Our parents were convinced you needed company. Also, dinner in that fancy place takes forever, and they were sitting with Mr. Ramirez, and I didn't want to listen to them talk about work."

"Oh, I'm sure no work talk was going to happen whatsoever."

"Yeah, I was probably mistaken. That doesn't sound like our moms at all."

We both laughed.

When we reached the front of the line, the server gave us buns and meat—double for Tanner—and we moved to the buffet line for toppings, condiments, and potato chips.

I added cheese and ketchup to mine.

"Is that all you're having?" Tanner asked.

"I like simple burgers."

Tanner piled everything onto his, tomatoes and pickles, lettuce and onions, large quantities of ketchup and mustard, along with a mountain of chips on the side. "I like big ones."

"I can see that."

"Not even lettuce or tomato? You're a runner. Don't you like vegetables?"

"I like some of them. Just not on my burger."

"You're killing me."

"I know. Moore the Bore."

A shadow flickered in his eyes. He opened his mouth.

A gust of wind hit us. It picked up the chips and the precarious stack of toppings on Tanner's plate—a top bun coated in condiments, lettuce, rings of onion—and carried them through the air.

The wind deposited half his chips in the pool, where they immediately began to sink. The onions and lettuce landed on a pool chair, barely missing an e-reader someone had left. And the bun landed condiments-first on the cheek of an old lady sitting at a table nearby. It stuck, the ketchup acting like glue. And it slowly slid and plopped onto the deck beside her, leaving a trail behind on her cheek more obvious than the snail's on the tablecloth.

chapter Thirteen

Port of Call: Ketchikan, Alaska

~

I was torn between laughter and wanting to throw myself behind the bar to hide.

Tanner did laugh, but he also snagged a stack of napkins and trotted over to the lady.

"I'm so sorry, ma'am. It sure is windy out here, isn't it? I didn't know I needed to guard my meal. Please, let me help you." He knelt beside her, extending the napkins.

She took them with a smile.

Seriously? How did he get away with absolutely everything? And why was my annoyance at that fact tempered by the thought that he was being rather sweet?

He chatted with her as she wiped her face, then he retrieved the lettuce and onion. He stared at the pool like he might jump in and go diving for soggy potato chips like sunken treasure, but an employee with a pool net stopped him.

This was severely messing with my brain. I would have expected him to laugh. Throw more chips in the air to see where they landed. Hide behind a pillar to watch anyone slip and fall.

I retreated inside to eat my burger in a wind-free environment. A couple minutes later, Tanner joined me, having replenished his burger toppings.

I no longer knew what to say.

"Now I know to keep a hand over my plate when it's windy out," he said as he plopped into a chair.

"See," I said. "There's an advantage to my simple meal. Lower center of gravity, less available surface area to catch the wind."

"Why are you and science always plotting against me?" His eyes twinkled.

"Don't get on the wrong side of science. It never ends well. Like eating around you."

He laughed and devoured his repaired burger, and I contemplated the urge I'd had to thank him earlier. But the moment, and the privacy of our individual balconies, had passed.

"You held up your deal today, Fun Coach," I said. "Have you thought about your college major homework? Your grades were fine. Why do you need this, anyway?"

"According to my parents, good grades are not the same as having a solid life plan." He spoke lightly, but a shadow crossed his face.

I was hit by a strange urge to march downstairs to the dining room and defend him. And I wanted to ask more, but I wasn't sure if we were that far along in this, what? Partnership? He didn't seem inclined to elaborate.

"This isn't too challenging for you, is it?" he asked.

"Of course not. I don't give up."

"I know you don't." He sounded almost admiring.

His gaze warmed my cheeks. "Are you ready for the next step?"

"Hit me. Wait. What is the next step?"

I pulled up the list I'd made on my phone. "I'm going to regret this question, but other than football and Ping-Pong, what are you good at?"

"I know you're so tempted to mock me."

"I really am. But you've been moderately helpful so far in the Fun Coach department, so I'm upholding my end of our truce."

"Moderately? You wound me." He grinned. "I'm great at helping old ladies. And naturally, I'm great at star club."

I narrowed my eyes. How had I nearly forgotten about that? His supposed charm had distracted me from plotting my coup. I needed to get my brain in check.

"Next question," I said. "Why'd you pick the mentoring program for your volunteer work?"

"Hanging out with kids sounded fun. Since I basically am one." He gave me a pointed look, and okay, fair, I had told him that on multiple occasions.

"What do you guys do?" I asked. "Jordan and her Little Sis paint their nails and listen to music and look at clothes online, on top of whatever the official stuff is."

"Play video games, throw a football, talk about life. And yeah, there's a booklet with topics and stuff. I also teach him how to charm old ladies."

The image of him and a junior high kid helping an old lady across the street appeared in my head far too easily. But what I said with a smile was "That poor kid." I checked my list. "Okay, if you could have a meal with anyone, dead or alive, who would it be?"

He paused with his burger lifted to his mouth. "This is supposed to help me choose a major?"

A family passed us, and the little boy said, "Hey, it's Bird Girl and Bird Boy."

Tanner fist-bumped him, and I shoved three chips in my mouth so I had an excuse not to answer.

When they were gone, I continued, "I read some online quizzes. Like, would you want to eat with a famous person from history who did something cool or a successful businessperson or a celebrity? It supposedly gives insight into the type of person you admire or the type of success you hope to have in life."

"Did you make that up?" he asked. "Benjamin Franklin. No, wait. Don Shula. Yeah, Coach Shula, final answer."

I sighed.

"What about you?" he asked.

"Neil Armstrong, I guess."

"Cool. What about a fictional character?" he asked.

"What?"

"If you could eat with a fictional person? Who would it be?"

"Um . . . maybe the crew of the *Enterprise.* Does that count? Captain Picard's."

"Naturally," he said. "Captain Kirk was far too rebellious. Mine would be the Doctor, because we could go anywhere in space or time."

"You like the Doctor?"

"Doctor Who?" he asked with a crooked grin.

I smiled and ducked my head to hide it. But my heart skipped a beat. The more he surprised me, the harder it was to know how to interact with him.

"Don't look so shocked," he said. "A person can like sports *and* science fiction, S'more."

"I know they can."

He pointed at me with a potato chip. "I refuse to stay in your little box."

I liked my boxes. They were neat and orderly and perfectly stacked in my mind, which made life less stressful. Him refusing to stay in his was complicating things—and making me realize I may have been unfair and was going to have to think about him differently.

I cleared my throat. "Back to the college stuff. How do your teachers describe you?"

"They usually just ask about my latest touchdown catches or sweet blocks."

"That's on every evaluation you've ever gotten? I thought part of teaching was finding nice things to say about everyone, no matter how far you have to stretch the truth." I was smirking.

"Maybe you aren't meant to be a teacher," he said. "Maybe people who are drawn to teaching are the ones who naturally see the good in everyone, the potential. And you aren't one of those."

"I know you're implying something, but I would be a great teacher, thank you. That's what I plan to do."

"Really?" He studied me.

"Really what?"

"What do you want to teach?" His interested gaze appraised me.

I shifted in my seat. "High school math. Or physics."

Physics. That made me think of Mr. Lin's email. Today's excursions had distracted me from it. Throwing out the plan on vacation was one thing. Upending my home routine for my senior year? I still wasn't convinced it was worth it.

"Huh." He studied me before his smirk returned. "My teachers say I'm charming and funny and creative. I'm a leader among my peers." He sat straighter and puffed out his chest.

"Yeah, but what are you leading them into?" I muttered.

"And I'm sometimes disruptive and loud, but since they love me, it's okay." He sat back with a satisfied expression.

"So far, cruise ship magician sounds like a decent option," I said. "Where do you see yourself in five years?"

"You sound like the guidance counselor."

"What did you tell him?"

"Catching the game-winning touchdown in the NCAA championship game," he said confidently.

"Right. Make that eight years."

"How old would that make me?"

"No wonder you couldn't beat me in math." I definitely should have ordered room service by myself tonight.

"Eight years is a long time. Do people plan that far ahead? Where do you see yourself in eight years? I know, I know, we're not talking about you. But it might help me"—he waved a hand—"visualize."

"Fine," I said. "I'm planning to study math, maybe at UCLA or UC Irvine. Or one of the Claremonts if I can get a scholarship. Get a master's, probably. Then teach."

"Not Caltech or MIT?"

"I'm not smart enough for MIT. And it sounds cold. I don't do winter."

"Wait, did you share something real with me, S'more, and answer a personal question? Wow, I need to mark this date." He pretended to pull out his phone and then said, "Ohhhh."

"Oh, what?"

"LA schools. You don't want to move."

His attention fixed on me, serious, perceptive, the teasing gone. My stomach squirmed the way it did every time I thought about moving away. Starting college, in a new place, with new people, unfamiliar restaurants, and roads. Far less scheduled than high school. Having to create a whole new routine.

I cleared my throat. "I told you, this isn't about me."

"You said you had fun today." His subject change was abrupt.

Apparently we were done working on his college project. "Yeah . . ."

"You spent most of the day not in control. My driving, the zip lines. That didn't freak you out?"

"It did. At first."

"Only at first?"

"I guess it was sort of fun. And the zip lines are safe. Your driving, not so much."

"We didn't crash. Why this need for control? You realize that's an illusion, anyway, right? Like, even when you were driving. The engine could have stopped, or another cart could have hit us, or an earthquake could have swallowed the hillside, or a rabid moose could have charged out of the forest and impaled us on his antlers."

"I'm glad you waited to mention these possibilities until after we were done."

His face was earnest. "I'm just saying, even when you think you're in control, you aren't. No one is."

"There are lots of things you *can* control. Ways to create order and stability."

"True, but that doesn't work with everything. At some point, life happens. Chaos. Surprises."

I knew that too well. "All the more reason to manage as much as you can."

"Hmm. Maybe." He pushed away from the table. "Are you done? Come on."

"Where are we going? Is this a test to see if I'll let you be in control of the evening?" I stood and followed him out.

"Let's explore, see what we can find."

What else was I going to do? Might as well join him. See? I could be fun and spontaneous. Although, I was glad for the limits of a cruise ship with only so many options.

We wandered past bars and clubs, agreed to skip the ballet show in the main theater, and came to the art gallery. People sat in chairs facing a row of framed paintings, and a guy with a microphone stood in front of them. Most of the crowd held paddles and glasses of white wine, and I felt underdressed in jeans and a hoodie.

Tanner tugged my arm, and shrugging, I joined him taking seats in the back.

It was an auction. I sat on my hands to make sure I didn't accidentally buy a three-thousand-dollar nude painting in front of my parents' coworkers.

The first painting they brought out and set on the center easel was in vivid tones, showing a man with an umbrella walking down a rain-drenched street with reflections in the pavement. It was pretty in a generic way. I liked the colors.

It was followed by a modern art bulldog in primary colors that looked like a portrait a rich person would commission of their prized pet. Then came a semi-abstract piece of a couple dancing the tango.

The people in the crowd raised paddles with numbers, and the auctioneer called out their bids and the winning bidder's number. He wasn't as fast as the typical auctioneer but still moved quickly. Surely two-thirds of these people were just here for the free champagne.

"They certainly have an interesting variety," Tanner muttered as the next painting was displayed, renaissance in style, but of a court jester and a pig in a fancy hall.

"Next we have Mungo the Magnificent and Her Porkiness, Miss Baconbits," Tanner said under his breath. "Done in the old French style. Do I hear ten dollars?"

"Shhh." I tried to contain a giggle as someone paid significantly more than ten dollars and Tanner whistled softly.

Once Mungo found a home, they brought out an image of the backside of a woman bathing.

"And here we have a watercolor portrait, painted by a perv who shouldn't be looking in other people's windows when they're taking a bath."

I swallowed a laugh. "How does this work, anyway? Do they ship the paintings home? Or carry them on an airplane under their arm?"

"That one would be super awkward," Tanner said as the bathing woman was removed. "Farewell, Francesca. May your next bath be more private."

Francesca was followed by a cartoon Tasmanian devil on a white background.

"Ah yes," Tanner said knowingly. "This is an exclusive, of a rare creature in its native habitat."

"Its native habitat is blank?" I gave in and asked.

"Obviously it's a creature from the North Pole, and the white is snow," he said. "Come on, join me. The next one is yours."

It was uncovered.

Tanner snorted.

This one was completely abstract, with blobby, rounded shapes, some of which appeared to have faces. And tentacles.

He poked me.

"All right, fine." I kept my voice down. "This piece is commonly mistaken for a portrait of amoebas, but is in fact a rendering of the life forms found by the Mars Rover's latest mission. Scientists at NASA were forbidden from speaking of life on other planets, so they expressed their findings the only way they knew how. You, too, can be in awe of the first signs of extraterrestrial life, as it's perfect to hang in your billiard room."

A loud laugh exploded from Tanner.

Everyone turned to stare at us, and my face got hot.

"Excuse me," said the proper British voice of the auctioneer. "You in the back."

Tanner grabbed my hand and tugged. I stumbled to my feet and let him drag me away, down the hall and around a corner until we reached a dark, quiet area. When we sagged against a wall, well out of hearing range, his laugh burst out again.

I couldn't help it. I cracked up, bent over and bracing a hand on the wall.

"I can't believe I got kicked out of an auction," I said.

"Better than accidentally buying something. Though now I want that last one so I can tell everyone it's a portrait of Martians while I'm playing pool." He laughed again. "That was awesome."

In the past, I would have yelled at him for getting us in trouble, for disrupting a serious, formal occasion. But we hadn't hurt anyone. Tears were leaking from my eyes, and I couldn't remember the last time I'd laughed so hard.

He braced a hand on my shoulder. "I didn't know you had it in you, S'more."

I wiped my eyes and looked up. He was close, his eyes crinkled, a smile splitting his face as he gazed down at me. Those champagne bubbles were in my chest now.

Tanner might occasionally mess around too much, but he knew how to have fun. And that was something I was starting to realize I needed more of.

Chapter Fourteen

Port of Call: Juneau, Alaska

~

When we sailed into Juneau the next morning, foggy clouds were hugging the tops of mountains on both sides of the bay. Skinny waterfalls threaded the hills, forming ribbons of white from top to bottom. The ocean was a deep green. Like Ketchikan, the town sat at the base of the mountain. Through the clouds, I saw wires leading up the hill, a tram or cable cars.

I leaned over the edge of our balcony to watch the ship crawl toward the dock and stop inches away. Impressive. Thinking about the engineering of this vessel and the chance to see similar feats up close was almost enough to make me reply to Mr. Lin's email.

My mom was taking a whale watching cruise with coworkers today, but my dad had been happy to join a dogsledding trip since he got seasick on smaller boats. He, Tanner, Mr. Woods, and I clutched coats, gloves, and hats as we disembarked into an area where flowers exploded from planters, and everything was bright and clean. Foggy, damp air swathed the forested hills, and puddles covered the ground. The temperature was mild in town, but we'd need the warm clothes soon.

After last night's art auction, I wasn't sure how to act around Tanner. I'd had more fun with him than I'd expected, but it was the first time I'd been kicked out of anything in my life. Guilt had set in when I returned to my room, along with the hope that my parents hadn't found out about it because a coworker had been annoyed that Mom's teenager had interrupted their quest to purchase abstract Martian art.

We boarded a bus to a small airfield, where a helicopter waited to fly us to a nearby glacier for sledding. I might not have picked this excursion, but Tanner had been excited about the idea, and I wanted him to have fun. Plus, it sounded quintessentially Alaskan, and I liked dogs, so there we were.

Tanner took the seat next to me, bouncing with excitement.

It was a short ride to the airfield. The pilot assigned seats in the helicopter based on weight. Tanner flashed me a grin when the pilot told him to sit up front, and I climbed into the back. Headsets let us hear the pilot over the thumping.

I'd never been in a helicopter. It was more disconcerting than an airplane because it was so small, at the mercy of winds or storms, but surely they'd cancel the excursion if conditions were unsafe.

At first, the skies were foggy, and rain drops gathered on the windows. But as we rose above the town, the clouds cleared to allow glimpses of green mountains that soon turned rocky, many topped in snow.

Then the glacier was beneath us, massive, spreading between the peaks, nothing but ice and rocks as far as I could see. It wasn't solid white, but shades of gray and brown and blue, and the surface was rough rather than smooth like an icy pond.

I fought a shudder. It was pretty, yet so huge and remote and frozen. What would it be like to be stranded out there? We were a tiny speck in the endless sky. There was so much land, we could crash and never be found. Or fall into a crevasse inhabited by a carnivorous Sasquatch that might string me up and eat me if I didn't have a lightsaber to fight it off.

The helicopter was a constant vibration beneath me, and the pilot told us about the Mendenhall Glacier, a thirteen-mile river of ice that was a small part of an enormous ice field.

We landed in a lower valley, with soft snow instead of jagged ice. From the sky, I saw long rows of little tents. White buildings blended into the landscape. At this altitude, it was sunny, the sky a pure, bright blue. The reflection off the snow made me glad for sunglasses.

We exited to a blast of cold air. A chill bit my nose, and I tugged on my beanie to cover my ears. Tanner did the same, then reached over and yanked mine over my eyes. When I wrenched it up, he was laughing.

It felt different. Not like taunting laughter, just plain good humor, and I found myself returning his smile. I reached for his hat, but he danced out of my way.

"Too slow, S'more. I thought you were supposed to be the fast one?"

"Oh, so you admit it."

"I'm going to need more proof after that sad display."

The barking and howling of dogs filled the air as we crunched through shallow snow. The sound sent a swell of excitement through me.

Our families had been to Big Bear a few times, where we rented a cabin. Usually, I didn't see the purpose of snow. It was cold and wet and made it hard to run—I never planned to mention the time I'd gone running there, slipped, and fallen on my butt in front of a group of old people who hadn't even glanced at me. Skiing was an activity with injuries waiting to happen, and if you fell, which was guaranteed, it was hard to stand without looking like a baby giraffe on roller skates. Usually I stayed inside with a book. Especially after that sprained ankle incident.

But this place was beautiful, sparkling, brilliant white stretching into the distance, like a field of diamonds or starlight.

We approached the tents and rows of mini-igloo doghouses.

"What do you call a cold bear?" Mr. Woods asked. "A brrrr. I know, I know, my jokes are getting un-*bear*-able."

"What do polar bears eat on picnics?" my dad added. "Brrr-gers."

"Not you, too," I said.

Mr. Woods laughed. "Good one."

"Maybe we leave them on the glacier?" Tanner suggested.

We met our musher guide, a woman who had competed in the Iditarod, a thousand-mile dogsled race across the state.

"New eight-year plan," Tanner murmured.

"Hard pass for me."

She introduced us to the dogs who would be pulling us and

let us pet them. They weren't all the classic gray-and-white Huskies I'd expected, but a mix of brown and tan and white. They wore adorable little booties, which I immediately took a picture of to show Jordan.

I knelt in the snow next to a black-and-white dog and rubbed his ears, and he licked my face. Tanner crouched beside me to pet another.

"Are you guys going to get another dog?" I asked him.

We couldn't have one because Mom was allergic and wasn't willing to risk even a hypoallergenic one, but Tanner's family had had a golden retriever until a few years ago. They'd always put her outside when we visited, and Mom took allergy meds beforehand. I'd enjoyed Saturday morning walks with Caleb and his dog. I would miss those days in the park, throwing a Frisbee and watching his dog chase birds. The breakup had ended more than I'd realized.

Tanner rubbed the belly of a tan dog. "Probably not. I've been asking for one, but with me leaving for college soon, and my sisters gone, my parents say they don't want the work. They don't believe I'd take care of it. Did you know dogs take dedication, responsibility, and maturity?" he asked in a mocking tone.

I might not have trusted Tanner to lead the Astronomy Club or make menu decisions at fancy dinners, but why had I never noticed that his parents didn't trust him, either?

He wasn't 100 percent irresponsible. Someone had obviously decided he could be trusted to mentor an impressionable thirteen-year-old. But a pet was too much? The urge to apologize hit me, though I wasn't sure why.

"Do you want one, once you're on your own?" I asked instead.

"Absolutely. I'll teach it tricks and we'll entertain people at the park. What about you? Don't tell me you're a cat person."

"Nah. I mean, I like cats, but dogs are loyal and dependable and you can take them places."

"And go on long runs with them?"

"Exactly. And my dog would growl at people who encroached on my personal space."

He smirked. "And hunt doves for you?"

"Oh, I'm making any potential dog try out. If it can't catch wild birds, it's not a match."

"Does the same apply to guys?" he asked.

"Why, were you auditioning?"

Why had I said that? I froze, staring at the dog, my cheeks flushed against the cold air.

"I wasn't aware there was an opening." His voice was light, like mine had been, but I was too afraid to look at his face.

The breakup had been barely a week ago. I was doing all this to get Caleb back. The idea of Tanner as a guy in my life shouldn't have been even a glimmer in my mind.

After we played with the dogs, our guide showed us the sled. Ten dogs were harnessed to two small metal and Kevlar contraptions. They were little more than frames sitting on skis with small chairs. It was wild that people used these to travel across long distances, with nothing to protect them from the elements.

She told us that dogs had been used to pull sleds for thousands of years, and mushing was the state sport of Alaska. The animals were bred for it and loved to run, and had thick fur to protect them against the cold. The lead dogs followed vocal instructions, and each dog was intentionally placed in a certain position, with a specific job. They used their different strengths to work together.

I'd never thought of things quite like that before. Jordan and I were different, and we had a great friendship. Yet with Caleb, I'd gravitated toward someone like me. Our guide was saying sometimes opposites work best together.

I glanced over to find Tanner studying me.

Lightning bounced around my insides like blaster fire in a metal room.

What was he thinking? And why was the sun so hot?

My dad, Mr. Woods, and I started in the front chair and perch, while Tanner joined the guide in the back.

The dogs strained at the harness, eager to run, and I didn't blame them. The energy inside me could have used that outlet, too.

The guide yelled a command, and the dogs took off, racing across the snow, pulling us behind. It was a little bumpy over a path flattened in the snow, heading out across the glacier. Rocky, snow-topped cliffs towered above us. A chilly wind off the ice brushed my nose and cheeks, and a swishing sound filled the air.

We covered ground quickly, the camp falling behind with nothing but snow and ice ahead.

A thrill surged through me. This was not something I'd ever considered doing, but it was amazing.

We stopped to switch positions, and when it was my turn to mush after Tanner, he lingered long enough to tuck my long hair into my jacket, his fingers brushing my neck. I shivered and climbed onto the rail, bending my knees to absorb the light bumping as we took off again.

Even though the dogs were trained, I felt at their mercy. I recalled what Tanner had said. I did like to be in control, to know what to expect. Trusting cute dogs wasn't too hard—odds were good that it would go all right. But that's what I did, weighing the likelihood of trouble with the severity of that trouble, multiplied by a factor of unexpected. Yes, the LA freeway was probably more dangerous than wild animals, but it was familiar, known, and therefore a less terrifying risk.

After we'd all taken turns and had returned to camp, our guide pointed us to a pen full of puppies. I promptly sat in the snow surrounded by the little balls of fluff, and Tanner plopped beside me. The puppies swarmed us. One chewed on my glove, another licked my ear. I took off my gloves so I could stroke their silky fur.

Tanner clutched a white one while three more scampered over his lap. His smile could have melted a glacier. His cheeks were red from the cold, and his eyes sparkled beneath his beanie. Something weird twisted in my chest.

I was not mentally prepared for this view. I needed a warning. Red alert. Attractiveness overload imminent. Surely it had nothing to do with Tanner. Any objectively cute guy's hotness was exponentially magnified when he held a puppy. It was basic math. Not a commentary on my feelings for Tanner Woods in any way whatsoever.

I buried my face in a puppy. "Did you have fun today?"

"I'm supposed to be the one asking that," he said.

"Yeah, but you wanted to do this."

"You didn't?"

"Sure, but you were so excited, it wasn't like I was going to pick anything else. Was it everything you'd hoped?"

His gaze softened and held mine. "It was perfect. Thanks. I'm not used to . . ."

"What?"

He nuzzled the puppy. "People choosing something because it's what I want."

My heart clenched. Solely because of the puppy. Not at the thought of the youngest kid, always at the mercy of his older sisters, parents who didn't trust his judgment. To make him happy, I gathered every puppy within reach and piled them on him until he was buried and laughing hysterically and my face hurt from the cold and smiling.

I may have also sneaked a few photos. Of the puppies. That might have just happened to include Tanner.

We reloaded into the helicopter, and our route took us past the glacier again. We flew low over a jagged area with ponds and streams in the brightest blue I'd ever seen. I knew it was from light absorption, but the shade was so intense, it seemed like something inside the ice had to be making it glow. Then we soared along a giant cliff of ice that fell to the sea. Icebergs floated in the water at the base.

Once again, it was stunning and dramatic, but I was relieved to be on land when the tour was over. Another bus took us to the ship.

"I'm going to check on your mom," my dad said.

"Can we explore the town?" Tanner asked.

I blinked. He was motioning to me. Why was he motioning to me?

My dad looked at me, and I shrugged.

"I suppose that's fine," his dad said. "Cell phones?"

We waved them, kept our windbreakers, and handed over the cold weather gear for our dads to take.

Then Tanner and I were alone, facing the city of Juneau.

Chapter Fifteen

Port of Call: Juneau, Alaska

~

I was in a strange town in a strange state with Tanner Woods, and it was all very strange, and it was no wonder I didn't get an A in English, because I seriously needed another word and a thesaurus.

Why had he suggested this? Because he wanted to see the town and knew they'd tell me to join him? Because he wanted to rob a crab shack and he needed my casing-the-joint skills?

Or because he wanted to spend time with me?

I wasn't sure why that idea made my heart skip.

We wandered toward the shops and restaurants lining the street across from the harbor, advertising everything from diamonds to T-shirts to smoked salmon.

Tanner entered a gift shop, wandering among the shirts. He hurried to rearrange some, and when he moved on, I peeked. He'd moved a generic Alaska one to the front of a rack to hide a shirt that showed two bears standing next to a van with a stick figure family. One bear was saying, "Hey look, a menu."

Had he done that for me?

When I glanced at him, he was tugging on a furry hat with ear flaps.

"Very nice," I said, and my voice might have sounded too high.

"Ooh, samples." He took off the hat and darted to a wall of food items. "Want to try some? I'll eat them first and tell you what to expect."

"I don't know . . ."

"Jam. That's safe." He spread it on a cracker and ate half. "Totally normal. Blackberry, maybe."

When he handed me the other half, his eyes were so hopeful. It was like toast. It would be fine. I ate it.

"Yes," he cheered. "Chocolate. Can't go wrong there."

I accepted that without a review from him first.

"Reindeer sausage?" He took a bite.

"I don't even like regular sausage. Do you know how they make it?"

"Fair enough." He finished it. "Ooh, salmon. This is your chance, S'more."

"Yeah, seafood that's been sitting out sounds like a great introduction to the cuisine."

"It's smoked. This stuff lasts forever. They could send it to space, and you like space. Pretend you're an astronaut."

"I don't want to be an astronaut until it's like in *Star Trek* with gravity and transporters and food dispensers. If you want food poisoning, be my guest."

"I do want it. I want all the food poisoning. Sketchy salmon, questionable caribou, dubious deer."

Now he was just showing off his thesaurus skills.

After he tried the salmon and briefly pretended to choke while I rolled my eyes, we moved on to examine kitchen stuff, jewelry, candles, mugs, giving each other a thumbs-up or thumbs-down on each item. It was easier and easier lately to forget years of disliking him.

I bought fuzzy whale socks and a candle for Jordan and a shirt for myself.

"Are you planning to buy anything or just play with it all?" I asked Tanner.

"I want to get something for my sisters. What about these?" He held up a shirt with an angry cartoon moose that said, "Don't moose with me."

I smiled, not at all charmed that he was shopping for his family. "They'll definitely know it's from you."

After he paid, he asked, "Want to get food?"

"Didn't get enough suspicious samples?"

"Nope, I need more poisoned preserves."

Eating out on land felt different than ending up in the ship's dining room at the same time. But I was hungry. "Sure. Something normal, please."

We stopped in front of a huge corner building with dark red panels called the Red Dog Saloon. Swinging wooden doors covered the entrance.

"What do you think?" he asked.

"Why not?"

He started to push the swinging doors with one hand, his other ghosting across my back like he planned to usher me in. But then he stopped.

"What?" I asked.

"Ladies first? Or should I go first in case there's an old-fashioned bar fight happening?"

A tingle spread through me. "Together?"

We entered side by side into a Wild West explosion. Sawdust covered the floor, old-time piano music drifted from the back, and the walls held enough taxidermy caribou heads to pull three of Santa's sleighs.

"Do you think one of those was Rudolph?" I asked.

"I feel like a gunfight is going to break out any second," Tanner said. "I love it."

We took seats at a slightly sticky table.

"Why don't you try one thing?" he asked. "What's the item on the menu you've never had that sounds the least scary?"

"That doesn't mean anything. Just because something sounds okay doesn't mean it will be."

"If you don't like it, you can spit it out. I'll take a bite too, and make a huge show of spitting it out so no one will notice you."

"You don't have to do that."

"I don't mind."

"Trust me, I know you don't mind making a scene. But it's rude to insult their food. Plus, it would make people look at us."

He shrugged. "If people are looking at you, you should give them what they expect."

His expression was blank, his tone flat. I knew he liked to

make people laugh, but I was starting to suspect there was something deeper than that. A saloon didn't seem the place to ask.

After Tanner's jab about chicken nuggets and chocolate milk, I didn't want to give him the satisfaction, but chicken tenders were the safest option. He didn't comment on my order.

While we waited for our food, we pointed out the craziest decorations. It felt like I was with Jordan, with a friend. Then we posted pictures and videos from the excursion.

I stared for too long at a picture I'd taken of Tanner holding a puppy. It was causing strange sensations in my stomach. It could have been a freaking ad for Alaskan tourism. Tourism and toothpaste, with his teeth gleaming white as the snow in his giant grin. If a puppy adoption group used this picture, people would be fighting each other off with chew toys to adopt the dogs.

We showed each other our favorites. He had a great one of me and my dad, and I'd gotten one of his dad looking back, with the running sled dogs behind him.

I immediately got a text from Jordan. *Tanner AND puppies??? How has your brain not exploded?*

Me: *It might have . . .*

Jordan: *It doesn't look like you're having the worst time.*

Me: *I haven't wanted to murder him for . . . maybe a day?*

Jordan: *Wow. Is that a record?*

I laughed.

Tanner looked up.

Guilt surged through me. He was helping me. I'd had fun.

He'd been less obnoxious than usual lately. How many days had passed since I'd found him annoying? Surely we were in record-breaking territory.

"Hopefully this will make Caveman see what he's missing," he said, something flickering in his eyes.

Right. Caleb.

Letting Tanner assume my mind was on my ex was better than him knowing he'd been the one I was texting my best friend about. I'd thought about Caleb's dog today more than I had about my ex-boyfriend.

It hadn't occurred to me earlier, but today was Saturday, our day to go to the park. Was he walking the dog without me? Missing me? He'd liked my zip line post, but he hadn't commented.

Our food arrived, my chicken and Tanner's fried fish.

Tanner dunked a fry in ketchup. "What's up with the food thing?"

"What do you mean?" I tested the ranch dressing to ensure normalcy before dipping a chicken finger in it.

"Do you really have no interest in trying anything different? Do you have allergies?" He didn't sound judgmental, just curious, and he wasn't shoving a snail in my face or mocking my meal, so I decided to answer.

"No allergies that I know of. I just like simple stuff."

"But what if you haven't discovered your favorite food yet because you haven't tried it? What if there's something better out there, waiting to be discovered, and you miss out on something you might love?" He was leaning toward me across the table, his face earnest.

"What if I'm happy with what I know? Why bother looking elsewhere when I already have something good?"

"Are you settling for fine, though, instead of looking for great?"

He held my gaze, our meals temporarily forgotten. Every detail of the room except Tanner's face had become a blur. My heart thudded in my ears.

Were we still talking about food?

He leaned back, the intense expression fading. "Have you ever had Thai? Or Cuban? Or gyros?"

I swallowed before asking, "Do you like those?"

"I like everything except apples."

That was a random single food to hate. "I had ramen once. The real kind, not the stuff in Styrofoam."

His eyes twinkled. "Wow. Impressive. And?"

"I know you're mocking me. *And* I got food poisoning."

"Oh. That sucks. So any food you've never tried is automatically suspect now?"

"I know what I like. Why risk trying something I don't like when I know I'll be happy with the usual?"

"If you say so. I hardly think one bad experience should affect your life, but . . ."

More than food had led to bad experiences. But I didn't want to press my luck by telling him about the other situations.

"Did you like it?" he asked. "Before you got sick?"

"I guess so, but it's hard to remember, since I associate it with, uh, what came after."

He nodded thoughtfully instead of making a joke. "That would be hard to get over. My mom used to give me blue Gatorade when I was sick, and now I won't touch it even if it's the end of a three-hour practice and that's the only thing available. Oh, apples and Gatorade, then."

The lack of mocking, the understanding, were totally breaking my brain.

After we finished eating, we wandered outside.

"What else do you want to do today?" he asked.

"Could we check out the tram?"

He fake gasped. "Is this Savannah Moore, wanting to try something new?"

I shoved his arm and he staggered, pretending I'd pushed him hard, and laughed.

"No really, is that your ideal date? Riding a tram?"

My heart stuttered, and I tried to keep my voice light. "Is that what this is?"

"Of course not. I was just curious if Caveman ever took you on a tram."

"I don't think there is one in LA."

"If he wanted to make it happen, that shouldn't stop him."

I rolled my eyes.

"Seriously, though. What's the best date you've ever been on?"

Why the sudden interest? "Um, I don't know. I like doing things together. Having someone with you to share an experience and stuff you like."

"What would be your ideal day?" he asked.

"I'd go for a run. Maybe watch a movie. I like the tar pits and the Natural History Museum. The observatory or the zoo. Milkshakes, obviously."

"Obviously."

He was waiting, so I let the words keep coming. "I guess there are places I wouldn't mind seeing. I've always wanted to visit the San Diego Air and Space Museum."

"Why haven't you?"

"Don't laugh, but the idea intimidates me? I get overwhelmed with not knowing what to expect. Where to park, how bad would traffic be, what food they'd have. I don't love going into new situations unprepared. You probably never worry about that."

"I tend to jump right in. Which often leads to problems, so your way might not be the worst."

My face was hot, and I cleared my throat. "What about you? What's your ideal day?" I made sure to enunciate so he didn't hear *date.*

"Hmm. Kind of the same. Work out. Watch football. Be with people I like and do something fun. Doesn't matter what it is. It can be low-key. Maybe that's why it didn't work with the girls I went out with."

"They weren't fun?"

"I don't know. There was always something missing once I got to know them."

"Are you saying you needed more than fun? Like, something deeper and serious?" I gasped. "Who are you and what have you done with Tanner?"

His lip quirk said he recognized my using his words against him. "They expected me to provide the fun. To be on all the time, like I was a source of entertainment. And yeah, I'm an entertaining guy."

"You think you are, anyway."

"It's a fact, S'more. But that's a lot of pressure. If I ever wanted to be serious or I had a bad day or wanted to chill, they'd get, like, disappointed. I couldn't be real."

"I'm sorry. Everyone needs people you can just be you with. Did you—" I stopped. Was digging deeper wise?

"What?" he asked.

"Did you ever try to be real? Share or open up?"

"You ask hard questions." He elbowed me. "I guess I didn't. Not really. And they never asked hard questions, so." He lifted a shoulder. "Could you be real with Caleb? Is that what you liked about him?"

"Sort of? I don't know if that's why I liked him. He was dependable and serious. We liked the same things." I sniffed. "I thought we did, anyway."

"Now what didn't you like?"

"What?"

"Other than the way he broke up with you, which clearly shows bad judgment, and his appalling obliviousness to sarcasm, what didn't you like?"

I barked out a laugh. "Yeah, there was the sarcasm thing. He didn't catch half of my jokes and always took me seriously. At first I would explain myself, but the last couple months I didn't bother."

"What else?"

"I don't know . . ."

"No one's perfect, right? You're great at pointing out when I annoy you. This might help you process."

I didn't know if I wanted to process. I wanted to undo what had happened. Was that the same thing? "Um. He bent the pages in books."

"That animal," Tanner said.

"Oh, okay, he would always ask the same questions, like, all the time. How are you, how's your day, what's new. Even if we'd spoken an hour ago."

"S'more hates small talk. Noted."

"It's just so unnecessary. And when I'd respond with *same as an hour ago,* he would nod like my reply fascinated him. Sometimes he didn't like my ideas, but he never had his own. We never even said I love you. A few times I thought he might be preparing to say it, and I freaked out because I didn't want to say it back." My voice had grown more animated, and I couldn't believe I'd admitted all that aloud.

"Feel better?" Tanner asked.

"I do, actually." Lighter. Like a spaceship jettisoning its rockets. Like dropping baggage.

"Excellent. Now, are we talking or are we riding this thing?"

"You're the one who brought it up," I said.

That had been yet another strange conversation. But, not terrible?

The base of the tram wasn't far from the cruise ship, in a small red-and-white building with lots of windows. I studied the cables, the red-and-white cars, the engine.

Tanner craned his neck to watch the cars overhead. "Of course, the new thing you want to see involves science."

"Hey, you asked. We don't have to ride it."

"Are you kidding? Of course we're riding it. I don't want to have anything in common with Caveman, so I will take you on a tram."

I snorted.

"You could build something like this. Like your bridge and your rocket? Or a working tram can be your next LEGO project."

Or something I'd work on in the physics program? The idea took shape in my head, so when Tanner's hand pressed my back to steer me into the tram line, I barely contained a jump.

Why did this feel like a date?

We boarded the car, which hung from overhead cables. Benches lined the walls of the cabin, but we stood at the back window. As the tram rose and swayed, our arms pressed against each other. Tanner didn't move away. I didn't, either.

The town spread out below us: cars and buses, buildings, and two cruise ships. What was the angle of this cable? We seemed to be traveling vertically up the forested mountain, with the bay below. Soon the giant ships looked like toys.

"Why doesn't this make you nervous?" Tanner asked.

"What do you mean?"

"You don't like new foods. You don't want to drive off the road or see bears. But a tiny car hanging on a wire going up a mountain doesn't bother you?"

I shrugged. "The engineering is solid. I know how it works. Does it make you nervous?"

"Nah, I only get nervous when other people are upset with me or when it's been a whole day and no one has texted me. So the cruise ship, the zip line, the helicopter, were fine?"

His answer was more revealing than he realized. "I prefer the ship. It's large and sturdy. But yeah. When I understand something, it's easier to trust."

"Hmm." We studied each other in our reflections in the window for several seconds, long enough that I started to wonder what he was thinking.

And long enough for me to consider the words I'd said. Was I only talking about the tram?

Our conversations had too many possible double meanings today.

Life was easier when we were making fun of each other. Or not speaking at all.

The cable car deposited us on a ridge halfway up the mountain, and we followed a sky bridge to land. I craned my neck to study the mechanisms as the car hovered above us.

A big building had snacks, coffee, and a gift shop, plus outside viewing decks with vistas of the mountains and the entire channel, water and hills stretching forever.

"Now what?" I asked.

"You just wanted to ride the tram, not explore?"

"Yep."

Tanner laughed.

"But we can explore if you want," I said.

We *had* come all the way up here. There were lots of people, a building. It wasn't too remote. Surely the bears stayed away, right?

Or they knew to find a buffet.

A trail led away from the visitors center along the ridge, so we wandered down it, taking our time to enjoy the views. Purple and yellow flowers bloomed in a meadow, and a large bird, an eagle or a raptor, soared overhead.

I wanted to be able to enjoy the fresh air and views without worrying that every movement was a bear or imagining us getting lost in the wilderness. Why couldn't my normally logical brain stop jumping to the worst conclusions whenever nature was involved?

Tanner maintained a running commentary about how great dogsledding had been, and I found myself relaxing. He made me feel safer, like if I was with him, nothing bad could happen.

I must have jumped when I saw a shadow, because he slowed, studied the area where I'd mistaken a rock for a man-eating animal then asked, "Why this fear, S'more? The bears. For real?"

His voice was soft. His eyes were shadowed under dark brows, but gentle. He seemed to want to know, and I found that I needed him to understand.

"My mom divorced my bio dad when I was five, but he had visitation rights."

"Bio dad? Oh right. I always forget your dad's not, like—"

"He is my dad now, in every way that matters."

"Of course he is. Bio dad. Makes sense. Sorry, go on."

"I was six, and it was my weekend with him. This was before we moved to LA. We were supposed to stay at his place, this small apartment in San Diego, and go to LEGOLAND. But he decided last-minute to take me camping."

"Ooh, no LEGOs *and* a sudden change of plans? Major fail, bio dad."

He said it so seriously, not like he was making fun of me but like he truly agreed it was awful, and I laughed briefly.

"Yeah. So we had this tent at a state park. I woke up in the middle of the night, and I had to go to the bathroom. But he wouldn't go with me, told me to go alone."

Tanner made an angry, strangled noise.

"I was terrified, but I went. Found the creepy building, you know, those awful campground ones with metal toilets and spider nests and ghosts of campers murdered in the woods."

"Oh, yeah, all of those are definitely haunted."

"When I was done, I got lost trying to find our tent. There were so many paths and trees, and so many noises. Rustling in the bushes. Now, I know it was probably squirrels or raccoons, but I was six, and it was dark, and I was scared." I shivered, and Tanner reached out and rubbed my arm.

"I was convinced a bear or wolf was going to eat me, and I panicked. Ran to the nearest tent and shook it until the people came out. Thankfully, it was a nice older couple, not a serial killer. I was sobbing, and they tried to find where I came from but I couldn't talk. A park ranger got involved, then the police, and they questioned my dad. That was the last in a long line of plan changes and disappointments, and my mom had been trying to get full custody. After that, he decided he was done, which was fine by me."

Tanner's hand was still on my arm. "That's awful. I'm sorry that happened to you."

"Thanks."

"Do you ever see him now?"

"Sometimes I get a birthday card like a month early or a month late."

"It's great that you got an upgrade in the dad department."

"I definitely did," I said. "So yeah, I know there isn't a bear around every corner, but my mind goes back to that moment when I was alone and scared, and I can't stop it."

"That's why you don't want to go camping for the meteor shower."

I shuddered. "I know you're right, that it would be an amazing view."

"I'm sorry, did you admit that I was right?" His smile and his voice were gentle.

"I'm not saying it again," I said. "Besides, the observatory is much—"

"Safer. Closer. Less likely to have wild animals, unless you count Brady or a bear learns to navigate the 405."

"Exactly."

He nodded thoughtfully. "Thank you."

"For what?"

"For telling me. For trusting me."

My chest twisted. "Thanks for not laughing."

"S'more. Savannah. I wouldn't, not about something like that. You know that, right?"

He bent close to study me, his eyes a clear gray. His voice was rough, and I bobbed my head. To my surprise, I did know. We studied each other until a flash of movement made us turn.

A bald eagle had landed on a tree stump yards away. We froze. It was elegant and majestic, with a wicked curved beak and intelligent gold eyes. It lifted off, graceful, and soared away, and Tanner and I looked at each other again with soft smiles.

I thought of our earlier conversation about an ideal day. Or date. Or whatever. Not that this was a date. But it would have made a pretty perfect one.

Tanner had me pose for a selfie with the view behind us, pressed his cheek against mine. I jumped, then tried to smile. His face was warm, and the slightest bit of stubble on his jaw rubbed my cheek as his face split into a grin.

Another eagle took flight inside my chest.

We went back to the visitors center. The sun was getting lower, but there was still lots of light, gentle and warm, muting the colors in a way that felt like magic.

"Want to hike down instead of taking the tram?" he asked.

I'd seen people hiking on an official trail when we rode up. "Why not?"

The trail was steep, leading through dense rainforest with thick, humid air. Rocks and roots jutted up through the dirt path, and patches were thick with mud. I took bags of Goldfish from my backpack and handed one to Tanner, which made him laugh.

The trees blocked the light, making the air cool, and green light enveloped us. Something about telling Tanner my fear, or maybe his presence, allowed my worries to fade. We walked in pleasant silence until my phone buzzed.

I pulled it out to find a text from my mom saying *Where are you???*

The multiple question marks made me stumble. I saw the time at the top of my screen.

Oh no.

chapter sixteen

Port of Call: Juneau, Alaska

~

"We're going to miss the boat!"

"What?" Tanner asked.

A supernova of panic flared in me. "The on-board time. I didn't think about it because it stays light so late."

Understanding dawned on his face. "Let's go."

We took off running downhill.

I fumbled to call my mom as we ran. "We're coming, we're coming. I'm so sorry. Please don't let them leave."

"Savannah, slow down," she said. "Where are you?"

"Can't slow down. Can't talk. I'm coming."

I didn't bother trying to return the phone to my pocket, just clutched it tight as I raced down the trail, trying not to trip on a root or slip in the mud.

What would happen if we were too late? The ship wouldn't wait; they'd made that clear. Our guide earlier had said that

Juneau was the only US capital you couldn't drive to. We'd have to take a boat or plane to get anywhere. But we were minors. Surely it was illegal to leave kids behind, right? We could sue the ship for child abandonment.

Even if lawsuits were an option later, I didn't want to be stranded in Alaska alone.

My feet raced along the path, too quickly given the steepness. I skidded on a wet area, grabbed for a branch or anything. Tanner reached for me, but not in time. I twisted. Rather than right myself, I fell face-first into the mud. Wet dirt slimed the side of my face.

"Whoa, you okay?" Tanner stopped.

"Fine." I grunted and spit out a disgusting mouthful.

"If you want a mud bath, try the spa. Today, we have a two-mile record to beat."

"This isn't funny, Tanner."

I scrambled to my feet, wiped my phone off on a clean patch of pants, and tried to use my sleeve to clean my face. Never mind. It would take too long. I spit once more and took off.

"We'll be okay," he said.

"Less talking, more running."

The trail deposited us in town, closer to the hills than the water. We sprinted down the street, heading toward the port where the ship waited, too far away. There weren't many people to dodge. Though it was light, the town was emptier.

Sure, because everyone from the cruise ship was safely aboard, waiting for the captain to keep the schedule. My legs burned from the hill, and I focused on breathing.

Tanner glanced at me. He was panting. "You okay?"

"Yeah."

Okay to keep running, anyway. In all other ways, I was far from okay. I was fearing what might happen, I was sick with guilt, and I was annoyed with him.

"Sure you can keep up?" he asked.

I knew what he was doing, challenging me to push me on. And I knew this wasn't his fault. But old habits had me wanting to blame him, as if the familiar sensation of being annoyed at Tanner Woods offered a life raft in the sea of worry. He'd been the one who'd wanted to stay in town, the one to suggest the hike, when the tram would have gotten us down the hill an hour ago.

"I can't believe I let you talk me into this." The words burst out before I could consider them.

"Yeah, yeah, I know. It's always my fault." His words huffed out.

Somehow his lack of arguing made me feel ill. More ill, since I was already close to puking. But I didn't reassure him.

We rounded a corner, and the ship was ahead. In port, not sailing away. We wouldn't have to swim and hope someone threw us a rope. We raced past workers at the terminal and onto the wooden dock, our steps thudding, then ran alongside the massive ship. Clapping and cheers came from above.

People were watching from their balconies, probably judging us, worried two teenagers were going to screw up their trip. Our pictures would be added to the wall of cruise ship offenders, or we'd be featured on the morning show again, this time asking people to keep an eye on us to make sure we got back. Bird Girl and Bird Boy were not to be trusted.

Our parents were standing at the base of the metal ramp, along with two employees in cruise ship polo shirts.

I checked the time. Fifteen minutes late.

We stumbled onboard, scanned our cards, and I slumped onto a nearby bench to catch my breath. My lungs were on fire. My legs were trembling. The Goldfish I'd eaten were threatening to swim out of my stomach. And the drying dirt on my face itched, but my shoes had already gotten enough mud on the carpet, so I didn't scrape it off.

"Savannah, what happened? Where were you? You aren't hurt?" My mom ran a gentle hand along the non-muddy part of my face.

I shook my head.

Tanner bent over nearby with his hands on his knees, chest heaving.

"I'm sure it was Tanner," Mr. Woods said to her. "Usually Savannah is so trustworthy."

I winced as I continued to focus on sucking in oxygen. My chest burned. "Lost track of time."

"That's unlike you," Mom said.

"It was all me," Tanner said. "I stole her phone and her watch and made her hike off in search of reindeer."

Mrs. Woods crossed her arms. "Once you're recovered, I expect a better explanation than that."

Mr. Woods was shaking his head. "I should have expected something like this. When will you learn to be more careful? And dragging Savannah into it."

Technically he hadn't dragged me, but my chest burned and my throat was tight and even though my heart hammered at me to say something, to stand up for him, I didn't speak.

My dad put his arm around me. "What matters is you're okay and you made it. We were worried."

I leaned my head against his shoulder before jerking it away so I didn't dirty his shirt. "I'm sorry." I turned to the employees who were closing up the security area. "Really, really sorry. Thank you for not leaving us."

The nearest man gave me a kind smile. "The onboard time is an hour before we leave the dock, so the captain does have a little leeway. But please be more careful. We can't always guarantee the ship will wait."

I ducked my head and nodded.

Tanner was uncharacteristically silent. Where was his usual charm, making people forget he'd ever caused trouble? He definitely was avoiding me.

I didn't blame him. I mean, I *had* blamed him. For this. Which is why I didn't blame him now for being mad at me, because that had been terrible of me.

I still didn't know what to say as our parents shuffled us upstairs to our rooms. Despite the light lingering in the sky, it was late, but I was too wound up to sleep. My heart hadn't stopped racing. After showering the mud off, I went to the balcony as the ship sailed away and watched the silver sunset over dark mountains and inky water. I remained alert for the sound of Tanner emerging onto his balcony next to mine.

My stomach churned. Guilt ate at me, not just for being late, but for getting mad at him, when it had been equally my fault.

It was habit to pit us on opposite sides, to assume if something went wrong in my life, it could be traced to him. But we'd been on the same team today. He hadn't forced me into anything.

Then I'd let his parents blame him, when I could have stood up for him.

An invisible fist was squeezing my lungs. I felt slimier than a mud puddle, and I wouldn't blame Tanner in the least if he decided we were done.

Turned out panic, guilt, and body surfing in a mud puddle did not make for a good night's sleep.

I'd waited until the sky was dark and I was shivering and there was nothing to see but blackness, but Tanner had never come out, so I'd eventually given up and gone to bed.

Now, we walked into the town of Skagway, which was nestled in a gap where mountains met the sea. It looked like a hidden frontier town. Our families were taking a train ride into the Yukon Territory.

Tanner was quiet, trudging between his parents.

I owed him an apology.

It was going to be awkward.

At a historical train depot, two green-and-yellow engine cars were followed by a string of old-fashioned ones with red roofs and dark panels. We boarded the caboose that Mr. Ramirez had reserved for employees, along with him, his wife, and several other coworkers and their families.

The interior was classic to match the outside, with wood

paneling on the walls and large windows. My parents and I sat at one table—with me at the window and Mom on the aisle. I was surprised she hadn't invited herself to her boss's table, but maybe she wanted to keep me close, make sure I couldn't get out, as if I might jump off the moving train, get lost, and once again nearly miss the boat.

Tanner and his parents were across from us, and he looked as tired as I felt. I hoped he hadn't been up late getting yelled at, otherwise my apology was going to have to be even grander.

The train emitted a loud whistle, and we were off, slowly easing away from the station and town before picking up speed.

The tracks led along a silvery river. The hillsides were covered in shades of green, and clouds hid the tops of the mountains. We rose steadily, winding through the hills. When the train went around a corner, through the window I saw the front part of the train ahead of us, curving with the track. Sometimes the track ran along the edge of a cliff and a whole valley spread beneath us. I'd never seen so many trees in my life.

We sat and watched the view, lulled by the rocking and the clacking. A docent was supposed to give a talk about the railroad and the area, but we were free to move around and go onto the platform.

"I'm going to check out the outside," I said.

"Be careful," Mom said.

It wasn't like I could get separated from the train and be late.

The back door led to a small platform. Since we were in the caboose, there was nothing behind us but the even tracks, stretching into the distance and disappearing around the last curve. A flimsy gate and metal rail enclosed the small space, rattling slightly along with the sound of the wheels. Cool wind rushed around me.

The fresh air somehow made the views more impressive, the speed faster, and the nature more all-encompassing. I liked the row of railroad tracks, a solitary sign that humans had conquered a tiny part of this wilderness. People had come before me and succeeded and returned, which was a good sign I wouldn't end up trapped here forever.

The door cracked, and Tanner peered out. He joined me, standing as far away as the platform allowed, which wasn't far. He had to have known I was out there, which meant he wasn't avoiding me forever. That made me happier than it should have.

We stood in silence, except for the clacking, as we rattled past a deep valley with a rushing river at the bottom. What was he thinking? Why wasn't he talking?

My stomach turned over. We were alone. Nothing to do. Trapped. I had no excuse.

"Hey," I said.

He raised an eyebrow.

Ugh. Why did I have to find words for this? I should have prepared something to say. Or texted him while we were walking through town. Except text apologies were nearly as high on the jerk scale as parking lot breakups.

"I, uh." I peeked at him then the mountains then him again. I gripped the metal rail as we went around a curve. "I need to say I'm sorry. For yesterday."

He stared at me, not making this easy. His eyes were the same stormy gray as the clouds.

I swallowed. "I shouldn't have blamed you for making us late. It was both our fault."

"It was."

He wasn't giving me much. I forged on. "So, I'm sorry for blaming you. And for letting our parents blame you, too."

He held my gaze. And nodded. "Thanks."

I released my breath.

His lips quirked. "Is this the first time you've ever apologized to me?"

"Quite possibly."

"I might need a minute to recover." His focus shifted to the view, and he huffed what sounded like a laugh.

"What?" I asked.

He shook his head. "It's just, I thought that was what I always wanted."

"An apology from me? Almost missing a boat and getting stranded in Alaska? Watching me face-plant in a mud puddle?"

He shifted to face me. The wind was cool, and the tracks rattled beneath us as the train hurtled on up the mountainside. His face was solemn.

"You to get in trouble," he said, and his voice was rough.

"Excuse me?"

"Not, like, really in trouble." He ran a hand through his hair. "All I ever hear about is how smart you are, how responsible, how hardworking. How you passed the driver's test on your first try and will get into colleges without a sports scholarship. My parents are always saying they wish I was more like you. They think you're this perfectly behaved angel who never does anything wrong."

"Not after yesterday, they don't." My tone was wry.

"I always thought, if the two of us were having fun together, my parents would see it as kids being kids. Like your participation would legitimize what I was doing. Show them it wasn't all that bad. And sometimes I hoped if we both got in trouble, they would see you were human and stop comparing us. When I say it out loud, it sounds awful."

It kind of made sense. There had been many times I'd assumed he'd been trying to annoy or embarrass me, when I'd thought he was childish or ridiculous and wondered why he wouldn't leave me alone. No, I didn't want to jump off a cliff into the ocean or eat twenty Otter Pops at a time or race shopping carts in the store.

But he'd never tried to get me to do anything illegal. Or horribly dangerous. Or that would hurt anyone. My mind had seen it that way because I never wanted to risk anything at all. Now, I looked back and saw a wild boy being a kid, wanting to have fun, not some evil attempt to lead me into a life of crime.

He shifted closer, so I had to crane my neck to see him. "Like I said, it wasn't as satisfying as I'd hoped. I just felt bad, because you were right; it was my idea to hike. So I'm sorry, too, for yesterday, and for all of it."

"Oh. Thanks, I guess. Wait, now it's my turn to record this moment to prove that Tanner Woods is capable of apologizing."

His crooked half smirk and piercing eyes melted my insides.

"I always figured you were either trying to annoy me, or you thought I was boring and needed to have fun."

"I never thought you were boring. I wanted you to have fun,

and I found those things fun. I wanted company, and you were there, so I thought you'd enjoy them, too."

"If it makes you feel better, my mom wishes I were more like you, with an actual social life. She always wanted to have that house where kids were coming and going all the time, where friends randomly stayed for dinner, or stopped by unannounced."

"She might not feel that way if she had to feed half the football team. My mom says once I have a job, I have to reimburse her for years of groceries. I'm ninety percent sure she's joking."

We stopped talking as the train plunged into a tunnel and blackness enveloped us. When we emerged, I blinked at the brightness. We left the tunnel behind, and I watched the black hole in the side of the hill get smaller and smaller.

"Is that why we hated each other for all these years?" I asked. "Because our parents liked the other too much?"

Tanner's head whipped toward me. "You hated me?"

"Um. Maybe?" It sounded mean to say now, especially with how he asked the question, like he was genuinely surprised. "You were always mad at me for getting you in trouble, and you admitted you didn't like being compared. You didn't hate me?"

"I was annoyed by you. You did get me in trouble a lot. It was fun to challenge you. But I never hated you." His eyes were intense, serious, locked onto me.

Huh. A ball of light inside me was expanding slowly to fill me with warmth and something fizzy. "I'm sorry. For those times I ratted you out. It wasn't cool of me."

"I would have been caught, anyway, and I was kind of asking for it."

We were silent, and I had to look away, watching the trees whip past instead of him and whatever weird reaction he was setting off inside me.

"Are we good now?" he asked. "Do you still hate me? I hope not, because we're stuck together for another week, and I'm not spending it with Dottie or Mr. Ramirez, nice as they are."

"I suppose I can tolerate you a little longer."

"I'm glad."

The look he gave me made the explosion in my chest worse.

I cleared my throat. "We should go inside. I want to hear the talk."

"What happens on the train caboose stays in the caboose?"

"That sounds wrong."

He laughed and opened the door, pausing long enough that I had the option to go first or to let him.

I felt like I was tumbling down one of those cliffs. Was it possible that years of hatred had been misunderstandings? Just two kids with different personalities and naturally competitive natures who didn't understand each other?

Mind. Blown.

chapter seventeen

Port of Call: Skagway, Alaska

~

While Tanner and I were outside, our parents had shifted tables, so our dads were together with Mr. Ramirez, and our moms were with his wife. Tanner and I took an empty one, and he broke out the playing cards until a guide came on the speakers.

She talked about the Klondike gold rush coming through Skagway in the late 1800s, and how the people had to carry many loads of supplies up this trail on foot or horses. How they hurried to build the railroad in two years to reach the gold fields, and how it was listed as an engineering landmark.

Tanner was oddly quiet. I figured he'd been contemplating our conversation until he said, "Can you imagine coming here, hoping to strike it rich, and then carrying all your stuff?"

"You mean the terror, not having a road, no one to call for help? Lots and lots of bears?"

"That's what made early people so interesting. The courage it took to do things we take for granted." His eyes were gleaming.

"You like history." My words came out like an accusation.

"What? I do not."

"You totally do. Nerd." A smile took over my face.

"No way. Memorizing all those dates? That class is the worst." He leaned back and tried to look casual.

"Didn't you get an A? There's more to history than dates. Like you were saying, there's the people who lived it. Their stories. What it was like. Making it come alive."

His eyes narrowed playfully, and he pointed at me. "Don't get ideas. I'm not majoring in history. Do you have any idea how many boring books I'd have to read? I bet the tests are like giant lists of dates and you have to say everything that happened in the entire world."

"I don't think that's accurate."

"I'm pretty sure it is."

"You liked when the ATV guide talked about Ketchikan, too. Oh, and that project when we wrote plays about the explorers and you wanted to star in all of them. Or field trips to the missions when you volunteered for the demonstrations." I'd always assumed he liked being the center of attention. But knowing it might have been more than that made me smile.

"Keep trying," he said. "I'm not studying history for four years."

I mock frowned at him. "Fine. I will find something."

"I know you will. You're incapable of failing."

I blinked at him.

"It's a compliment, S'more. Can you accept those?"

"Usually. But it's weird coming from you."

"I'm going to do it all the time, to mess with you."

He smirked, and we rolled our eyes at each other, but it was friendlier than before.

The guide was now pointing out an abandoned cantilever bridge spanning a deep gorge.

"Nice," I said. "Look at the beautiful angles. It's fascinating, how they could build something like that back then. And the engineering is so elegant. I like the trestle bridges. They're classic. But that one is incredible."

"Now who's the nerd?" he asked.

"I never tried to hide that fact. I wish I'd seen this before our bridge project in physics. I would have built one."

He opened his mouth but closed it. Studied me.

"What?"

"You like building stuff, that's all. Are you going to miss physics?"

I straightened the forgotten deck of cards. "Mr. Lin wants me to do this program next year. Extracurricular physics and engineering. Projects and field trips and a competition." The thought of the names and places and events in that email was making my heart race.

"That sounds cool," he said. "Are you going to do it?"

I slid him the cards, hoping my hands weren't shaking. "I haven't decided."

"Hmm." He studied me but didn't say anything else, and I almost asked what he was thinking before deciding I'd rather not know.

We had reached the mountain pass and were now in Canada, above the trees and into a subalpine environment with rocks and grass and flowers. They served box lunches, with a sandwich, chips, and bottled water.

"Are you planning to eat that?" Tanner asked.

"Yes. Why?"

"I was hoping this was on your do-not-touch list so I could eat two of them."

"It's a turkey sandwich. Why would I not eat a turkey sandwich?"

He tore open the bag of chips. "I don't know. Maybe one betrayed you once."

"You've seen me eat sandwiches." I paused. "You can have my pickle, though."

"Sweet." He reached over the table and snagged it, grinning.

Sharing food and interests. Apologies. Compliments.

I had entered an alternate dimension or parallel universe. Today couldn't possibly be real.

The train reached an area of small lakes, the water right alongside the tracks, a pale but brilliant aqua blue. The scenery here physically stopped my breath. Maybe nature, like Tanner, wasn't the worst.

We'd traveled out of the clouds and into blue skies. The track led along the shore of a huge lake backed by mountains. The peaks and trees reflected in still water. We stopped alongside the lake, where a big red barnlike depot waited, and the spire of an old church was visible on a nearby hill.

We got off and ambled toward a trailhead, where a sign informed us we were in bear country. That was not a country I wanted to visit.

I could just wait on the nice, comfy train. . . .

Someone near us was holding a small canister and inspecting it. When he shook it and held out his other arm, the guy with him grabbed his hand.

"Dude. That's bear spray."

"Yeah, it keep the bears away."

"It doesn't work like bug spray, man. You spray the bear, not yourself."

"Why would I spray the bear?"

Tanner and I sped up to pass them so we could hide how hard we were laughing. Before I knew it, we were partway up the trail. The bear spray had worked to repel my nerves, at least.

It was a mild climb, with scattered pine trees, and when we reached the top, Tanner spread his arms and raised his eyebrows at me in challenge.

The view was gorgeous. We climbed onto a boulder. The lake stretched so far into the distance, I couldn't see the end. Mountains framed both sides, ringed in pine trees, like they were cupping the clear turquoise water.

My breath suspended in my chest as I took it in. No unease crept in, only peace.

Tanner stood beside me in silence before wrapping his arms around me, trapping mine at my sides. He lifted me off the ground.

"Bear hug," he said.

"Oh no, the bad jokes are contagious. Make it stop."

"Want me to put you down?" He took one step toward the edge of the boulder, nowhere near falling, and I swatted him as best I could with my arms stuck.

"I'd never drop you," he said in my ear.

His hold was sturdy, and I was locked in, and I believed him.

"Aw, you two are so cute," said a woman coming up the trail.

Tanner put me down, smiling, and the idea wasn't as terrible as the last time someone had said it.

Canada was messing with me again.

We headed down the trail and Tanner stepped in front of me, his back to me, with his arms out. "Want a ride? So you don't slip again? Jump on."

Definitely an alternate dimension. I let him give me a piggy-back ride, his arms strong on my thighs, my hands clasped at his chest. Despite my height, I felt tiny.

We passed a kid and mom wandering the trail, the kid straggling behind.

Tanner stopped, and I slid off his back.

"Hey, buddy," Tanner said. "That's a big backpack you've got."

"It has my comics and my Spider-Man and my jacket and my rocks."

Sounded legit to me.

Tanner knelt by him. "It will be easier to walk if you wear both straps. It distributes the weight better. Spider-Man is heavy. He's a lot for one shoulder."

The boy inspected him as if debating whether Tanner looked like someone who would give trustworthy advice then tugged the other strap on and stood taller.

"Perfect," Tanner said.

They marched off, and I studied Tanner while trying not to let him notice. I was getting an idea for his eight-year plan, but I wasn't ready to share.

After we reboarded the train, it continued along the lake-shore, where actual waves lapped. The color was insane, a tur-quoise too vivid for words. The next stop was in a small mountain town with a sandy beach and strong wind. Native art decorated the buildings. We found ice cream and wandered around. It was hard to imagine that people lived here, so far from any large cit-ies. That was a huge nope from me.

For the return trip, we loaded into a bus. Tanner plopped down next to me like it was natural. The drive was nearly un-inhabited, with more lakes and flowers. I'd never considered how much empty space there was in the world, living in a city that sometimes seemed endless.

The bus stopped to let us photograph a moose that was am-bling down the road, and the driver gave us facts about the ani-mals. My attention caught on the fact that moose were actually deadlier than bears, because they would charge a person who got too close.

Fantastic. Another animal to worry about.

Tanner leaned sideways so his shoulder bumped mine. "Can I ask you a question?"

"You just did, and you only get one per day."

"What if I use tomorrow's in advance?"

"Was that a question? Because now you're up to Tuesday's." His face was solemn, so I said, "Yeah, go ahead."

"Why don't you like new things? For real."

His voice was an in-between. Serious yet light. Like he wanted to know but wouldn't be upset if I chose not to answer.

My stomach clenched. Facing the question itself was a scary

new thing. But he'd opened up today, and he hadn't teased me about the other truths I'd revealed.

"You know how I told you about my bio dad? It wasn't just the camping trip. He and my mom had this whirlwind romance, adventures and traveling, but then after she had me, he didn't want to settle down. So it was more than a few changed plans. He'd go on trips without us whenever he felt like it, make plans and change his mind. Not show up for big events."

"What a jerk."

"Yeah. And I always liked boundaries, even when I was little. Knowing what to expect. He'd try to make things sound like a fun adventure. Some kids might have found him fun. You probably would have. I just found it stressful."

"It's not fun if the other person is miserable. It was on him to learn enough about you to know how to make you happy."

"That was exactly it. I didn't understand this at the time, but now I see that he didn't take time to think about me. They weren't adventures because he thought I'd like them. It was all for him."

Tanner chewed his lip. "Okay, it makes sense that you like stability. But not eating new foods or running new routes or anything?"

I fiddled with my phone, which was nothing but a camera in the wilds of Canada. "Things go wrong."

"Things always go wrong. That's life."

"Yeah, but when I stick to my routines, I know what to expect. What's likely to go wrong."

His forehead wrinkled like he wasn't buying it. "I need examples here. Like the food poisoning?"

"Yeah. Or, I hate scary movies, and usually I refuse to watch them, but at a sleepover once, everyone else insisted. For months, I couldn't walk past a sewer without being convinced a clown was going to come out of it."

He laughed.

"Let me guess, you love scary movies?"

"Nah. I mean, I'll watch them. The jump scares and creepy stuff don't bother me. But it feels like cheap storytelling."

Apparently I needed to get used to him surprising me. "What do you like, then?"

I couldn't believe that after all these years, I didn't know.

"Pretty much anything. Comedies, sports movies. And I do like science fiction. Stuff with cool visuals, sets, costumes. No need to look so surprised, S'more. I'm more than a pretty face and muscles."

Was he reading my mind? "I never said you weren't."

"I'm pretty sure you have said that."

"Okay, maybe I have. But I apologized to you once today, and I'm not sure the universe can handle a second one."

He grinned. "What else went wrong?"

"Oh. Um." It took work to get my brain unstuck from the fact that he was a nerd, too. "Allergic reaction to a new shampoo that made me sneeze all day. Or my mom bought a different brand of bread once because the regular one was out, and it tasted like cardboard. One time Caleb's older brother drove us to the Science Center and took a new route, even though I told him not to, and we were late for a speaker I'd been wanting to hear. And once, Jordan talked me into wearing heels when we went out for dinner, and I got blisters right before a big race."

He blinked a few times. "Wow. Okay. But couldn't you get blisters from running shoes? Or be late on your usual route if there was an accident?"

"Yeah, but the known is safer and more manageable."

"Is it, though?"

"I know, you think I'm boring."

"I never said that."

"You say it all the time."

"Name one time?"

"Um. Moore the Bore. In front of everyone, while I was getting dumped."

His face darkened. "That wasn't me."

"Oh please. I'm supposed to believe the guy who's been giving me nicknames for years and was standing right there didn't come up with that one?"

"Yes," he said with conviction. "Because it was Kody. I told him to shut up. And then I ordered him to throw that football to distract everyone. So they'd watch me instead."

I narrowed my eyes. "I thought you were being insensitive and rude while I was having a terrible day."

"I was trying to help. I wanted to throw the football at Caveman, but I figured I might knock him out and I'd get in trouble."

"So . . . you decided to help me by bowling for trash with your body?"

"Exactly. Give everyone something else to talk about."

It was sweet in a weird way. "Sorry to tell you I don't think it worked."

He sighed. "Yeah. Moore the Bore caught on, even after I told them to stop."

"And it really wasn't you?"

"Nope. And the words you're looking for are, 'I'm so sorry I blamed you, Tanner. Please excuse my ignorance and forgive me for falsely accusing you of things you didn't do.'"

"You have to admit, you do like to give me nicknames."

"Cool ones, not rude ones."

"Then . . . sorry for assuming."

"Was that so hard?"

"It truly was."

His lips quirked. "I'm sorry, too. I knew we didn't get along, but I had no idea I was making your life so miserable."

"Really? *No* idea?"

"Okay, maybe some idea. And maybe sometimes it was fun."

I poked him and he grabbed my hand.

"Truce?" he asked. "For real, not just for the trip?"

Our gazes held. I nodded.

He slowly released my hand, and my heart stuttered. Tanner was the first one to dig deep enough to learn these things about me, even given Jordan's amateur psychologist tendencies. Caleb had certainly never asked anything so insightful.

We stopped at the border between Alaska and Canada and took pictures at a sign saying *Welcome to Alaska*. Tanner put his arm around me as we posed, and, nestled against him, I felt safe and happy. Like I fit.

I was not going to analyze that thought. Nope. Shoot it out an airlock, fire it into the sun.

Once back in Skagway, we wandered through the frontier-style town with its wooden buildings and wide streets.

"Are you imagining it with dirt and horses instead of cars, and a gunfight on the main road?" I asked Tanner.

"Sadly, I don't think those happened as often as movies want us to believe," he said. "But yes, I was."

I was seeing a whole new side of Tanner. Had it been there, buried, for years? Surely I hadn't missed all this?

We were walking toward the ship when my phone buzzed with a message. The sensation felt foreign. I'd almost gotten used to not having it on the ship.

I pulled it out to check, expecting a comment from Jordan on the fact that I'd posted a picture of Tanner and me crossing international borders.

But it wasn't from her. It was from Caleb.

Chapter Eighteen

Port of Call: Skagway, Alaska

I stumbled, my eyes glued to the phone screen, and stopped.

"What is it, Savannah?" Mom asked.

"I'm going to read this message real fast. I'll catch up."

"Tanner, will you wait with her?"

I lifted my eyes. We stood on a sidewalk leading straight from town to the port, with colorful wooden buildings on one side, a green hill on the other, and our enormous ship clearly visible straight ahead.

"Mom, the ship is right there. I'm perfectly capable of walking a few hundred feet by myself."

She blinked. "Oh. Okay. But don't take too long."

"I won't be late again. I promise."

My phone was burning a hole in my hand. What did the message say?

Tanner studied me and I avoided eye contact. Was he hurt that I didn't want him to stay? Why did I care?

The others continued on, and I fortified myself with a deep breath before opening the message.

Hey Savannah, your vacation looks like lots of fun. I hope you're having a good time. Talk to you soon.

I stared at the letters. That was all? I wasn't sure what I'd expected when I saw his name, but . . . more than that? Those were words you'd say to anyone. An acquaintance, your friend's grandmother, the clerk at the grocery store.

The words didn't miraculously multiply into something longer and more illuminating. They were an equation, but the worst kind—one I couldn't solve.

I sent a screenshot to Jordan with a row of question marks and trudged to the ship.

Tanner was standing by the gangway.

"Waiting to get stranded with me in case I was late?" I asked.

"Nah, I knew you wouldn't be late. I wasn't with you." His smile said I was forgiven for yesterday. "But I was fully prepared to fake an emergency and delay the ship if necessary."

"Playing in trash again?"

"Jumping in the water and pretending I was drowning was the leading contender. Everything okay?" He nodded to the phone in my hand.

"Huh? Oh. Yeah. Caleb messaged me. To say hi and that he'd talk to me soon."

Tanner's expression went very blank. His eyes darkened. "Did he apologize for dumping you?"

"Not exactly." Okay, not at all.

"I know you dated for a long time and this"—he waved a hand—"is to get him back. But please respect yourself enough to not listen to anything he has to say until he apologizes, because what he did sucked."

My stomach squirmed. "Maybe he didn't want to apologize by text."

Tanner hummed. "Or he sees you having fun and regrets losing you. But think about what I said."

I heard him. I did. He was right—Caleb's methods and timing for the breakup did suck. It had been a jerk move, and I did need to know he was sorry for how it happened.

But if he apologized . . . Everyone made mistakes. Shouldn't I be willing to forgive him? To not do what he had done and throw away the last nine months so easily? Besides, it wasn't like he'd asked me to get back together. He was just saying hello.

My phone buzzed again.

When I looked down, Tanner asked, "Caveman again?"

"Jordan." My lips twitched. "She says he better apologize and I shouldn't talk to him until he does."

Tanner grinned. "I knew I liked her."

"Really?"

"Sure. She seems cool."

"Oh. She is. Way cooler than I am."

Tanner's frown returned. "Why did you let him convince you you're boring?"

"I know I'm not adventurous and cool and fun like Jordan."

"There are lots of ways to be cool and interesting. You build rockets. You run. You throw yourself over high bars with a pole."

"Yeah, those make you popular in high school. I'm telling Jordan I hear her." I tapped out my reply.

"And Caveman?"

"I . . . I'm going to wait to reply to him."

"Good for you. Make him work for it."

It was more because I didn't know what to say. I didn't want to sound desperate, like I was waiting for Caleb to reach out to me. And I didn't want to have to demand an apology by text. That was pathetic.

But I did want to talk to him. And I did hope he was sorry.

We'd been dating for nine months, friends for two years before that. We played a big part in each other's lives. Moving forward without him would be like losing a piece of my life.

Tanner and I boarded the ship, and because it was late and a train into the Yukon totally counted as my new thing for the day, I grabbed a quick pizza dinner and went to bed. I was still contemplating the message, and also the facts I'd learned about Tanner. My brain was so full, I was worried it might go into a total meltdown if I didn't force it to rest.

And a tiny part of me was disappointed at how quickly Tanner had said goodnight.

"Why did I let you talk me into this?" I asked.

"Because it's awesome. And because we're helping our parents."

"If Mr. Ramirez is basing the promotion on who's willing to risk hypothermia, that's definitely an HR violation."

We stood in our bathing suits, wrapped in big fluffy towels, on the lowest deck of the ship, along with our parents and several of their coworkers. The ship was stopped near the entrance to Glacier Bay, where we'd be cruising for the rest of the day. But first, the company was holding a polar bear plunge.

And somehow Tanner had convinced me to participate.

The way he turned everything into an adventure, wanted to do and see everything, knew how to seize the day, was rather infectious. I was infected. I probably needed to see a doctor.

"Corporate America would be better if more things were decided by contests," Tanner said. "Want a job? Gotta beat the other applicants in a cage fight."

"That's easy for you to say." I jabbed his arm muscle.

"Fine, what about a race? They can drop off potential candidates two miles from the office, and the first one to reach it is hired."

"Hmm. I could at least beat you in that."

"Oh, you think so?"

"Everyone knows football players can't do distances."

"I kept up fine in Vancouver."

"Because I let you."

He laughed, and I suddenly realized how close we were standing. We were huddling for warmth, that was all. The open hatch was letting in chilly air.

Not everyone here was participating—my dad wasn't. He was our designated cameraman. I suspected many would chicken out and were here to watch their coworkers make fools of themselves. But Mr. Ramirez was determined, which meant our moms were, too.

I had to admit, I agreed about it being awesome. I felt strong and bold just thinking about what I was about to do. Who could call someone boring and stuck in their ways when they were willing to plunge themselves into a frigid ocean?

Mr. Ramirez stood in front of the group. "I'm grateful for all of you who are here this week. I hope you and your families are having a wonderful experience. And thanks to the crew for arranging this team-building exercise."

Tanner snorted, and I smiled, as the others clapped. Nothing built a team like joint risk of frostbite.

"There are no bonuses involved for participating," Mr. Ramirez continued. "You'll just win the admiration of your coworkers. Since I never want to ask any of you to do something I wouldn't do, I'll go first."

We dropped our towels. The shock of cold air made goose bumps sprout on my skin. The water was a forbidding light, cool teal. A small temporary metal platform with three stairs led down to a small deck. If the ship made port anywhere without a dock, we would have boarded the lifeboat tenders here. Today, there were no small boats waiting, only icy water.

I tried not to stare at Tanner's shirtless chest. It wasn't like I'd never seen it before, at family lake trips or beach outings. But today it was pulling at my attention.

Snap out of it, Savannah.

Mr. Ramirez hurried down the steps, onto the platform, and leaped off. Others followed. One of the ladies from accounting made it to the edge before stopping, laughing and waving off the teasing as she returned to the indoors. Our moms went together.

Tanner squeezed my hand. We ran three steps and jumped.

I had enough time to see him do a flip before I plunged beneath the water.

The shock was intense and instantaneous. A cold that stole my breath, stopped my heart. Jolted my brain until I was awake, alert, alive.

I surfaced and Tanner came up beside me. We both yelled.

I flailed my arms to stay afloat as the icy water sent prickles through me.

Tanner floated on his back briefly, hands behind his head like he was in a tropical sea. Then he flipped over and sucked water into his mouth and spat it out in an arc.

"Gross," I said. "Seals pee in here."

"I bet I could stay in longer than you," he said.

My toes were already going numb. I'd never taken his dares in the past. Not publicly, anyway. I plotted in private how to get better grades or beat him for an award or circumvent his terrible ideas for projects. But this was like one of his past dares—I had no need to prove myself in something that might result in me losing fingers.

"Yup," I said. "I bet you're right."

"Aw, you don't want to make a bet, S'more?"

"I'll let you have this one, since you care more."

"So nice of you. I do care."

We joined the line to climb up the hanging ladders. My shoulders hunched, and I was shaking.

"Ladies first." Tanner offered me a smirk.

This time, I'd take it. As soon as I was out of the water, Dad thrust a towel at me. I immediately wrapped up. My nose and ears felt like they were made of ice. Were they turning blue? My teeth were rattling, and I couldn't stop shivering.

"Smile," Dad said.

Tanner's arm came around me, so I was cocooned in his towel as well as mine, and I beamed even though my half-frozen hair was dripping down my neck and I could barely feel my lips. The extra body heat felt nice. Because it was warm. Not because it was Tanner. Not because that muscled torso was pressed against me.

After my dad lowered the phone, Tanner's arm tightened briefly. Before I could look up at him, he let go and stepped away. The chill instantly returned.

Dad handed me the phone. The photo was great. We were grinning and wet, and the water behind us looked cold, a chilly teal. Fog was visible on the mountains. Tanner scrolled to see that Dad had also captured a video of us running and leaping. Our clasped hands were clearly visible before Tanner did his somersault.

"See?" Tanner leaned close to see the screen, his arm resting against mine. "Awesome."

My lips curved up.

This was way outside my usual box, but once again, I was glad I'd done it. Each small step made the next one easier, and they were pushing the walls of my box outward, inch by inch.

Chapter Nineteen

Cruising Glacier Bay

~

The ship plowed a line through blue-green water dotted with small icebergs. My mom unironically loved the movie *Titanic,* and I was hoping not to have any sort of reenactment as we sailed into the depths of Glacier Bay.

After the polar plungers defrosted, the six of us had reconvened on the front deck in warm clothes. Icy mountains topped with snow towered above us on both sides. The ship stopped in front of a wall of jagged blue and white and gray ice.

Our parents fought their way to the railing, but Tanner and I hung back in the middle of the deck, where there was more room.

On the speakers, a park ranger explained how the glacier was formed, how it moved, what it was made of—not just ice, but rock and sediment, too, slowly inching toward the sea thanks to its own weight and gravity.

We got to see what the ranger called calving, when a chunk broke off the wall and fell to the sea, accompanied by booming and a splash. Everyone cheered.

Staff brought around trays of pea soup. I accepted a mug without thinking then stared at the greenish . . . yellowish . . . brownish concoction. I stirred it with the spoon. Small chunks of orange dotted it. Carrots? And something pink. Meat?

I wasn't a huge fan of peas, but I was feeling brave after the polar plunge. It was only soup. How bad could it be?

The texture, though . . .

"One bite," Tanner said.

"Does eating pea soup make me fun?" I scooped some up and let it plop back into the cup. "I'd have thought you ranked that with walking tours and pottery classes."

"It means you're getting into the spirit. Enjoying the experience. Immersing yourself." He waved a hand as if to show off the glacier behind us and almost smacked a stranger in the face.

I stirred again.

"On three." He held up a spoonful, waiting.

I scooped a small amount onto my spoon and edged it out of the mug.

"One." He raised the spoon, and I could tell he was trying not to laugh. "Two."

I lifted mine halfway and grimaced.

"Three." He took a bite.

I forced my spoon into my mouth, imagining the polar plunge, the spoon jumping in with no hesitation.

"You did it," he said. "I thought you were faking me out like you always do."

I wrinkled my nose at him. The soup was warm, and mushy, and a little salty, with soft chunks of vegetables. The meat was ham or maybe sausage.

The flavor wasn't awful, but as I'd feared, the texture was weird.

Tanner leaned his face close to mine. "Are you going to throw up? Do I need to make room for you at the rail?"

"Not unless it poisons me later."

"What do you think?"

"It's . . . fine."

He took another bite. "Was that really scary?"

"I guess not." I stirred again and took another small bite. I didn't know if I would ever order it for fun, but now I could say I'd tried it and survived.

"Pretend it's your new favorite." He raised his phone.

I held up the mug so he could take a picture with the glacier behind me.

"Hashtag better than milkshakes," he said.

"Hashtag I hope I don't get sick."

"Hashtag yum."

"Hashtag please stop."

He laughed. "I'm proud of you."

"Shut up."

"No, I am. It does look a bit sketchy."

"You say that after I ate it?"

His smile faded. "Is it possible you build things up in your head to be bigger deals than they actually are?"

"Absolutely. But just because something is a big deal in my head doesn't make it less valid as an obstacle."

"Fair enough." He ate more and studied the view. "We have to figure out how to get around that obstacle." He tapped my temple with two fingers as my mind latched onto *we*. "If you want, I mean. If you're happy, as soon as we get home, you can go back to your usual stuff. But you were the one who called it an obstacle, so I thought . . ."

"What?"

"Maybe you weren't one hundred percent happy? Or you wanted to find a way to, I don't know, like, overcome all of it? Not that you need to."

His rushed rambling was sort of endearing.

Did I want to overcome anything? The idea of the physics program drifted into my mind, along with my reluctance to agree. Stepping outside the safety of my box was scary. New things did feel like obstacles. But Tanner might have had a point that the real obstacle was my brain. Did I want to let it win and keep me from things I might enjoy?

Strangely, Tanner had helped a lot this week. Everything had been easier to face with him and his enthusiasm, his optimism, his humor. Not pushing me, just encouraging me and providing company so I wasn't alone with my thoughts. I spent enough time with them, and they weren't always the cheeriest of company.

I stood at his side, and even ate two more bites of soup before handing it to him to finish.

He put our empty cups on a passing waiter's tray and tucked his gloved hands into his pockets. "So do you always eat at the same places?"

"Pretty much."

"You eat the same breakfast every day. You don't want to try a custom omelet? Fresh waffles?"

I shrugged.

"Hmm."

I tugged on my beanie. "What?"

"I'm just thinking. Don't worry, I won't hurt myself. Does Jordan like the places you always go?"

"Of course she does."

Wait. Did she? I thought she did. But had I ever asked her?

Tanner hadn't argued with me. Hadn't tried to convince me to change anything. And yet, here I was, evaluating my life as if he had. I narrowed my eyes at him, but he was watching the glacier.

My eating the same foods at the same places didn't hurt anyone. Unless Jordan didn't like them, and I was being a bad friend by never letting her try somewhere new.

Maybe I'd sample breakfast foods in the morning. Tanner would finish anything I didn't like. And I hadn't heard of anyone on the ship getting quarantined to their cabins this week because of food contamination or projectile vomiting, so it was probably safe.

The ship made an impressive 360-degree turn to give everyone a view of the glacier before sailing away. We went inside to warm up, this time with hot chocolate instead of blended peas. Then the ship stopped at a second glacier, bluer than the first, with interesting patterns in the ice, layers of rock and dirt and little caves. Seals rested on small, rocky islands.

Tanner and I chatted about the view, the polar plunge, what we'd do in Denali in a few days during our post-cruise tour, and it was so comfortable. I had the strangest urge to rest my head against his strong shoulder.

The park ranger had talked about how the glaciers moved slowly but over time changed whole landscapes. It sounded like my life lately. I didn't know if I wanted to change, or move, but life and gravity were slowly shifting me.

The question was, would I like where I ended up?

The other question was, should I keep fighting when change might be inevitable, whether I wanted it or not? Would it be better to control that change, to take steps myself instead of letting gravity do it for me?

Because a primary lesson of physics was, gravity always won.

After dinner at the buffet, I let Tanner drag me to one of the smaller theaters, where I realized the show wasn't a performer—it was the audience itself.

Karaoke night.

Nope. Nope nope nope.

I dug my feet in outside the door. Inside, someone was murdering a Beyoncé song.

I crossed my arms. "I jumped into a freezing bay today. Isn't that fun enough? And ate pea soup, which is totally riskier than swimming in icy water."

"We can just listen," he said. "I won't make you sing."

"That's what everyone says at karaoke night, and the next

thing you know you're in front of a crowd holding a microphone and the lyrics to Katy Perry's 'California Girls' are coming up on the screen."

Tanner blinked at me. "I feel like there's a story there. Are you speaking from personal experience? Because I desperately need to know."

He very much did not need to know about Jordan's last birthday. "It doesn't matter. Anyway, how am I supposed to trust you here when you volunteered me for the magic show?"

"I did ask if you had stage fright first." He placed a hand over his heart, his face growing serious, his eyes boring into mine. "I won't volunteer you tonight. I promise. I'm trying to help you have fun, but I would never force you into something you truly didn't want to do."

We stared at each other, and I was vaguely aware of people edging past us into the room, but they were blurs. Tanner's face was the only thing in focus.

He had a point. Everything we'd done so far this week had either been my choice or he had suggested it but left the final decision to me. He hadn't shoved me into the glacial water or tied me into the ATV or carried me onto the magic-show stage kicking and screaming. Even as kids, he'd invited, asked, bribed, dared, but eventually left me alone to do what I wanted.

He searched my face, making my heart flutter.

Then he blinked, and his usual twinkle returned. "I cannot, however, be held responsible for you volunteering yourself once the spirit of karaoke takes hold of you."

"Yeah, right."

He raised his eyebrow in mocking doubt. "Do not under-estimate the power of the karaoke."

He grabbed my hand and led me into the room. He started toward empty seats up front in the center, glanced at me, and changed course for a booth on the side. I stumbled for a step, grateful that he knew I'd be more comfortable on the edge. He didn't release my hand until we were seated.

It had been a long time since I'd held hands with a guy. When had Caleb and I stopped doing that? I couldn't even remember. Had his hand felt so solid, so comforting and thrilling and right?

Unlike the dark jazz club, this room was bright, with neon lights above the small stage. Servers circulated with alcoholic beverages, so the karaoke could be entertaining to watch.

In a quiet announcer voice, Tanner gave commentary like he had at the auction. "Interesting choice from our next partici-pant. Dave did not, in fact, realize that 'Every Breath You Take' is a classic stalker anthem. Mr. Carter failed to recognize that this is a family-friendly affair. Janet is far too good and needs to remember that karaoke is more enjoyable when it's early rounds of *American Idol*, not finals of *The Voice*."

Tanner went onstage three times, dragged up by Dottie, Mrs. Ramirez, and a group of strangers. He never declined an opportunity to put on a show—or possibly, he never declined an opportunity to make others happy. He couldn't say no, didn't want to let them down. I'd always seen that tendency in a nega-tive light as opposed to noticing the positive effect he had on people.

A guy stumbled through "The Devil Went Down to Georgia," until fiddle music took over, and that was the first rule of karaoke, dude—don't pick something with a long instrumental section.

"Dance," his friend called.

"Please don't," shouted someone else.

"Dance, dance," people were soon chanting, and once he did some sort of hoedown, I was inclined to agree with the one who'd told him not to.

I wanted to tell him it was okay to sneak out the back and hide in his room for the rest of the cruise.

When Tanner stood and asked me to join him, I didn't think, and was moving toward the stage before I realized I'd decided to stand. My brain screamed *abort, abort* while my feet were apparently saying *why not.*

The crowd chanted, "Bird Girl and Bird Guy," and okay, it was a little fun that they were cheering for us.

Despite Tanner's warning, I had underestimated the power of the karaoke.

I took the second microphone as Green Day lyrics appeared. Our moms' old favorite. I shook my head as my gaze met Tanner's, but a thrill went through me. We belted out words with the confidence of kids subjected to lots of nineties music. Jordan would have been proud.

At the end he dipped me, like he had in our dance lesson, earning us an ovation from the crowd. We collapsed into our seats against each other, breathing hard and laughing. I'd laughed more on this trip than I had in ages.

After two more songs, it sank in that we were still leaning

against each other, the sides of our heads resting. I started to stiffen, decided I was comfortable if he was, and stayed.

But now I was aware of every breath, the way my shoulder hitched against his, my hands, which were awkwardly resting on my legs. What was I supposed to do with them? What even were they for? Why had I never realized how weird *hands* were?

Tanner tilted his head so our faces tipped closer. "I don't think you're boring at all," he murmured.

chapter Twenty

Day at Sea

~

I was still trying to wrap my mind around the fact that I hadn't 100 percent hated karaoke as I laced up my running shoes the next morning. We were starting our day at sea with a 5K run/walk for charity.

"Remind me why we're doing this again?" my dad asked.

"Because Mr. Ramirez will be there," I said. "Forget good causes. It's all about sucking up to your boss."

"I know you're joking," Mom said, "but thank you."

Dad winked at me.

There were options for a mile or a 5K. Mom and Dad were doing the mile with Tanner's parents, even though they were capable of the 5K. Mom and Mrs. Woods regularly attended spin and Pilates classes, and my dad ran three mornings a week. But apparently a mile was enough to impress the boss. Tanner and I were doing the longer run, which involved multiple laps of the outdoor track on the upper deck. We joined Tanner's family there.

"I'll make sure to wave when we lap you," Tanner told his parents.

"I won't," I said. "I'll be in the zone."

Tanner laughed. Using the band on my wrist, I pulled my hair into a ponytail.

Tanner tugged it gently. "Your hair is long."

I'd always worn it that way. I got it trimmed once or twice a year, nothing more. Another easy decision—I liked it fine, so I didn't think about it.

As we stretched, Tanner asked, "Aren't you glad you tried those breakfast foods? They were better fuel than toast."

"I don't know if bacon counts as healthy fuel."

I'd tried a custom omelet, and Tanner had brought five different levels of bacon crispiness so I could find the right one. I'd refused the French toast because I was full from the omelet, and because bread soaked in eggs sounded weird. Tanner had put the toast beneath his giant cinnamon roll and eaten them together.

"Are you sure all that food was a good idea before exercising?" I asked. "If you puke, I plan to keep running."

"Savage," he said. "I approve. And I'll be fine."

The longer distance runners began first, and Tanner and I set off at a decent pace.

"So why running?" he asked. "I understand the pole vaulting, since it's basically math and physics in athletic form. But you're tall. Did you ever try basketball or volleyball?"

"Coaches always wanted me to. When I hit this height in eighth grade, they were begging. I didn't mind either sport, but I didn't love them enough to play more than a season. Mom kept hoping I'd stick with one. She wanted to be one of those soccer moms who yelled a lot, and she can in track, but there's less opportunity."

"Can I come to your next track meet? I'll happily heckle the other runners or complain to the ref. Wait, are there refs?"

"There are line judges and starting judges, people to make sure you stay in your lane or don't start too early or no one trips anyone."

"Have you ever tripped anyone?"

"Not on purpose."

He twisted to look at me, glee on his face. "But on accident? Please say yes."

"Remember your mom's nice birthday dinner where you made fun of the giant road rash scrape on my leg?"

"I didn't make fun. I asked if you had a run-in with a gravel monster. It was a legitimate concern. What happened?"

"My feet clipped someone. We both went down."

"Ouch. At least football players wear pads."

"I remember plenty of injuries of yours. Strained hamstring, broken finger?"

"Yeah. It can be rough."

We had reached the starting area and dodged the walkers before our path cleared. "But you want to keep playing in college?"

"Um. Yes. Remember? That's what I plan to major in."

"That's not a thing."

"Well, then, where are you with finding something else? I feel like we aren't making progress."

"I have ideas. You just don't get to hear them yet."

I did have a growing idea. After spending so much time with him this week, I'd learned that he wasn't what I'd expected. That had made the task more challenging, but I was on the right track now. Metaphorically.

"It's hard to imagine not playing anymore," he said. "I know I'll never go pro, but I would miss it."

"What do you like about it?"

"It's fun to hit people. And I like catching touchdown passes so everyone cheers my name."

I waited, now that I knew him well enough to realize his first answer was rarely the real one.

He met my expectant gaze. "Oh, S'more," he sighed. "You're going to be difficult, aren't you?"

"Excuse me?"

"You don't let me get away with stuff," he said. "I like the sense of being part of a team. Guys who have my back. Starting high school, I didn't know who I was going to be. I knew I wouldn't be like my sisters, and football gave me something that made me confident, gave me community. I love seeing it be that for others, too. When Roddy lost his grandma and a bunch of us spent a weekend playing *Madden* with him, or when Matt's mom had cancer and we pitched in to help the family. Plus, Coach really cares, you know?"

It was the most passionate I'd seen him. His words had

latched onto my heart like a tractor beam and were slowly but surely tugging it toward him.

I regretted every time I'd thought he was shallow or fake or incapable of taking anything seriously.

Our feet pounded rhythmically. Like in Vancouver, it felt weird to run with someone. Tanner's pace fit mine, despite his longer legs.

"You never answered my question," he said after we lapped our parents, and he waved exaggeratedly and I pretended not to see them. "Why running?"

"I like the rhythm. I get in the zone, and my mind relaxes. It's peaceful."

"What's the longest you've done?"

"I often run three or four miles at a time. I've been thinking about doing a 10K. The distance wouldn't be a problem, but I'd want to train for a good time."

"We should do it together."

I stumbled. "Train?"

His hand grasped my elbow until I regained my rhythm. "That, and the race. We could make a training schedule. Push each other, like we always do. It would be fun to have someone to do it with. One of those costume races would be awesome. Or a regular one," he added quickly.

"Oh. Um. Maybe?"

"Afraid I'd beat you?"

"Afraid I'd embarrass you."

"Lucky for you I don't get embarrassed."

"I'm sure I could find a way."

"So. The race?"

It was weird to consider that pushing each other could lead to positive results. Though, I guess it had helped me study harder for my liberal arts classes, and led me to more hours at the Science Center.

He seemed to mean it, but that would require spending more time with him after the cruise, apart from our families. Did he want that? Did I?

"Maybe," I said again.

We reached our final lap, and Tanner sped up. I did too. I wasn't letting him beat me.

His longer legs gave him an advantage, but I was the official runner here. And I wasn't afraid to stoop to his level.

"Hey look, whales," I said, pointing over the edge of the ship.

When he turned his head, it slowed him long enough to let me surge across the line first.

He laughed as he joined me. "Well played, S'more."

"Still want to keep running with me?"

"Of course. I have to beat you next time."

"Good luck with that."

Other people had heard me and were rushing to the railing beyond the track, darting in front of runners. Walkers doing the mile veered off course to look as well.

"I heard whales," someone said.

"I don't see anything."

"Was that a spout?"

"That was a wave."

"No, I think it's a bird."

Laughing, Tanner and I grabbed cups of water from a table.

"You broke their hearts," he said.

"And yours."

"And you aren't even sorry."

"I'm sorry I got their hopes up to see whales."

He shoved me and I laughed, unsticking hair from my neck.

Our parents were waiting to tell us great job. Mr. Ramirez gave us fist bumps and moved on to chat with other employees.

"Mr. Ramirez is happy," I said. "My day is complete."

Mom shook her head at me, smiling.

"Oh, the day is just getting started." Tanner wagged his eyebrows at me.

"What do you mean?"

"Go shower, then meet me in the main lobby in an hour. Wear tennis shoes."

I narrowed my eyes. "Should I be prepared for revenge? Another race since you lost this one?"

"You'll see." He wore a slight smile. I couldn't read his expression.

I looked at our parents, who shrugged. Weird.

When I reached our room, I checked the schedule, but I didn't see likely candidates for another activity. Flower arranging class, VIP shopping tour. Nothing Tanner would consider fun.

I showered and washed my hair. Tanner was right—it was getting long. The color was somewhere between dark blond and light brown. Boring. Unlike Jordan, changing her style every week, I'd never had the courage to try anything different. I rolled the ends under, played with it, studying it in the mirror.

And made a spur-of-the-moment call to schedule an appointment for later.

A dozen people were waiting when I arrived in the central lobby.

I sat beside Tanner. "What's going on?"

He smirked. "You'll see."

An older man with a Northern European accent met us and introduced himself as the ship's chief engineer. "Today I am happy to be taking you on a tour of the ship's engine room."

No way. I whirled toward Tanner, who grinned.

"Are you serious?" I asked him.

He nodded. "I signed us up as soon as I saw it. I thought you might like it."

Something bright and twinkly unfurled in my chest. I didn't know what to say.

The engineer gave an overview of the ship's size and cruising speed and draught. Then we followed him to the lowest level. Tanner's hand pressed against my back to steer me down the hall as I practically bounced along.

We went through a hatch and down metal stairs to a level not open to the public. It resembled a NASA control room, with a bank of computers, a whole wall with diagrams and lights showing engine statuses, one wall of screens displaying multiple camera views of engine areas. And, okay, if Mr. Lin's program got me access to more places like this, it might be worth the unknown, the comforts I'd have to give up.

The engineer talked about how a relatively small crew monitored and maintained the systems. Sadly, none of them wore red Scotty shirts. Then we got earplugs and went through another hatch, to the actual engine room, where the roar of machinery was audible even through the earplugs.

The engines were enormous, everything taking up several decks. Parts spun and whirred. Pipes, ducts, wheels, gauges, and unidentifiable machines filled every square foot. We saw pumps that used seawater to keep the engines cool, and the propeller shaft, and the engineer talked about the Azipods. If I'd had scuba gear, I would have taken another polar plunge to see them in action. Was there a bridge tour, also? Because I'd love to see the controls to those.

I had to stop myself from pointing at every single machine and asking what it was. I hung on every word. Tanner stayed at my side, hands in his pockets, a faint smile on his face.

Warmth flooded me. This was incredibly thoughtful. Why was he going out of his way to do something so nice?

The tour lasted an hour, and when it ended, Tanner and I made our way to the coffee shop. We ordered drinks and sat by a window that revealed nothing but gray skies and pewter water.

"What did you think?" Tanner's voice and face were oddly vulnerable, like he cared that I had enjoyed it and was worried I hadn't.

I cupped my warm mug of hot chocolate. "It was incredible. Thank you. Really."

One of the most wonderful gestures someone had ever done for me had come from Tanner Woods.

"The group was small. How did you get us a spot?"

His eyes darted away. "I know people. And I'm very persuasive."

I studied him. "I have no doubt both of those statements are true. But honestly?"

"You can sign up at the excursion desk."

I waited.

"Oh, fine." His shoulders slumped. "It books fast, and I signed us up the first day to ensure a spot."

The first day. After we'd agreed to spend time together, but before we had started, what? Getting along? Having fun together? Becoming, dare I say it, friends?

Definitely before we'd cleared the air about the past.

He'd noticed enough about me to do something incredibly personalized.

He was avoiding my gaze, and now I was doing the same as a storm whirled in my chest. The air between us felt charged and electric.

I cleared my throat, my voice rough. "I really enjoyed it. Thank you."

"You're welcome." He finally looked at me.

The light from the window softened his edges, made his eyes mysterious gray shadows. His cheek twitched like he wanted to fully smile but wasn't sure how to finish the expression.

It drew my focus to his lips, always curved up at the corners like he knew a secret. My heart thudded.

I dragged my eyes back to his to find them aimed at my mouth.

Heat flooded me. What was happening? Was I wondering

what it would be like to kiss him? Surely he wasn't thinking the same thing.

Half of me wanted that, half wanted to run, and half wanted to melt into a puddle under the heat of his gaze. And yes, that was too many halves, but Tanner had reduced me to violating the laws of mathematics.

I took a sip, leaned back, made myself look away.

"So did it inspire you?" he asked. "To do the program for Mr. Lin?"

"It might have given me a nudge in that direction. The list he sent did include amazing facilities that I'd get to see in person. Why are you smirking?"

"I'm not smirking. I'm smiling. Because I like how you get intense when you're interested in something. You go all in, really try to understand it."

"Oh."

"Why—" He stopped.

"Why what?"

"Why haven't you already agreed to the program? It seems like you'd love it."

I set the cup down, spun it in slow circles. "I probably would love it, once I started. But the thought of traveling, of visiting new places, of messing up the schedule I had planned for senior year . . ."

"I know my opinion isn't worth anything, but I think you should do it. Stop thinking small for yourself. Go all in, in life, in what you love. Dream big and see what's out there."

The idea sounded huge and terrifying, like the Alaskan

wilderness. Almost too much unknown to contemplate. Yet, something sparkly stirred deep inside me.

"I'll think about it. Any other ideas for the day, Fun Coach?" Now my voice sounded too high.

He didn't answer immediately, giving me time to return to the serious topic if I wanted, but when I didn't, he asked, "Trivia competition after lunch?"

"If it's aimed at the average age of the ship's guests, most of the questions are from before we were born."

His eyes twinkled. "Then we'll compete with each other to see who can make up the wildest answers possible."

"That worked so well at the art auction." I leveled a finger at him. "I'm not getting kicked out of anything else."

"Oh come on, that was fun. The art was ridiculous." He stood and offered a hand.

I took it to let him pull me up, but he kept it all the way to the elevator, his grip warm and solid. And I let him.

chapter twenty-one

Day at Sea

~

Usually I wasn't a fan of surprises. Past results hadn't gone in my favor. A monster truck rally with my bio dad instead of a trip to the zoo. Tanner winning the Astronomy Club election. Getting dumped in front of half my classmates.

But somehow, lately, when it came to Tanner, I was coming to fear them less. To almost be curious how he would subvert my expectations this time.

Trivia took place in a lounge, with a host asking questions that also appeared on a screen, and a tablet at each table for selecting answers.

Mr. Ramirez and his wife were sitting across the room. He waved at us. So did Dottie with her colorful walker, today accompanied by her husband.

Once we started, Tanner focused. More than I usually did. He knew every sports question, including about athletes from before we were born. He also knew a surprising number of historical ones, proving I'd been right that he liked the subject. And he answered the health questions, confirming the direction of my idea for his college major. I tabled the thought while I handled math and science and a surprising number of music ones, thanks to Jordan.

I was seeing sides of Tanner this trip that I had never suspected existed. All these years, I'd labeled him. Annoying. Loud. Goofy. Jock.

But I'd been forced to add funny, perceptive, observant, kind.

The box I'd put him in was utterly destroyed, lying in wreckage. And it wasn't a terrible surprise.

First place went to Dottie, who honked her horn in celebration. Her husband gazed at her fondly.

"She's been on a million cruises," Tanner said. "I bet they use the same questions and she memorized the answers."

We came in third, just behind the Ramirezes, which was good. I didn't know if it would help our moms if their teenagers seemed smarter than their boss.

Mr. Ramirez came over to congratulate us. "Glad to know the public education system is strong. Your parents should be proud."

"Tell them that, sir." Tanner grinned, but a muscle jumped in his jaw, so slight I was certain no one else saw it. Why was I noticing? And why did I want to press my fingers to it and ask him what was wrong?

"I hope you two are having a fun trip."

"Yes, sir," we said.

"Thanks for making our parents come," Tanner said. "And for the train ride. It was great."

Mr. Ramirez beamed, and it occurred to me, possibly for the first time, that Tanner wasn't sucking up or trying to make himself look good. His manners were just a result of his genuine desire to make people happy.

He was more complicated than the engine room.

And I was a sucker for a complicated problem, a mysterious equation to be solved.

When Mr. Ramirez left, I checked the time.

"Got somewhere to be?" Tanner asked.

"Yes, actually."

He cocked his head. "Do tell."

"Nope, you'll have to wait and be surprised at dinner."

"Ooh, mysterious. I like it."

Mysterious didn't usually describe me, but it was kind of fun.

"Buying art? More pea soup? Please tell me you're not springing for Wi-Fi so you can email Caveman."

Caleb. I'd barely thought about him in two days, which was weird, since he'd texted me—and I hadn't responded, because we'd been on the ship.

"Not emailing," I said. "You'll find out soon enough."

I returned to the cabin to grab my mom, who had heard me make the appointment and wanted to come. Together, we went to the spa.

My heart was racing as I entered the white room. This had sounded like a better idea a few hours ago. I tugged on the end of my ponytail and fought the desire to walk right back out.

Soft music, trickling water, and faint incense intended to create a calming atmosphere were failing in their mission—facing this was as nerve-racking as facing bears.

We went to the salon, and I sat in a chair and stared in the mirror, my long hair falling halfway down my back.

A tall woman with pale blond hair whose name tag said Ingrid stood behind me and ran my hair gently between her hands. "What are we thinking today?"

Usually I asked for a couple inches off, to trim the split ends. I gulped. "Something new, I think. But nothing too short or drastic. I've always had it long. And it's really straight."

Ingrid gave me a book full of pictures. Most I would never consider, short and spunky or half shaved, and many required waves or curls, which I had no hope of attaining.

When I didn't say anything, Ingrid asked, "What if we give you a trim and layers?"

"Okay. But make sure it's long enough to pull back when I run." My attention caught on a picture. "And maybe this?"

Mom peeked, and I wasn't sure what she would say. I'd never been adventurous with my looks, so I'd never learned her opinion on piercings beyond one in each ear, or tattoos, or edgy fashion.

"I love it," she said.

"Really?"

"Really. It's just hair. If you hate it, it will grow out or we'll fix it."

"Cool."

Ingrid washed my hair, and the scalp massage relaxed me. Her fingers were magic. But tension crept into my shoulders again when we relocated to the chair so she could comb my hair.

Haircuts are a nightmare scenario for introverts. You're

trapped in a chair, frantically searching for conversation topics, hoping not to accidentally say the wrong thing and annoy the person standing behind you holding a sharp, pointy object with easy access to the major artery in your neck.

Thankfully, Ingrid was content to work in silence, which was fine by me.

When she started cutting, I nearly shouted *stop*. A large amount of hair covered the ground, several inches, plus more for the layers. But if I left now, I'd be lopsided.

She brought out the dye—deep blue for stripes on the under layers. Mom was getting regular highlights, and they left us to marinate.

"Hoping a new look will impress Mr. Ramirez?" I asked.

"I have been rather distracted this week, haven't I?"

"Yep."

"I'm sorry."

"It's fine. I'm having fun."

"You and Tanner seem to be getting along."

My heart fluttered. "No one else to hang out with. And you told me to be nice."

"Mmm."

When we were done, Ingrid washed out the dye, blow-dried my hair, and spun me to face the mirror.

It was me, just trendier. Instead of long, straight hair all the same boring color, now layers swung at different lengths, and the blue streaks peeked out. Not obvious or glaring, but hints of fun. I snapped a picture to send to Jordan later, knowing she'd love it.

"Happy?" Mom asked.

"I am."

"What prompted this?"

"I thought it might be time for a change." I fingered the end of a blue strand.

"Well, you look beautiful. You always do, but I like the color."

"Hopefully Dad does, too."

"Is he the one you're thinking about?"

My face got hot. "Who else would I mean?"

Mom shrugged and smiled as Tanner's face flashed through my mind.

The hair matched my dress for our second formal dinner. This one was ruffled and longer and would have been a much safer option for going onstage with devil birds in front of hundreds of people.

My head felt like it had lost a few pounds. Layers swung against my collarbone as I swiped on mascara and lip gloss. I could conquer the ship.

We left, but I realized I forgot my phone.

"I'm going to run back real quick," I told my parents. "I'll meet you there." I went inside, grabbed the phone, and rushed into the hall.

Just in time to run into Tanner bursting out of his room.

"Oh, good," he said. "You're late, too. I was—" He froze. His gaze traced my face, and I swore I felt it physically touching every inch. His throat bobbed.

"Wow. You look amazing." He reached out to run his fingers

through a blue streak in my hair, and they brushed my bare shoulder.

I shivered. "Thanks."

"Kind of subtle punk rock. It suits you. Quiet, but with hidden unexpected depths."

My mouth was suddenly dry.

He continued to stare at me. Time in the hallway froze.

His hand was still resting on my shoulder, barely. I tried to swallow.

"You, um, you look nice," I said.

Tonight, he wore a blue dress shirt with the sleeves rolled partway up and a gray vest, and the dressy outfit made semi-casual had stolen all coherent thoughts from my brain. We matched, like we'd planned it.

He offered his elbow. I slipped my hand through it, feeling solid muscle under his sleeve.

Despite my heels, he was taller. I liked it. Slower than normal, we strolled down the hall. Every inch of me felt on edge, thrilled, but also like I might float away.

"Aren't you two adorable," said an older lady near the elevator. "Here, let me take a picture."

Tanner handed his phone to her and slid his arm around my waist like he'd done it hundreds of times, gently pressing me against him. Without thinking, one of my arms snaked around his back and the other hand came to rest on his chest.

A slight exhale came from his throat, and his hold on me tightened.

"Smile," the woman said.

I didn't know if that was possible, if this energy sizzling

through me would let me. Every point of contact between us felt welded together, like it would take actual physical force to separate us.

When the lady extended the phone, Tanner moved to take it. But he moved slowly, his fingers trailing across my back as he reluctantly removed his arm from around me.

"Thanks," he said, his voice cracking.

I could no longer meet his gaze. I stared at the carpet. My face was on fire, and my heart was racing.

He cleared his throat. "We should, um."

"Yeah."

This time, as we continued to the dining room, we kept two feet of space between us.

What was happening? Surely any butterflies I'd been feeling were simply from the objective fact that Tanner looked good in dress clothes. That was a simple, quantifiable fact. No actual emotions could be involved.

We joined our parents and sat across from each other at the end of the table. I immediately reached for the bread basket to give my hands something to do.

"Savannah, dear, you look beautiful," said Tanner's mom. "I love your hair."

"Thanks, Mrs. Woods."

Don't mind me, I wasn't recently imagining what it would be like to feel up your son.

A menu lay by my plate, and I busied myself reading it. Tonight's theme was "A Taste of Alaska," and it included many intimidating items.

"You survived the soup," Tanner said. "And that terrifying omelet. Are you up for something else?"

His voice sounded light, and I peeked at him. I couldn't let him believe a simple photo had affected me in any way.

"If you order snails again, I'm leaving."

He grinned, and my insides did the foxtrot.

"Crab legs?" he asked, naming one of the appetizers.

A waiter had just walked by with those, and they looked all pinkish-orange and crunchy, like they'd been removed from a giant crab five minutes ago. Or from an alien life form.

A man at the table across from us was cracking one with his bare hands, and my stomach heaved.

"Please, for the love of Alaska, don't make me look at those."

"They do look like aliens, don't they?"

How did he keep doing that?

"What about the main course instead?" he asked. "You like steak, right? They have elk. That sounds cool. Or surf and turf. Regular steak plus lobster, so if you don't like the lobster, you can eat the steak."

"And you'll finish the lobster for me?"

"Naturally."

"I guess I could try that."

Since I was being adventurous in the meat selection, I had no hesitation in ordering a plain dinner salad and baked potato on the side.

"Oh, Savannah," said Mrs. Woods. "How was the tour of the engine room?"

I spun to face her. "Amazing! We saw the control room and

the lowest levels. It's so complicated and impressive. And we learned about how they steer and how the propellers work."

"Sounds fascinating," Mr. Woods said. "These ships are marvels."

"Tanner, what did you think?" my mom asked.

He grabbed another roll. "It was loud." He wore a disinterested expression and kept his tone light.

"You seemed to enjoy it," I said.

His gaze flickered to me, shadows in his eyes. He hesitated. Shrugged. "I didn't understand it like you. You're the one who's good at that science stuff. Can I have the butter?"

Now that I knew him better, I was starting to understand what he was doing—lowering everyone's expectations. Why? So he couldn't disappoint them by failing to live up? I thought back over many conversations this week. When his parents talked about his sisters or anything academic or serious, and he played dumb or interrupted to make jokes or did something outlandish. Provided a show, a distraction, a flashy performance to hide anything real underneath.

It was so obvious now. How could his parents not see it?

"You could learn from Savannah, you know," his dad said. "I wish you'd apply yourself like she does."

"He applies himself in lots of ways." My voice rang out before I could stop myself.

chapter twenty-two

Day at Sea

~

Every set of eyes at the table locked onto me. What had I done? I hadn't meant to sound so argumentative.

But now the attention of two sets of parents was more glaring than the magician's spotlights. I couldn't back down.

"It's hard work to stay in shape for football, not to mention nutrition and learning plays. He almost beat me for most service hours this year, and our GPAs are the same. And you should have seen him at trivia this afternoon," I said. "Even Mr. Ramirez was impressed."

His parents' eyes widened. My mom was nodding, while my dad was looking at me.

"She's the one who was impressive," Tanner said. "I just had fun pressing the buzzer. And it came with free Cokes."

I met his gaze, but I couldn't read his expression. "You're not giving yourself enough credit."

"I had some lucky guesses. And they asked a lot of football questions. Can you please pass the butter again, Mrs. Moore?"

My mom handed it to him and cleared her throat. "Well. I'm glad you two had fun."

Conversation resumed, and once the others were talking, Tanner asked quietly, "What was that?"

"I could ask you the same question. What's up with pretending to be dumb all the time?"

"Who says I'm pretending? You never thought so before."

"That was before I knew you."

He stopped slathering butter on his roll and met my eyes. "And you do now?"

"Better than you realize."

"So you've, what, appointed yourself my defender?"

Had I? "If you aren't going to defend yourself, then maybe, yeah."

We were leaning toward each other across the table and hissing our words to keep quiet, but conviction filled my voice.

His expression flickered from frowning to something soft and warm, before going blank. "Thanks, but don't waste your effort on a losing battle."

I was about to argue, when he said, "Save your energy for that battle instead."

The server stopped at our table with his tray of silver domes. When he uncovered mine and placed the plate in front of me, I almost told him to take it away.

The orangey shell with a tail at one end was split on top so white meat bulged out of the opening. I wasn't the only one who had ordered surf and turf. Multiple lobster tails adorned the table, as horrifying as the crab legs.

"I greatly prefer it when my food doesn't look like an actual animal," I said.

"But you aren't a vegetarian."

"I don't mind eating animals. I just want it not to look like one."

Tanner laughed. "One bite? Or eat the steak first and see how you feel."

I could do that.

The steak was regular cow, no Alaskan mammals involved, and the potato was normal with my usual cheese and bacon. Between bites, I eyed the lobster.

At least there wasn't a head attached. Or those little antenna things. Then I definitely would have made a run for it. Or tried to throw it back into the ocean.

Tanner was eating his, digging the white meat out of the shell. I didn't want to watch and yet couldn't look away.

"What does it taste like?" I asked. "Don't say chicken."

"It's kind of soft and sweet. Have you ever had shrimp?"

"No."

"Oh. Well, the meat is like that. You can cover it in butter."

A small cup sat beside the tail. The butter had been melted when the food arrived, but now the top had started to congeal.

"That didn't sell the snails, and I'm not sure it's selling this."

I poked the meat with my fork. A bite flaked off easily. I glanced at Tanner.

"The offer stands to cause a distraction if you need to spit it out," he said. "I could spill my drink or throw a roll at someone."

It was sweet that he was willing to risk his parents' wrath by causing a scene during a formal dinner. Or it was more of that intentional distraction stuff.

Here went nothing. I studied the bite on the fork and, like the polar plunge and the pea soup, shoved it into my mouth before I could chicken out.

It wasn't awful. A little sweet, like he'd said. Not chewy, which probably would have made me spit it out. I swallowed.

"Well?" Tanner asked.

"It was scarier than the soup? But not terrible?"

He laughed. "Are you gonna eat more?"

"You already had a steak and all of yours."

"I require lots of calories. But if you want to eat more . . ."

Now I kind of did, to prove myself. I forced down two more bites before the sight of the orange tail hit me again, and I shoved my plate toward him with a shudder.

He chuckled.

I took another piece of bread. Chewed.

The bread lodged in my throat briefly. It felt . . . tight. Hard to swallow. I sipped my water. The roof of my mouth itched. I sucked up an ice cube and rolled it around my tongue.

"Dessert?" The waiter cleared our plates and presented us new menus.

An itch distracted me. I rubbed my arm. Red bumps had formed on the inside of my forearm.

Was it getting hard to breathe?

"Um. I think I shouldn't have had that lobster."

"Savannah?" My mom turned to me. "What's wrong?"

I scratched my collarbone.

"Oh no," Mom said. "That looks like hives. What did you eat?"

"Is this the first time you've ever eaten shellfish?" Mrs. Woods asked.

"Probably?" I rubbed my neck, finding more bumps, and swallowed hard again.

"We better get you to the medical facility." My mom stood.

My gaze met Tanner's stricken face. "I'm so sorry, S'more."

Mom put her arm around me and guided me through the dining room, winding around tables. Many were topped with stupid lobsters, and it was like an obstacle course taunting me. I stumbled along, the room blurring, my brain numb.

"Do you feel sick?" she asked. "Dizzy? Can you breathe?"

I pressed my lips, which tingled but weren't swollen. I could breathe, right? In and out, in and out. "Just itchy, I think."

"Hopefully the symptoms will stay mild. I'm so sorry."

"Why are you sorry?"

"You're my child. I should have known about any food allergies."

"How could you, though? I've never tried it before. Seriously. Don't blame yourself."

I rubbed my itchy arms again.

Thanks to my first-day tour, I knew exactly where the medical facility was, on the ship's lowest level. Score one for being a curious nerd. It had several small rooms with curtains, and one room full of rows of medicines. Half were probably for sea-sickness. The place looked like a mini hospital.

I was ushered into a room with a faint antiseptic smell lingering in the air.

The doctor was a woman older than mom with a Boston accent. She settled me onto a bed, took my blood pressure, heart rate, and temperature, inspected my arms and my mouth.

"Allergic reaction," she said. "So far, it's not severe enough to require a shot. I'll give you an antihistamine, and we'll see if that helps. I'd like to keep you here for a little while to make sure it doesn't get worse."

I swallowed the pill she gave me and sank onto the pillows. Mom smoothed my hair out of my face and took my hand.

Nothing good came of eating food that looked like animals.

I must have drifted off, because the next thing I knew, Tanner was sitting in the seat Mom had been in. His big frame looked cramped in the small chair, and he was jiggling his foot and tapping on the arm.

I blinked a few times and rolled my head toward him. My brain felt fuzzy. But my arms no longer itched, and I could swallow without a problem.

"Tanner?"

"Hey!" He yanked out his earbuds, put down his phone, and leaned toward me. A slight smile flickered and faded. He reached for my hand but stopped. "How are you feeling?"

"Fine. Just sleepy from the drugs. How long have you been here?"

His eyes darted away. "Not long. Just got here. So, uh, your mom could take a break."

He was totally lying. My lips pressed together to contain a smile.

"What are you listening to? Shouty music?"

"Yep, what else?" He still wasn't meeting my gaze, so I snatched an earbud and jammed it into my ear.

He fumbled for his phone, and before he turned it off, I heard a man's voice, talking.

"Tanner Woods. Is this a podcast? An educational one?"

"Of course not. I should get the doctor, let her know you're awake." He reached over and took the earbud from my ear, jammed them into his pocket.

I wanted to smirk as he stepped past the curtain. But the humor faded. He'd absolutely been sitting there for a while. What time was it, anyway? And what did it mean that he'd spent the whole evening at my side?

The doctor appeared. "Hello, Miss Moore. Feeling better?"

I nodded.

She checked me out again. "Breathing okay? Mouth normal? No more hives?"

"I think I'm fine."

"Excellent. You're free to go. If any of the symptoms return, or you experience any dizziness or swelling, don't hesitate to come back."

Tanner stooped to pick up something under the bed but hid it from me, then offered his hand to help me off the bed. After we exited the medical office and stood in the quiet hall, he handed me a cup.

"What's this?"

"Milkshake. Since you missed dessert."

My insides warmed.

"I kind of drank some of it," he said. "And it might be a little melted. You slept for a long time. So your mom said, I mean. Since I just got here."

"Uh huh. Right." The first swallow revealed mint chocolate, my favorite. "How did you get this?"

He waved a hand. "Oh, it was easy."

I stopped, sipping and watching him, waiting.

He paused farther down the hall and turned to look at me. "I went to the ice cream place for three scoops of mint chip and then took it to the coffee shop and convinced them to blend it with milk and extra chocolate syrup."

The ice cream place was on deck eleven, the coffee shop on deck three, which meant he'd gone on a scavenger hunt across the ship, sweet-talking people into helping him. For me. And he'd remembered my order.

I stared at the cup. "Thank you."

"I felt bad for pressuring you into eating the lobster."

"Hey." I chanced a peek. "I know this wasn't your fault. You didn't force me to eat."

"Of course it wasn't. It was the lobster's. He was clearly a questionable crustacean."

I laughed softly. My heart clenched at the knowledge that he had, in fact, thought I might hold him responsible. I was sad that he'd think that of me, and also sad for him, that he blamed himself so easily.

"Clearly," I said. "I will forever be suspicious of lobsters from this point forward."

"The milkshake was supposed to be an apology milkshake, but if you're saying I don't have anything to be sorry for, I guess I should take it back." He reached out a hand.

I hugged the cup to me and shielded it with my body. "You wouldn't dare. But I do like that idea. Anytime you do something from this point forward that requires an apology, I will expect a milkshake."

"Good to know you're easily bribed. Does the size of the milkshake have to match the size of the offense?"

"Why, are you planning to do things that will require bucket-sized milkshakes' worth of apologies?"

"Absolutely not. But I'm an idiot, so I can't make any promises except to try not to ever have to bring you an apology milkshake."

Our gazes held. Was there a future where Tanner and I spent enough time together that we not only fought, but cared enough to make up after an argument? I found myself hoping there was.

"You are okay, right?" His eyes traced my face, serious now.

"I am. And since we're apologizing . . ." My face flushed as I recalled the rest of dinner. "I'm sorry if I said anything you didn't want me to. About trivia and all that."

"Why did you?"

I sucked the milkshake and debated what to say. "I think you underestimate yourself and let others do it, too. Actively *make* them underestimate you. It worked on me for years, and that's my fault. But I guess I got, I don't know, defensive. On your be-half."

He studied me, speechless. Wow. I'd broken him.

I looked away. "I should tell my parents I'm okay. I'm sur-prised my mom isn't here."

He walked me to our hall and gave me a quick side hug. Was that something we did now? Or was it a result of my near-death-by-lobster? He was affectionate. It meant nothing. Right?

He waited for me to unlock the door. "Sleep well, S'more."

It seemed like he wanted to say more but didn't.

My heart tumbled around in my chest, and I hugged the nearly empty cup. "Thanks for the milkshake."

I wanted to say more. But my mom was calling, "Savannah, is that you?"

"Night," I said, and slipped inside, cradling the cup like it was something precious.

Chapter Twenty-Three

Port of Disembarkation: Whittier, Alaska

My immune system had officially defeated the lobster and no further medical attention was required, so we went through the disembarkation process the next morning. Porters had picked up most of our bags the night before, each one carefully numbered, and when we got off, we easily found them in a sea of thousands of suitcases. Whoever organized that should be put in charge of managing LA traffic.

Then we loaded onto a fancy coach for the ride to Denali National Park, where we'd spend three nights at a lodge for a post-cruise tour. After many days of more adventure than I'd had in years, I welcomed several hours to sit and relax. I took a window seat, and Tanner sat beside me.

"Good thing for you I prefer the aisle to stretch my legs," he said, "or I'd be calling you a window hog."

"There are lots of other empty seats," I said, then immediately wished I hadn't because I didn't want him to move. Because I didn't want to sit next to a stranger, of course. Not because his presence had lately started to fill my insides with a warm buzz.

What was wrong with me?

"Not getting rid of me that easily, S'more." He bumped his shoulder into mine. "Just means we're a good match. Seat-wise."

Because we obviously weren't a match in any other respect. Right? That was unimaginable. Except . . . it wasn't.

My imagination needed help.

The ride to Anchorage took about an hour. The road hugged the shore of a bay lined with trees, framed by mountains, and the sky was gray and rainy.

Now that I had time to think, the events of the previous evening were sinking in. At first, I'd been in shock. Then I'd been sleepy from the drugs. But now it was hitting me how much worse the situation could have been, how much more severe a reaction I could have had, how a single lobster could have sent me to an Alaskan hospital.

The sensation of my throat tightening, my skin itching, took over. I rubbed my arm.

Tanner took my hand, pushed up my sleeve. "How are you today?"

"No more symptoms. I just feel it in my head."

"That makes sense. When I was in eighth grade, I sprained my ankle on a sharp cut while running a route. After it healed, I didn't think I was nervous, but when it came time for another similar route with a quick turn, I hesitated. I kept replaying that moment, and I cheated, not making the cut like I was supposed to."

"What happened next?"

"After the coach yelled at me?" He smiled. "I thought about what I wanted, which was to keep playing football. I couldn't give it up, which meant I had no choice but to move past the worry. I loved football more than I feared injury."

He wasn't usually a long-term thinker, and I respected the commitment. I lacked that devotion to seafood and was perfectly happy to give it up.

"I also thought about everyone else making fun of me," he said. "The threat of humiliation is very motivating."

Moore the Bore. I understood that.

He twisted, making our legs bump, and left them touching as he studied me. "So physically you're good. But for real? Are we continuing with the new things?"

"I don't know." I picked at a thread on my jeans. "I'm definitely going back to chicken fingers and turkey sandwiches."

"That's fair. What about everything else?"

Logically, the allergic reaction had been a random event. The rest of the week had gone fairly well. Other than getting called Bird Girl. Or eating mud while nearly missing the boat. But I'd survived. And I'd had some amazing experiences.

What was the other option? Over the next few days in Denali, we had a bus tour planned, whitewater rafting, exploring a land full of bears. I could stay in the lodge and eat toast and bananas for three days.

"I'll be there with you," Tanner said. "I'll protect you from sea life."

"Denali is landlocked."

"Then I'll protect you from land life."

"You're going to fight a bear?"

"If I have to." He flexed, which was apparently a devious way of emptying my brain of all rational thought.

I cleared my throat. "Let's hope that's not necessary."

"What scares you the most? Other than bears."

"Rafting, maybe."

He nodded. "No engineering involved. No boats or trams or trains. At the mercy of the river."

"Exactly." A raging river was unpredictable, something I had no control over. Even wilder than driving an ATV or zipping down a line. Or spending time with Tanner.

"That's the last day," he said. "You have time to work up to it." He lifted a shoulder. "Or skip it."

The low-level nerves about the wilderness of Denali lingered, a ball in the pit of my stomach. But the idea of trying a few things didn't send my heart rate spiking, didn't make my hands shake. I'd conquered other activities. I could do this, too. Just not the food.

"Okay," I said. "I'll keep going."

He leaned into me. "Of course you will, S'more. Don't let the lobster get you down."

"I won't be defeated by shady shellfish."

We fell silent as a guide talked about the region's ecology, the tides in the bay, the area's wildlife. We stopped in Anchorage for lunch—thankfully, lasagna and salad and no animals that wanted to kill me. Though the city wasn't large, it had the tallest buildings since Vancouver. Sadly, the glimpse of civilization was fleeting.

Tanner and I took the same seats for the remaining four-plus hours to Denali. Our route led away from the water, and outside were endless hills, trees, and rivers, with few towns.

Tanner broke out his earbuds.

I reached over and grabbed his phone. "I need to know what you were listening to last night. I heard voices."

"Sports. That's all."

"It didn't sound like sports. What kind?"

"Football."

"It wasn't live, because it was a Tuesday in June. And it didn't sound like announcers."

"You know what announcers sound like?"

"Yes. I actually do enjoy watching football."

He was studying me like he didn't know what to say. "I thought you hated it."

"Why would I?"

"You roll your eyes when I talk about it and refuse to accept it as a college major."

"Because it's not a major. And it's not because I don't like the sport. It's because it's all you talk about."

Except I now understood the reason for that—tied to dinner last night and how he'd deflected. Football, like humor and stunts, was a shield.

"So. Let's listen to this *football* of yours." I held his gaze.

His eyes were wide in fake innocence.

He sighed. "Oh, fine. It wasn't football. Itwasapodcast."

"Wait, did you say *podcast*? Didn't you make fun of me for listening to podcasts? I believe your exact words were 'those are for nerds.'"

"That doesn't sound like me."

275

I raised my eyebrows.

"Okay. I mocked it. But then I saw this one and tried it and I actually like it."

"What is it?"

He loaded it and handed me one of the earbuds. I scooted closer, though the earbuds were wireless and I didn't need to. He also shifted, so our arms touched, and voices filled my ear.

It was a history podcast. A funny one where they gave random and hilarious facts and told little-known stories about strange events.

Tanner was tense, like I might comment, and kept fidgeting with his phone case. When several minutes passed of us listening and watching the view in peace, our shoulders pressing closer when we laughed, he finally relaxed. After the episode ended, he shut it off.

"I knew you were a history nerd. You can't deny it anymore." I smiled to show I wasn't mocking. I nudged him with my elbow.

"Please don't tell anyone." He looked truly concerned.

"I won't if you don't want me to. But why not? Didn't you tell me to own what I like? That as long as I liked it, others' opinions didn't matter?"

He sniffed dismissively. "No one would believe you, anyway."

I twisted away from the window to face him fully. "They are distractions, aren't they? The jokes and stunts. You're trying to make everyone think you're dumb, even though you aren't."

"You're being nice to me. This is weird."

"You joke around in class and act like you don't care, but your grades are good. You call it *star club,* but you cared enough

276

to run for president. Unless that was just to mess with me. Is all of it a cover?"

"Nah. I really am a show-off who gets bored easily and likes attention."

Maybe so. But he'd also learned to use that to protect his heart against people who made assumptions about him based on that behavior.

People like me.

I wanted to grab his hand.

His shoulders slumped. "There you go again, not letting me get away with things. It's what people expect, especially my parents. I could never compete with my sisters. Could never keep up with their debates, never understood half their conversations. So it was easier not to try."

"Because they were older," I said.

He shrugged. "They, and my parents, love to debate deep issues and discuss current events."

"So Charlotte would have been eighteen and Livvy fifteen, and you were eleven or twelve, and you thought you should have been able to debate politics? That makes no sense."

Why was I so determined to defend him? I was seeing everything from our past in a new light. Not him trying to annoy me, although he had, but him trying to figure out why his parents kept comparing him to me and he was, in his eyes, falling short. Not wanting to commit to a major because it wasn't going to be business or law, and he worried his parents wouldn't approve. The loud stunts when the mood got serious, to hide his discomfort or give people what they expected rather than risk showing his true self and having them think it wasn't enough. Because he hadn't seen himself as enough.

My heart cracked for him. He'd even wanted to help me when I was having a bad day, despite our history, even if it had been in a way I might not have preferred.

I put myself in a box because it was safer, but he'd allowed his family to put him in one, too.

"I'm sorry," I said. "I'm sorry for not seeing you."

"What's this, an apology and it's not accompanied by a milkshake? This is setting a dangerous precedent, S'more."

"That's only required when you're apologizing to me."

"So what do I get?"

His tone was lighthearted. He was doing it again.

"Tanner. I'm sorry if your parents ever made you feel you weren't enough. I'm sorry you feel you have to hide yourself. And mostly I'm sorry that it worked on me. But you don't have to do it anymore. You've ruined it, anyway. You admitted you listen to podcasts and you like history and you're good at trivia. I will never see you as a dumb, annoying jock again."

His throat bobbed in a few hard swallows. "Thank you," he finally said.

His eyes darted toward mine, and they were a black hole sucking me toward him in an inescapable trajectory.

We returned to the podcast and watching the views until my phone buzzed with a text. Service had been spotty since Anchorage. At lunch, I'd posted pictures from our days at sea—the polar plunge, the glacier, my new haircut—but I wasn't sure if they'd gone through. I'd read texts from Jordan with updates from her, including a picture she'd snuck of her student's cute older brother.

The new text was from Caleb.

"What does Caveman want?" Tanner was eying my screen.

"I don't know." I angled the screen. "Stop spying. He wants to make sure I got his last message. He says he knows I've had service since I posted pictures."

"Real genius, that guy. Wait. You never responded? It's been three days." Glee filled his voice.

"I got busy. And we were on the ship without service."

Tanner shifted to face me, his face lighting up. "Interesting." He drew out the word. "So you were doing all these new things to make him want you, and now you aren't even answering his texts? Good for you. Show him what he's missing."

"It's not like that." Was it? "I just . . . forgot."

"About the guy you supposedly want to be with?"

"I do." I didn't sound very convincing.

Tanner remained silent.

"What? You clearly have thoughts."

"Nope," he said. "No thoughts. This"—he made a circle around his face—"is the face of a guy with no opinion on the subject whatsoever. You should write him back now while you still can. Might not have service for long."

He put his earbuds in and shifted again, this time to angle himself away to give me privacy. Except it left me feeling like I'd ruined something, but I didn't know what.

chapter twenty-four

Post-Cruise Tour: Denali National Park

~

Cell service in Alaska was like Halley's Comet—it involved lots of waiting for a brief payoff. At least with the comet, you knew when it was coming.

The rest of Caleb's message said, *We should talk when you get home. I didn't like how we ended things.*

How *he* had ended things. Yeah, I didn't like that either, dude. But what did he mean? That he wished he hadn't broken up with me at all? Or that he'd done some self-reflection and was now properly sorry for making it a public spectacle?

Answering the first part was safer. I told him we'd had spotty service—which was true. My message didn't send until we reached the next small town. That reply didn't feel like enough, so I added that I hadn't forgotten about him. Even though I had. And I told him we were nearing Denali, then asked what he'd been up to.

That was casual, right? Something friends would ask? It didn't sound desperate or needy or boring.

My next text was to Jordan to tell her about Caleb's message. Her messages arrived sporadically, loading slowly, leaving me in suspense between each tiny bit of service.

Jordan: *Sounds like C is the desperate one. But I want to know more about Tanner. Because the two of you look hot enough to melt that glacier. Spill.*

Me: *There's nothing to spill. We're getting along, that's all.*

Jordan: *And you're enjoying getting along with him.*

I eyed him briefly.

Me: *I guess so.*

Jordan: *Maybe instead of Khan and Kirk or Anakin and Obi-Wan, you're the opposites attract story. Han and Leia. Mulder and Scully.*

Me: *Enough about Tanner. What does Caleb want to talk about?? It could be Math Bowl, right?*

Jordan: *He specifically mentioned the breakup. That will definitely be part of the conversation.*

My insides were tied in knots. I didn't know what I hoped Caleb would say. I wanted to talk to Tanner about it, except he hadn't removed his earbuds since Caleb had texted. That bothered me more than I wanted to admit.

Me: *I miss you. Wish you were here.*

Jordan: *I miss you too. But no you don't, because then you wouldn't have gotten to know your Han. Love you.*

I sighed and watched the highway. We were in the national park now, with sporadic small areas of development, but mostly just the road stretching endlessly. Eventually I lost all cell service and put in my earbuds, wishing I was sharing with Tanner again.

The lodge in Denali where we were staying had fancy wood cabins on a hill above a river. On the opposite bank, another row of mountains looked down on us, and in the distance, there was nothing but endless peaks.

Wooden boxes overflowed with bright flowers, and hewn log benches were strategically placed so you could admire the views. A central area held shops and a couple restaurants, along with a firepit. We were staying down the hill from the main lodge, and our room had heavy curtains to block out the light since Denali only had a few hours of darkness per night this close to the summer solstice.

It was beautiful, if you liked the whole rustic mountain vibe.

We got settled in time for dinner and went to one of the lodge restaurants, a casual place with a large patio.

"We should ask them how things are cooked," my mom said. "Make sure nothing touches shellfish."

"Yeah, S'more, it might be risky." Tanner's gaze met mine, and he raised an eyebrow.

I wasn't sure if he was teasing, and that hurt.

To prove something to him, and because I hadn't technically done anything new today, I ordered the caribou cheeseburger, staring directly at Tanner as I did it.

Then immediately second-guessed the decision. Look how well being adventurous with food had ended last time.

Caribou was basically a cow with antlers, right? Ketchup would hide any weird meat flavor. No antlers would be making an appearance at the table, so I could pretend it was normal. As long as I didn't think about eating one of Santa's pets.

Surely I wasn't allergic to caribou, too. Although it was possible there was a grand conspiracy among Alaska's wildlife to try to kill me. If it couldn't eat me like a bear, or charge me like a moose, it would poison me when I ate it.

"So, Savannah," said Mrs. Woods. "What are your plans for the rest of summer after we get home?"

Not what I had originally intended, that was for sure. Those breakup LEGOs were calling my name. I'd have a fleet of spaceships large enough to defeat the Borg by the time school started.

"Hanging out with Jordan. Volunteering at the Science Center. Preparing for Math Bowl. I might work on college applications or visit campuses nearby."

"You should go with Tanner. He needs to start thinking about that. And figure out what he wants to do."

Before I could say *he's seventeen, he has plenty of time*, Tanner said, "It doesn't matter. I'm not attending a four-year college, anyway."

"Since when, young man?" his dad asked as I stared at him.

"I'm going to be a personal trainer. Don't need a fancy degree." He was using the light, fake, unconcerned voice I now recognized as a lie or a cover.

Tanner had asked me to help him pick a college major when he had no intention of going? Or was this another show? He'd mentioned wanting to keep playing football and getting a scholarship and going wherever I went.

What was real?

I narrowed my eyes at him. He ignored me.

"Interesting," my mom said. "How did you choose that?"

He lifted a shoulder. "I can spend all day in the gym. Science is how much protein powder to add to your shake, and history is how many reps you did in your last session."

I watched his parents. Surely they would challenge him, ask more questions, dig deeper.

Mr. Woods frowned. "We'll discuss this later."

Tanner was saved by the food's arrival, but I kept studying him. He couldn't hide the hard edge to his jaw, despite the fact that he was extra loud through the meal, making jokes and chatting with the server. Presenting the façade he wanted people to see, so no one got close enough to notice the good guy inside. The smart, thoughtful guy who chased down milkshakes and distracted me from my fears and believed I was worth more than a parking lot breakup.

What would our relationship have been like if I'd seen the truth sooner? Would we have competed, challenged each other, argued about everything? Or could we have become friends, looking forward to family events and enjoying each other's company?

As we finished dinner—thinking about Tanner had made me forget I was eating a weird burger—he was still fidgety, moving the salt and pepper shakers around, playing with his straw. Our parents wanted to return to the rooms, but Tanner was barely containing his pent-up energy.

"We're going to explore the grounds," I announced.

"Okay, just be careful," my mom said.

"You want to explore?" Tanner asked when we were alone.

"You looked like you needed to work off some energy."

"Oh." He studied me intently. "How could you tell?"

"I know you. Or I'm starting to."

His gaze on me had weight. There was so much I wanted to say and ask that I didn't know where to begin.

The sky was spitting light sprinkles, but breaks in the clouds showed blue skies and occasionally illuminated patches of mountain. We walked toward a wide, gray river rushing fast. Rows of pointy pine trees stood dark against a hill covered in a dozen shades of green. Boulders rested along the shore, then a rocky beach, and a trail led along the river.

It was dramatic and ethereal and the air was laced with magic.

I was walking too close to him. Our arms kept brushing. The backs of our hands. Each contact sent a shot of energy straight through me. Yet I couldn't move away. I was a magnet drawn to his North Pole. It must have been our proximity to the actual North Pole. That was the only explanation.

I peeked up at him.

Once the tension had eased from his posture and he no longer looked like he wanted to tackle someone, I nudged his arm with my elbow.

"So what was that at dinner, that personal trainer stuff?" I kept my voice light.

"I have a confession. I didn't really need your help with a college major." His voice was light, too.

"Excuse me?"

He lifted a shoulder. "I wanted to help you this week, but you were suspicious. I figured if I offered a trade, you'd be more likely to let me."

I stopped, planted my hands on my hips, and glared at him.

He stopped a few steps later and turned toward me. "Are you mad at me?"

I didn't know what to do with that. Was it sweet that he'd wanted to help? Yes. Even if it was because he'd felt sorry for me at the time. Was he right that I might not have been so willing to accept if I hadn't thought he needed something from me in return? Also yes.

Did I know him well enough now to suspect he wasn't being entirely honest?

One hundred percent.

"I am mad," I said. "But not that you asked for help or that you lied to me."

He blinked. "So what, then?"

"I'm mad at you." I stepped closer and poked his chest. "For hiding."

"Excuse me?"

I glared at him, inches from his face. "Oh, come on. You don't plan to go to college? There's nothing wrong with that or with being a personal trainer if it's truly what you want. But I don't think it is. What happened to playing football? To a sports scholarship? I think what you said at dinner was convenient because it conforms to their expectations. Expectations you accept even though you shouldn't."

"You're giving me too much credit, S'more." His voice tried

and failed to capture a breezy tone. "Personal training sounds like the life. What other job would let me show up in workout clothes and pay me to improve my bench press weight?"

To keep him from walking away, I closed my hands gently around one forearm. "Listen to me, Tanner." I waited until he reluctantly met my gaze. "Even if you weren't serious, I was. I told you I would help. Do you want to know what I learned?"

"Please, enlighten me, since you know me so well." His head ducked, and he left his arm in my hands. His gray eyes held a challenge.

"I do know you." I was surprised to find I meant it. "That's why I think you should go to college, play football, and study physical education. Then you can teach PE and coach one day. There. What do you say to that?"

He froze. Opened his mouth. Shut it.

I gave his chest a gentle shove with both palms, letting my hands linger briefly. "Stop underestimating yourself. And stop letting others get away with it, too."

A strangely vulnerable expression crossed his face. "How did you . . . ?"

My righteous indignation faded. I softened my voice. "I paid attention."

He ran a hand through his hair and looked away before meeting my gaze again, and his eyes were intense. "You . . . you're right, you do keep your word. And when you decide to do something, you put your whole heart into it. I've always admired that about you. You don't let anything stop you. Not even me."

A feeling like sparklers sizzled inside me.

His eyes drifted to the scenery over my head, a distant expression on his face. "I can picture it. Teaching kids about health and fitness and how to play sports."

"Ping-Pong and dancing and nutrition. Plus football," I said. "I bet with that major, you'd play games all the time and learn a bunch of sports and fitness stuff. Then you'd help kids learn to love being active and help them be healthy, and staying in shape would be like your job."

"You . . ." He blinked at me, his gaze heavy.

"If you want to skip college and be a trainer, do it." My voice was quiet now. "I know there's more to that job than hanging out with muscley dude bros and drinking protein shakes. But only do it if it's what you really want, what will make you happy. Not just what seems safe because you're afraid to dream bigger or because you're worried about what people might say."

A muscle jumped in his jaw, and I fought the urge to put my hand on his cheek and smooth away the tension. I clasped my hands in front of me instead.

"Or," I said, "put that craziness and energy and passion to use helping kids. Just maybe go easier on them at the Ping-Pong table."

He surged forward and grabbed my hands, prying them apart and squeezing. "I don't know what to say."

Now his full attention was on me, intense, eyes locked on mine, gray as the clouds. My breath caught in my throat. My grip tightened on his.

I swallowed hard. "Whatever. We made a deal. You helped me, I helped you." My voice was too high.

"Right. A deal."

"Why do you do it? Put on the show? Make jokes to deflect attention. You can tell me. It won't change my opinion of you."

He bit his lip, continuing to study my face. "Do you remember that history project in seventh grade?"

"The medieval one where you dressed as a knight for your presentation?"

"Yeah. I worked hard on that. I was proud of it, not just the outfit but the paper I wrote. And my parents barely noticed. They complimented yours. Talked about what my sisters had done at my age. So I decided, if I couldn't make them happy when I tried so hard, if I could never live up, I should take a different approach."

"The football and joking and wild stunts. Even though that makes them more disappointed? I've seen you this week. You love to make people happy. Doesn't that do the opposite?"

"If there was no way to please my parents, at least I could make everyone else happy. If I'm not trying, then failing doesn't hurt as bad. I hate conflict, but if it's not real conflict, then it's easier to deal with."

"Tanner . . ." I didn't know what to say. I wanted to hug him. I wanted to wrap him up in a cozy blanket and feed him chocolate. I wanted to tell him he wasn't disappointing to me. "You know . . . you don't have to make me laugh constantly to make me like you."

He was still holding my hands, and mere inches of space separated our faces. His thumb was rubbing absently across the back of my hand, and it was setting off explosions in my chest.

"S'more . . ." His head dipped toward mine.

My skin was on fire and my heart might burst. Invisible strings tugged me toward him. What would his lips feel like?

A dog barked nearby, shattering our bubble.

I let out a shaky breath and took a step back. My heart was racing. What had that been? Had Tanner seriously been wanting the same thing—to kiss me?

And why was I so disappointed that we'd been interrupted?

We kept walking, farther apart now like we were afraid of accidentally touching, even though my hand kept twitching with the urge to take his. But that was ridiculous. This whole evening was ridiculous. Surely it was nothing more than the magic of mountains under a summer sky.

We circled back to the central buildings, where a fire blazed in the large pit. Several people sat on logs holding long sticks with marshmallows. It was weird since the sky was still light, but with sunset at midnight, I supposed this was the only option unless you wanted sugar at three a.m.

"It's perfect," Tanner said. "S'mores with S'more."

Was his voice deeper than usual? Had that moment meant anything to him? Or had he just been surprised at the job stuff, and I was the only one of us reading more into it?

We found a table with a tray of graham crackers, chocolate, marshmallows, and sticks, and helped ourselves. Then we took the remaining log, which was barely long enough for two. Our thighs pressed close.

My stomach was an asteroid field, whirling and colliding. This wasn't much closer than we'd sat on the various bus rides, but that was before we had breathed the same air, studied each other up close. Before I'd realized all it would take to kiss him was a simple rise on my toes.

"I love a good s'more," Tanner said. "Plus, it's a fun word to say."

"Is that why you call me that?"

"Um, because it's your name. S. Moore. Do you not like it? I can stop."

"No, don't," I said too quickly, and his lips curved up. "I mean, it's not the worst nickname you've given me."

"It's a great nickname. S'mores mean summer and the outdoors and being with friends and campfires. They're crunchy on the outside but sweet and gooey on the inside, and they're delicious. They remind you of childhood and they make you smile. And they're addictive. Once you try one, you want more. It's right there in the name."

He had twisted to look at me. Flames gilded his profile and burnished his dark hair.

Air caught in my throat. Were we still talking about dessert? Why was that fire so hot? It could not be natural. They must have been burning something illegal.

"Now, I have an important question." Light flickered over his face.

Why did he have to be so freakishly good-looking? I couldn't breathe, couldn't reply.

"Golden, brown, or crispy?" he asked.

"What?"

"The marshmallows." He motioned to the tray resting across our knees. "You should be an expert."

A wild laugh fought to escape my throat. I shoved it down and tried to focus on the question and not his lips, begging to be tasted instead of the sugar.

"Golden brown," I said. "Hot enough so the marshmallow melts the chocolate, but if you catch it on fire, you have to start over. You?"

He clicked his tongue. "Yet another way we disagree. Burnt, all the way."

"Because you genuinely like it that way, or because it's faster and easier, and getting it golden brown takes too much patience?"

He pressed his lips together, and his eyes twinkled.

"I knew it. Give me that." I took his stick from him so I held both, jammed a marshmallow on each one, and carefully hovered them at the right distance. "I'll convince you this is the best way."

"Or," he said, "we can burn them and eat them immediately."

I shook my head.

"When did you learn to make these supposedly perfect s'mores?"

"It's my name, right? Part of the job description." My voice didn't sound as breezy as I'd meant it to.

He waited.

I sighed. "That camping trip with my bio dad. He wasn't interested, but another family at the campsite taught me. I can't believe we've never made these on any of our family trips."

"Our parents haven't tried to take us camping yet."

"I think my mom knows it might traumatize me."

I checked the marshmallows.

They were on fire.

Tanner laughed, a deep rumble, like he suspected he was the reason I'd gotten distracted.

Face hot—from the fire, nothing else—I got two more and started over.

When they were perfect, I pulled them away and Tanner readied the other supplies, holding the graham crackers so I could slide the marshmallows between them.

We clicked them together. "Cheers."

He took a huge bite and groaned. "Okay, fine, you win. It's better when you can't taste charred sugar. I shouldn't have doubted you."

"I'm glad you acknowledge my brilliance."

"That's one thing I never doubted."

He held eye contact, until I felt marshmallow oozing onto my hand and looked away to take a bite.

Like he'd said, once you had one, you needed more, so I made two more marshmallows. The sun was finally beginning to set. When we finished, we left the fire circle and stopped at a low bank overlooking the river. The water was liquid mercury beneath a watercolor sky full of cotton candy clouds, and the mountains glowed.

It was bursting with the promise of something otherworldly.

We stood side by side with our arms brushing, but Tanner turned from the view and toward me, staying close.

He shifted and I angled myself toward him to meet his gaze.

His eyes traced my face. Then his fingers followed, ghosting over my cheeks, down to my chin. He traced my lower lip with his thumb. I shivered.

He stepped closer, bending so when he spoke, his breath brushed my mouth.

"I really want to kiss you," he said.

I responded by rising onto my toes and kissing him first.

Chapter Twenty-Five

Post-Cruise Tour: Denali National Park

~

Our lips met in a gentle, testing touch that tasted of sugar and the scent of campfire smoke.

When I'd leaned toward him, I hadn't thought of anything beyond needing to feel his mouth on mine. After a second, his arms slid around my back, cradling me against him. He ducked his head so I could reach better, and my hands braced on his chest for balance as I perched on my toes.

Galaxies spun inside me, supernovas exploding behind my closed eyes. I was floating, soaring, through the vastness.

When we broke away, I was breathing hard. His face was open, stunned, blinking. His chest rose and fell as rapidly as mine. We stared at each other.

I had kissed Tanner Woods. And I had liked it.

In nine months of dating, kissing Caleb had never been like that. Never made me lose all track of where I was, melted my brain, turned my insides and my arms and legs to mush. Narrowed the universe to that single moment.

Caleb. I was supposed to want Caleb back. All my plans for the future, our safe routines and familiar patterns.

But right now my heart was beating *Tanner, Tanner, Tanner.*

My gaze dipped from his eyes, the same pewter as the river, to his mouth, as I considered doing it again.

He blinked and shifted backward, away from me.

"I'm sorry," he said. "I shouldn't have done that."

His words were a blast of glacier water to my brain Also, I was pretty sure I'd been the one to do it, or it had at least been mutual.

What I said was, "Right, yeah, of course, no worries."

No worries? Seriously? What was wrong with me?

I had been thinking *wow,* and not much else. But he might've had a point. With our history, this couldn't end well. We'd been overwhelmed by the beauty of our surroundings, or influenced by this week's forced proximity. Our families were too close. If we tried anything and it didn't work, things would be even weirder. There were so many reasons it was a bad idea.

But that kiss had been a compelling reason in favor, currently eclipsing everything else. Not to mention the whole evening, which had been one of the best and honestly the most romantic I'd ever had.

We walked to our rooms under a twilight sky in awkward silence. I would have gone ahead without him, except I didn't know if the grounds had bears, and I wasn't willing to risk encountering one on my own, no matter how weird this was.

We parted at our doors, glanced at each other and away. I had no idea what to say.

"Thanks for the s'mores lesson," he said. "And the career advice. I'm sure I'll have more for you to help me with soon, so get some rest."

Joking was his usual defense mechanism, but that didn't make it hurt any less that he didn't plan to acknowledge the kiss. I nodded, slipped inside my room, and gently closed the door.

The next day, we had a bus tour into Denali with our parents and several of their coworkers. Tanner was already on the bus when my parents and I boarded, sitting near the back by himself. My gaze found him like he was a magnet. Why did he look so good, in a blue shirt that hugged his muscles? Had he been awake as much as I had last night? Did he regret the kiss? Or did he regret apologizing for it?

I still hadn't decided which side of that line I fell on.

I would rather tie myself to the hood of the bus than sit next to him all day, but my parents took a seat together before I could join one of them.

Instead, I settled into the empty space next to Mrs. Woods and asked if she was enjoying the trip. We chatted until Mr. Woods boarded and smiled at me. Waiting for me to get up.

Fine. I could take a hint.

Next, I tried stopping at Mr. Ramirez's seat and channeling Tanner's charm. "Thanks again, sir, for the trip and booking these amazing tours. What made you decide on Alaska instead of a beach?"

"I've always wanted to see Alaska, which was part of it, but we also took an office poll." He did not, as I had hoped, invite me to join him.

"Oh, that's nice." His wife was now coming down the aisle. "Enjoy the day."

I moved on again and took a seat by myself, two rows in front of Tanner, who was staring out the window at the parking lot. If he'd seen my mega-awkward attempts to be friendly, he wasn't letting on.

The bus was filling up, and one of Mom's coworkers and his wife stopped next to me.

"Hello, Savannah. Would you mind terribly if we sat together?"

I forced a smile. "Of course."

I stood yet again. The only empty seat was next to Tanner. Mom's coworkers were all traitors.

Silently, I perched on the edge of the bench. Tanner was slightly turned so his legs would fit, and he shifted, trying to cram them into the small space and avoid touching me.

Whatever. I would show him that last night's kiss—and his subsequent rejection—hadn't affected me in the slightest. Hide the fact that I'd been awake all night reliving it, and my ridiculous brain had been wondering if a relationship with him was such a terrible idea, arguing with the more logical half that said I should pretend it had never happened and never speak of it again, like Frodo and the ring.

Except, that didn't work out so well for Frodo. I was probably setting myself up to get chased by undead dudes in black riding on grizzly bears.

Tanner was uncharacteristically quiet, and his long legs were now bent at an odd angle.

"Do you, um, want the aisle?" I asked.

He looked at me, serious and steady. "Sure. Thanks."

I let him out, then slid in toward the window.

"Window hog," he said as he sat again, stretching his legs into the walkway, and his voice almost sounded normal.

Okay then. I could pretend last night never happened if he could.

Except this vehicle was more regular school bus than fancy coach, and we could barely breathe without causing our knees to knock or our arms to brush. Every contact sent lightning through me. Cars were safe in thunderstorms, but what happened when the lightning was on the inside? I might make the vehicle combust if Tanner's shoulder grazed mine one more time.

I tried to make myself small against the window, but Tanner kept peering at the view, and I didn't want to let on that his nearness was affecting me, so I let him lean against me to watch as the bus left the safety of the highway and drove into the heart of the park.

"Sorry, is this okay?" he asked. "There's lots to see."

"Yeah, fine." My voice sounded too high. "I'm happy to switch anytime you want."

"Nah, I'm good, if you are."

"Great."

We fell silent. The crowded bus was a good excuse not to talk.

The vehicle seemed safe enough, but I hoped we weren't traveling off road and it wasn't going to break down and strand us in the middle of nowhere. I should have brought more food and water. Bear spray. Maybe gas, and spare car parts. A flare gun and a satellite phone.

The greens were rich on the endless hills, and we crossed several small rivers. A guide came on the speakers to tell us about Denali—six million acres, one-third of which was total, untouched wilderness. This was the only road in the entire park.

A ball of nerves formed in my stomach at the idea that there was so much wildness. No people, no buildings, no refuge from storms or cold or wild animals. I knew parks like this were good. The planet needed them, and preserving species was important. I didn't want to see it paved or developed.

I just preferred not to visit the wild places unless they had nice hotels. Or any hotels, even if they weren't so nice. Or just a permanent structure that a moose couldn't trample while I slept.

"I see why it's called the last frontier," Tanner said. "You should love that. It's like space."

I glanced at him. Were we doing the pretending now? "That's the final frontier. And I like it because I know I'll never go there."

"You could."

"I prefer to admire it from Earth."

The guide said that park rangers used dogsleds to do their jobs in the winter when the roads were too snow-covered for vehicles.

"Awesome," Tanner said.

"Sounds cold."

"Sounds hard-core."

"Until you freeze to death and your dogs eat you. Or vice versa. I'm not sure which would be worse."

We drove on through endless hills. Sometimes the road was enclosed by mountains and I'd forget how huge the place was, and then the view would open up and I could see into the distance that it kept going forever. A moose watched us from the trees. The guide pointed out sheep on a mountain. Without binoculars, I didn't see much more than white blobs.

Our first bear sighting was far up a hillside, a lone animal nosing around in the grass. A closer-up image appeared on screens throughout the bus from cameras mounted atop the vehicle. It was grayish brown, with a hump on its back.

Grizzly.

I swallowed hard.

The guide gave us grizzly bear facts. I could have gone my whole life without knowing they could stand up to eight feet tall, had a better sense of smell than a hound dog, and could eat ninety pounds of food a day.

"You don't have to be faster than the bear," Mr. Woods said. "Just faster than the guy next to you."

I was fast, so at least there was that.

"That's a common misconception," said the guide. "If you

run, the bears see you as prey and they're more likely to chase you."

So much for my advantage.

At our first stop, a short trail led up a hill, with views of mountains covered in patches of green, yellow, red, and orange. A shallow river wound through the valley. The air was cool and damp.

I could see for miles, which in a way was nice. No bears would be sneaking up on me.

"I'll guard your back," Tanner said.

"What?"

"You were totally watching for bears."

"I was not. I was admiring the natural beauty. Where bears might happen to live."

He let out a soft chuckle, and I shivered.

I gazed at the view for a while before glancing at him, to find him just looking away. When it happened again, a tingle shot through me.

A soft cry came from nearby. I whirled to see a boy sitting on the ground, holding his ankle. Tanner ran over and was the first by his side.

He kneeled next to the kid. "What happened?"

"I tripped."

The parents raced toward them from farther down the trail as Tanner checked the boy's ankle.

"It's probably a sprain, but you don't want to walk on it until you know for sure," Tanner said.

The dad bent to pick up the boy but grunted and clutched his back, leaving the boy on the ground.

"May I?" Tanner asked, then when they agreed, added, "Do you guys have a car?"

They pointed to an RV parked near our bus.

Tanner scooped the boy up easily. I trailed behind them on the path to the parking area as Tanner carried him like he weighed nothing. The calm, confident way he'd taken charge was impressive. And more than a little attractive.

Tanner asked the kid about his Batman shirt and whether he'd seen a bear yet and his favorite candy, and it was all very adorable.

After he settled the boy inside, the dad shook his hand, and the mom hugged him.

"Thank you for your help."

"He only darted away for a second. I'm glad you were there."

"It was nothing," Tanner said. "Glad I was around. Enjoy your trip."

They entered the RV, and we turned to find our parents watching. Mr. and Mrs. Woods were studying Tanner with puzzled expressions, like they didn't recognize their own son.

He was proving he'd be good with a gym full of kids, capable of handling emergencies. Even though I could take no credit for his charm or his skills or him being pretty incredible, I was proud.

chapter Twenty-six

Post-Cruise Tour: Denali National Park

~

"Not bad, Coach," I said when he'd rejoined me and the family was on their way.

"Kids love me, what can I say?"

We rambled slowly along the trail.

He chewed his lip. "I was thinking about last night. The job stuff. Or major, I mean. Physical education."

Right. Of course that was what he meant. Not . . . the other part of last night. Which I simultaneously wanted to repeat and also never think about again. "What about it?"

"I want to do it," he said, his face intense.

"Tanner, that's fantastic." I grabbed his hand and then immediately tried to let go but he wouldn't let me.

"I don't know what my parents will say."

"It's a great career, making a difference in lives, like the mentoring you do. Besides, wasn't that why you asked me to help?

Tell them it was my idea. Or I can be there when you talk to them, if you need backup. They saw what you did today, and they were impressed."

He studied me. "Will you keep helping me?"

"Of course. What do you need?" I didn't even have to think about my answer.

"How do I do it? Pick a school and . . . I don't know."

"You said you're hoping for a football scholarship?" I paused atop a low hill, and he stopped beside me.

"Yeah, but I'm not good enough for a big school."

"How does that work? Do you apply or do they recruit you?"

"Both. Either."

"So find schools you like and reach out to them, then also see who approaches you. Research programs and what classes they require. Maybe talk to the colleges about coaching, too. Like if you play, would there also be opportunities to learn about coaching. Ooh, or volunteer this fall, coach a kids' team. You'd be great at it."

When I stopped, he had a slight smile. His face felt close, his gaze warm.

"What?"

"Your planning skills are impressive."

"Oh. Thanks." A tingle skittered across my skin.

"I'm gonna need that plan in writing," he said.

"I can do that."

"You didn't do it for yourself, did you?"

"What do you mean?"

"Research programs and classes."

I studied the mountains. "I decided where I want to be."

"Close to home."

"Yeah. Why, do you think that's bad?" I couldn't read his face.

"All that matters is what you think. If you like LA and you find a college you like and a good program that helps you on the path to where you want to be, that's what matters."

"But you think I should look other places."

"Do you think you should look other places?"

I pointed at him. "Jordan uses that Jedi mind trick on me. I'm immune to it."

He smirked. "If you decide to look more, I can be your research buddy. Helping each other is working well."

It was. Maybe too well.

We seemed to realize at the same time how close we were standing. We jumped apart and walked to the bus in silence.

As we boarded, they handed out snack boxes. The box contained jerky, an apple, trail mix, crackers, and a cookie. We spread the items across our laps.

"Yes, I'm eating the cookie," I said before Tanner could ask.

"What about the elk jerky?"

"You can have that if I get your apple, since you don't like them." I plucked it from his box.

"Gross, take it." He unwrapped his jerky and extended it. "Try a bite."

I ate from his hand. The meat had a smoky flavor different from regular jerky. I must have wrinkled my nose because he took it back and grabbed mine, too. When we reached the trail mix, he shook out both bags into the box lid, plucked out the almonds and half the chocolate chips for himself, and left me the peanuts, raisins, and the other half of the chocolate.

"Perfect," he said, and it was.

Our next stop was along the rocky bank of a broad river. A small building contained a gift shop and displays about animals. Outside, a bench held a variety of real antlers, like some kind of disturbing animal graveyard.

Tanner held them to his head and had me take pictures of him pretending to be a caribou then a Dall sheep, making noises he thought the animals would make, which sounded a lot like an injured Chewbacca.

People were laughing. And . . . when had I started finding him charming and funny instead of supremely annoying? Before or after the desire to kiss him?

Which I was definitely not thinking about.

"Come on, S'more. You know you want to be a moose." He waved a giant moose antler at me, and it could've been a weapon. I wouldn't want an animal charging at me with those suckers.

I took it from him, and it was heavier than I'd expected. We each held one up, then he slipped an arm around my waist and we posed while someone snapped a photo of us as a two-headed moose.

His fingers were slow to leave my back. When he took the antler, his fingers lingered on mine. I avoided looking at him. Was he messing with me? He'd been the one to apologize for the kiss. Maybe this was all in my head and he meant nothing by any of it.

We wandered away, along the riverbank.

Tanner stared at the sky. "I bet the stars are great out here."

"Too bad it doesn't get dark enough to see them until later in the year. And that it's cold and bear-infested in the middle of the night. I wouldn't want to camp out here."

"S'more . . ."

"Yeah?"

"I've been thinking."

"That's dangerous."

"About Astronomy Club." His voice was soft, and he was staring at the view, not me.

"About how I was right, and I should have won?"

"Yeah."

"Wait, what?" I stopped.

He shoved his hands into his pockets. "It's always been your thing. You should do it."

I blinked. At him. At the hillside he was staring at, in case the words were written across the mountain and that would somehow make them make sense. "But you were right. Everyone voted."

"You came in second, though. If I step down, it's yours."

"Why would you . . . ?" I didn't know what to say.

"Did I ever tell you why I joined?"

"I've been wondering for three years, honestly. I figured it was to mess with me." Considering the first day he'd walked in, he'd asked if Astronomy Club was about zodiac signs.

"It might have started that way. Freshman year, my parents wanted me to do something other than sports. Again, there was that whole thing of them liking you, so I figured if I did a club you did, they were sure to approve."

"That's partly why I joined the service club sophomore year. That, and Jordan begged me to."

His lips twitched. "Well, I found I actually liked Astronomy Club. Although I don't appreciate the hard science parts as much as you."

"Your pathetic attempt at a rocket was evidence of that."

"Fair point. But I like the stars. Imagining what's out there."

Huh. "Yeah. Me too."

"So," he said, finally turning to me, and there were galaxies of unspoken words in his eyes. "You should lead. It means more to you. I'll say I'm too busy."

"Are you going to leave the club?" I found I didn't want to imagine it without him.

"Aw, would you miss me? Nah, I plan to stay. Just under new leadership." He gave me a mock salute.

A sensation like warm honey poured down my spine. "Tanner, I don't know what to say."

"Thanks is a good start. And that you'll get me an appreciation milkshake."

"I'll buy all your milkshakes from this point forward." The words were out before I realized I liked the picture they painted, of milkshakes being something we'd do together for a long time to come.

"I'll email Mr. Lin when we get home," he said. "So you'd better start planning."

"Thank you. And . . . we can talk about the camping trip. Since everyone else liked the idea. You'll have to help."

"Deal."

He folded my hand in his and left it there as our eyes met.

It might have been the most seen I'd ever felt.

Back on the bus, we didn't try to avoid bumping each other. Our sides pressed as if on purpose. It didn't have to mean anything. The ride was easier this way, so I didn't startle every time we touched, that was all.

We drove to a final lookout point, and the skies had cleared enough to let us see the enormous Denali in the distance. In the foreground were more green hills, but above them, the peak loomed, brilliant white and towering.

Even from far away, it stole my breath, made me pause in wonder.

The bus turned around to drive back. We saw more grizzlies up in the hills and a fox along the road.

Then the vehicle stopped and the guide told us to look out the left-hand side. A grizzly and two cubs were playing on the hill above us, scampering toward the road. When they reached it, the cubs continued on, but the mom stopped to meander along the gravel shoulder.

It was right outside the window. It seemed to be ignoring us, but I could see its bristly fur, its giant paws. I couldn't look away, like if I did, if I blinked, it would appear right in front of me, mouth opened, teeth bared, claws raised, Weeping Angel style.

Did the bear see this bus like a person saw a can of olives? All she had to do was find a way to rip it open, and inside were lots of plump, juicy morsels waiting to be devoured.

Olives were gross—too squishy and slimy—but whatever.

The point was, how secure was this vehicle?

Tanner's hand landed on my knee. "Breathe. It's fine. Look, it isn't even paying attention to us."

His voice was quiet, reassuring. The hand was meant to be but instead made every nerve in my body fire at once, radiating outward from the contact.

The cubs were playing on the hillside. And maybe they were cute, in a man-eating way. The mom eventually rambled after them and they moved out of sight.

I exhaled slowly. Everyone else lowered their cameras and settled into their seats.

I had survived my first grizzly encounter. Okay, it didn't fully count as an encounter because of the bus. But I was choosing to see it that way.

Tanner's hand remained on my knee as the bus moved on. I wanted to take it, lace my fingers through his. But after his reaction last night, I was afraid that would make him pull away, so I sat very still and hoped he might forget it was there, not that I could.

When we passed the visitors center and rejoined the highway, heading into the town, small as it was, I was relieved.

I was feeling tiny and insignificant. Awed. I couldn't deny Denali was beautiful and wild and impressive. But the familiarity of civilization felt safer, more comfortable.

"Maybe it's good to be challenged like that sometimes," Tanner said. "To remember how big the world is."

"I can remember that by looking at pictures or watching a nature show."

He laughed, though I hadn't been joking "Do you watch

nature shows? I thought the science shows you liked were about buildings and bridges and spaceships."

"I didn't say I did, just that I *could*."

He laughed again. "Come on, wasn't that impressive today? We should go hiking tomorrow. See it on foot. There are trails from the visitors center, not all the way into the park like today. A few miles, enough to experience it."

He expected me to say no. I wanted to. Today had demonstrated how much wildlife existed in the park and how small we were in comparison. But I didn't want to let him down, see his disappointment if I said no. He'd gone out of his way to help me this trip. I could take a risk and do this for him.

"Maybe a short hike," I said.

He pumped his fist. "Yes. It will be awesome. You'll see."

I wasn't sure I believed him.

At the lodge, Wi-Fi revealed messages I'd missed while being in the wilderness all day. I had several from Jordan.

And another from Caleb. He'd said we should talk, and once again I hadn't replied. I expected a thrill, a quickened heartbeat when I saw his name, but . . . nothing. I must have been tired, that was all.

I read Jordan's texts first, without opening Caleb's. She'd sent updates on her job, the conversation she'd had with the cute brother, and her sister's attempts to learn volleyball. While I was responding, I got an alert and clicked over to find Tanner had tagged me again.

It was a picture I hadn't known he'd taken, of me standing on top of a hill with all of Denali spread before me. The wind had blown my hair back to reveal the blue stripes.

I hadn't been posting as many photos lately. Because I had properly proved I was fun? Or because I'd decided I didn't need to? Caleb was writing, so obviously something was working.

When I opened his message, I dropped my phone. I caught it just before it hit the ground.

I made a mistake. I don't want to throw away what we had. Please respond, Savannah. I miss you.

chapter twenty-seven

Post-Cruise Tour: Denali National Park

~

The message might as well have been written in Klingon for all that I understood its meaning.

I immediately sent a screenshot to Jordan.

My phone rang a second later.

"You're calling me," I said. "Who does that?"

"Best friends in desperate times," she said.

"What's desperate about the times?"

"Caleb. He's desperate."

I snorted. "I don't know if that's the right word."

"Of course it is. Of course he is. He sees how cool you are, how much fun you're having with Tanner, how you're better off without him. He knows he needs to act fast. Therefore, he's desperate."

"But . . . isn't this good?"

"Do you think it's good?"

Why did people keep turning questions back on me? "I mean, yes?"

She hummed. "You don't sound very sure about that."

"It's what I was hoping for, until . . ."

"Until what?"

". . . until I kissed Tanner."

Her screech rang in my ear, and I had to move the phone away.

"It was a one-time event," I said when her screaming stopped. "It's not happening again. He apologized."

"You sound sad about that."

"I am not. He was right. It shouldn't have happened." But the reasons why were seeming nebulous, despite that message from Caleb.

"I need details," Jordan said.

"Which ones? Like how we went for an evening walk and made s'mores at a fire and kissed during the midnight sunset?"

"And you waited until the next day to tell me? Rude."

"It was like one in the morning, and we had no service all day today."

"That is news you can wake me up with anytime," she said. "In fact, I demand it. So how was it?"

"Um. Amazing? I might not hate him as much as I used to."

"And Caleb? Do you miss him?"

I'd expected more squeals of joy or shock or pretty much anything other than an interrogation. "It's hard to. I've been distracted."

She cackled. "By Tanner's—"

315

"Do *not* say tight end."

Instead, she asked, "Do you miss me?"

"Yeah. I keep seeing things you'd like and wishing you were here, or taking pictures to send you but then there's no service."

"I'm relieved to hear that mountain air and kissing Tanner Woods haven't made you forget me. Shouldn't that tell you something? Did you think about Caleb like that this week?"

"Maybe . . . some. When we played with the dogs. Or I was doing trivia and there were questions like in Math Bowl."

"Wow, sounds like you can't live without him." Her voice was dry. "Or you need your own dog and a new math partner."

Was that really all I missed about Caleb after nine months? Someone else who liked numbers and who had a cute pet?

"How did you feel last night when Tanner apologized for kissing you?"

I groaned. "Are you making me have a feelings talk?"

"Yes. I insist this time. Don't make me bust out the chart."

"Rude. Ummm. Disappointed. Kind of hurt. Like my heart was being squeezed and crushed." I scrunched my eyes shut and buried my head in my hands. "Ugh."

"Oh, Savannah. I'm giving you an enormous long-distance hug, and you're liking it."

"Yes, I am."

She was silent for a moment. "On the last day of school, during the breakup . . . how did you feel then?"

I froze. Allowed the misery of that day to wash over me for the first time. "Stunned. Definitely embarrassed. Maybe . . . scared. About the future."

"I'm saying this because I love you, but it sounds like the reaction was mental, because Caleb surprised you in front of people. But you weren't actually hurt, in your heart."

"You're either going to be a great psychologist one day or your patients are going to hate you."

"You can hate me now, as long as subsequent self-reflection shows you that I'm right and you come crawling back to thank me."

Now that I had distance from the breakup, I saw it more clearly. I hadn't been hurt. It had scared me, losing the comfortable, the familiar. Having the future I'd planned taken from me suddenly. But I'd been more upset about the nickname and the words Caleb had said about me than about the idea of not dating him anymore.

"Now," Jordan said, "I want you to consider whether your feelings toward Tanner, even if they were negative in the past, were always stronger than anything you ever felt for Caleb. And that's all I'm going to say. I gotta go to work. Love you. I can't wait for you to get home."

"Love you back. Hey, Jor?"

"Yeah?"

"Do I ignore what you want? You always go along with my preferences. Have I been a bad friend?"

"You're a great friend. And I understand."

"I know, but understanding and wishing you could sometimes pick what we do are different things. I want to be better about it."

"Ramen?" she asked.

"Don't push your luck. But I'm serious. I'm sorry. I've realized on this trip that I need to think about other people more, so I'm going to try. Miss you."

After we hung up, I paced the room, wishing I had time to go for a run or LEGOs to build or anything to distract me from her words and the possible implications if I admitted she was right about Caleb and Tanner and all of it.

Oblivious to my potential life crisis, my parents hurried me along to dinner theater. It was in a log cabin, with picnic tables covered in checkered tablecloths.

Caleb's message and Jordan's comments were burning holes in my mind.

And I hadn't responded to Caleb. What was I supposed to say?

Did I really have stronger feelings for Tanner?

I thought of all the times he'd annoyed me, exasperated me, argued with me, challenged me. And this week, how he saw me, went out of his way to help me, made me laugh and helped me relax, and dug deeper to know me than anyone else had.

I studied him surreptitiously as we took seats.

I didn't know if I wanted to tell Tanner about the message from Caleb. He'd made his opinion on Caleb clear. But then, he'd also agreed to help with my quest, knowing my initial objective. We had succeeded. I'd helped him find a path for his future that made him happy and hopefully would please his parents. In return, he'd helped me get Caleb back.

So why was I unsatisfied?

We ate a family-style meal of salmon and ribs. I was wary of the fish, so I took ribs, which were going to be messy. But then, I knew Tanner would smear barbecue sauce all over his face if I needed him to, just so I wasn't the only one making a mess. Which made me warm and gooey inside, like a marshmallow.

He sat closer than necessary, his knee touching mine, thigh pressing when he reached for seconds. His fingers brushed mine when we passed the potato salad, the rolls, the cobbler.

Was he doing it on purpose? He wasn't looking at me when it happened.

And I wanted him to, to see if the same pleasant shock was shooting through him as it did through me.

If I told him about Caleb's message, would he pull away again?

I couldn't stop replaying Jordan's words, wondering why Tanner rejecting me after one mistaken kiss hurt more than Caleb ending a nine-month relationship.

Actors in western clothes came out and performed a story about the Alaskan gold rush, accompanied by far too much singing. When the first song started, Tanner nudged me.

But I was barely paying attention.

Because it hit me—I liked Tanner Woods. Not as in, I didn't hate him anymore. As in, I *liked* him. A lot. His humor and the way he made everyone comfortable. The way he noticed details about people and wanted to help. The way he accepted me while also encouraging me to grow.

I had no idea what to do with this new knowledge rocketing

around inside me. I would never have believed it was possible. Did I want to act on it? Did he feel the same? With Caleb, we'd been friends, he'd asked me out, and it had made sense, so I'd said yes. There had been none of the whirling, spinning thrill of the possibility of it going well, or the terrifying idea that it would explode before getting off the ground.

After the show, as we left, and our parents were far enough away, I groped for anything to say to hide my monumental realization. "You can admit you liked it," I said to Tanner. "There was lots of history."

"Sorry you had to put up with the musical numbers." He returned my smirk.

"At least there was no spontaneous dancing."

As we walked to our rooms, the back of his hand brushed mine once. Then twice. It had to be deliberate, right? But I wasn't brave enough to take his hand, or to suggest we slip off alone again.

I tried not to peek over my shoulder as I went to my door, but I failed. And I found him doing the same, our eyes locking across the hall. Light exploded in my chest.

I shivered, fighting the confusing yet steady force that wanted to tug me those few yards toward him. Instead, I nodded to him and escaped into my room.

chapter Twenty-Eight

Post-Cruise Tour: Denali National Park

~

The sign was a huge indicator that this had been a terrible idea.

Tanner and I were decked out in hiking gear and rain jackets, with newly purchased bells attached to our backpacks. I was suspicious of the bell. How did we know that the bears didn't view it as a dinner bell, its ring telling them exactly when and where to come feast?

We also had snacks, water, and bear spray—which we knew not to use on ourselves. The bells and spray had hinted that we might encounter something large and unfriendly.

But the sign sealed it.

The title read WILDLIFE SAFETY, followed by detailed instructions about what to do if you encountered a moose, wolves, or a bear while on the trail. On foot. Without a bus surrounding you and lots of other people for the bear to eat first.

The first piece of advice for all three animals was STAY AWAY.

That was, in fact, very sound advice. And it was not too late for us to heed the warning.

"You know the best way to stay away?" I pointed to the wise sign. "Stay inside. Don't go marching off into their territory."

Honestly, it was asking for trouble. Why tempt nature?

Tanner laughed. "We'll be fine. It says to run away from a moose. You're a great runner."

"I am . . ."

"And wolves."

The sign told us to scold a wolf like a dog, yell, and throw rocks at it, and showed a park ranger with a dialogue bubble saying, "Bad wolf," which reminded me of Doctor Who but did nothing to convince me that throwing rocks at a wild animal was in any way a good idea.

"I have no trouble making noise," Tanner said. "And I have great aim."

"You claim the moose and the wolf are covered, but you left out the biggest one."

"They said moose are more dangerous."

"Really not helping."

The bear had the most instructions. First, it told us to be noisy.

"I'm good at noisy," Tanner said. "I'll sing karaoke as we hike. Ha. Bear-aoke."

"You sound like your dad. And that would definitely scare me off."

"That's what the bells are for." He wiggled his shoulders to make the bell on his backpack chime. "Then, 'make yourself look big,'" he read. "I got that covered."

"I don't think it means your head."

He placed a hand over my mouth to keep me from talking. "Then the bear spray. You can carry it the whole time, if you want."

Oh, I planned to.

I studied him, that new knowledge of my feelings burning inside me. Tanner was excited for this. Surely I could manage my panic for a few hours. We were already here. . . .

"Oh fine. Let's do it."

"It will be great, S'more."

He squeezed my hand as we started off—away from the visitors center and civilization and safety.

The trail led through a quiet forest. Soft dirt silenced our steps, and the damp air and trees swallowed the insignificant ringing of the bells. Soon, we came alongside a wide, rushing river. The sound was roaring and powerful and wild. Downstream, an impressive railroad bridge spanned the river, and we crossed a wooden suspension bridge for pedestrians.

It was early enough that portions of the trail and river were completely in the shadows, making the temperature cool, but sometimes we rounded a corner and sun made a hillside glow with green light. Towering mountains stretched into the distance.

We didn't encounter anyone, either because of our early start or because everyone else was wise enough to avoid the bears.

I couldn't deny it was gorgeous. As long as I didn't think about how alone we were, how there was no cell service, how we didn't have a map, how this park's ratio of animals to humans did not favor humanity. How if we got hurt or had problems we were on our own.

"Doing okay, S'more?"

"It's weird, right? How few people there are?"

"It is pretty quiet. I can sing anytime. Name the song."

"I don't know if my ears can take it."

To make noise, we chatted about movies and sports and when we might run a 10K. Tanner asked me to tell him about the bridges, which I knew was a distraction, but it was an interesting one. And it was sweet that he knew exactly what to ask.

After I'd given him an engineering lesson he probably hadn't wanted, I contemplated what he would get most excited to talk about.

"What have been your favorite parts of the trip?" I asked.

He enthusiastically relived the Ping-Pong tournament and our magic show fame and the shore excursions, then told me about Dottie trying to sneak him into the casino after trivia, while I'd been getting a haircut, and soon I was laughing.

Being with him felt so easy and light, and I could barely remember the time before the trip when I'd wanted to avoid him, or my past reasons for disliking him.

The trail led uphill. My thighs burned comfortably. The air was chilly, and I kept my hands in my pockets and my hat pulled over my ears. We climbed above the first row of trees. The river was now far below, a dark blue ribbon. The landscape went on forever—trees and mountains, turning blue as they stretched into the distance, many topped with snow.

We stopped to admire the view in silence, standing side by side, our shoulders touching.

A slow, not unpleasant ache unrolled in my chest.

"What are you thinking?" I asked before I could stop myself.

He turned toward me, inches away. "That I'm glad I'm here, and I'm glad it's with you, S'more." His voice was low, serious.

I shifted closer. "Me too."

"I've had a great time this trip," he said. "I hope you did too, and that it wasn't too scary."

"I did enjoy almost all of it."

"I know, playing with those cute puppies was challenging."

My lips quirked at the memory of him covered in wriggling balls of fur. "It really was."

He brushed hair off my temple and tucked it under my hat. His fingers trailed down my jaw. His cheeks were pink, and his eyes were bright. He captured my hands, which were cold, and brought them to his mouth so he could warm them with his breath. It sent heat straight from my hands to my chest, un-curling like steam above hot chocolate.

One moment we were looking at each other, and the next we were kissing. I didn't know who moved first. My lips were cold, but his quickly warmed them. His hand rested on my neck, and I gripped the front of his jacket.

The rush of wind and the expanse of wilderness had moved inside me, glowing with sunlight.

When we pulled apart, we didn't talk. He tucked me against him, my arms circled his waist, and we gazed out at forever.

The trail continued along the ridge, displaying the views. We walked single file, and I kept glancing at the back of Tanner's head. I didn't know what that kiss had meant. Did he share my feelings? Or had the magical effects of Denali momentarily overwhelmed us?

We turned to head back the way we'd come. Downhill gave my quads a break.

"Not too fast," Tanner said. "It doesn't look muddy, but I don't want you falling ag—"

I gave him a light shove and he laughed.

The trees were thick on all sides, with light playing in the layers of leaves. Rustling came from the bushes ahead.

A dark shape moved among the trunks.

My heart clawed its way into my throat as the details came into focus.

Grizzly bear.

chapter Twenty-Nine

Post-Cruise Tour: Denali National Park

~

I froze. My fists clenched so tightly I was worried I'd make my palms bleed. Wait. Could bears, like sharks, smell blood? I forced my hands to relax so I didn't draw its attention.

I was supposed to grab something, but I couldn't think. Tanner reached over to ease the bear spray from the outer pouch of my backpack.

"Hey, Bear," he yelled. "I'm sure you're a nice bear. I know this is your home. But it would be great if you could move along now."

The bear stopped and looked at him.

What kind of idiot advice was that sign giving, telling us to make noise? What if the bear hadn't noticed us until Tanner started yelling? It was like advertising Dessert Buffet on a cruise ship to people who hadn't known it existed. The feeding frenzy was going to descend, leaving our bones picked cleaner than a cake pan.

Tanner waved his arms. I should join him. Logically, if the sign said to do it, it made sense. But I was stuck in place.

"Don't make me spray you, Bear!" Tanner brandished the bear spray. "I'll do it. And I'll tell you my dad's bear jokes, which will be even worse."

The bear was enormous, brown fur brushed with lighter tan on the hump behind its head. Dark eyes studied us from above its narrow nose. The brush hid its paws, and I was glad for that because I didn't need to know if they were the size of my face.

"What color socks are you wearing?" Tanner called. "What? None? You prefer bear feet?"

It studied Tanner, unimpressed with the bad joke, before lumbering away. Leaves and branches rustled, and then all was silent.

I continued to stare after it. What if it was tricking us? Pretending to leave and setting a trap on the trail to lie in wait? Were bears masters of the ambush? They seemed like they might be sneaky.

Air was frozen in my throat, and my heart pulsed in every extremity.

"Wow. Did you see it? It was so cool." Tanner's voice sounded distant. "Oh. Hey. Are you okay?"

I shook my head. Tried to. My throat was too dry to form words. And my legs felt shaky, like they might collapse at any moment. The world tilted.

"Whoa, there, S'more. Hey. Savannah. Breathe." Tanner's hands came to my cheeks, forcing me to look away from the woods and meet his eyes. "Take a deep breath. Slow. In through your nose. Like this."

His nostrils flared as he inhaled slowly.

I gulped. Sucked in a little air. Swayed. I couldn't. There was no oxygen. I was floating in space and I was going to suffocate.

Tanner breathed again, exaggerating the motion. I concentrated on the gray of his eyes. Tried to match his slow pace of inhaling.

He shifted his grip to my shoulders, which were hunched around my ears, and his thumbs kneaded the muscles.

When he inhaled a third time, I managed to mimic him. Air went in, got stuck.

"Out slow." Tanner blew air out through his mouth, and it wisped against my face.

I did the same.

After two more breaths, the world stopped spinning. My body still trembled.

Tanner slid his arm around me. "Do you need to sit?"

His arm remained around me for several steps as I stumbled down the trail.

He guided me to a rock, kept a hand between my shoulder blades, and continued his measured breathing for me to copy. I tried to keep pace with it.

Feeling was returning, prickles coursing through my body. I had to fight to keep breathing normally, instead of wheezing like I'd broken my personal mile best. Every sound from the forest made me twitch.

"Easy, S'more. It's gone. You're okay."

I didn't know how long we sat there, the cold damp seeping into my backside, the fresh air in my lungs slowly bringing the world into focus again. Tanner's hand anchored me, and he kept repeating similar words reminding me he was there and I was alive.

Finally, I nodded. "I'm good."

He continued rubbing my back for a few more minutes before helping me to my feet. He smoothed hair out of my face, left his palm against my cheek.

I met his eyes, though I wanted to look away. My face was hot. He'd stayed calm and done exactly what you were supposed to, while I'd frozen up and been utterly useless.

Tanner kept hold of my hand and sang loudly the whole way back, our school fight song and rock songs and snatches of karaoke favorites with made-up lyrics, to scare off any wildlife. I wanted to run—anything to rejoin civilization as fast as possible—except the advice about not acting like prey looped through my head and helped me keep my pace normal so a bear didn't decide my speed made me look tasty.

When we spotted the visitors center, I gave in, raced to the paved area, and collapsed onto a bench.

Tanner crouched in front of me and took my hands. "We made it. You're okay."

I didn't feel okay. I felt like screaming or fainting or maybe vomiting. Or all three.

My mind remained on the trail, every detail branded into my memory. I couldn't do this anymore.

"I'm done," I croaked.

"What?"

"The new things. No more. I'm finished. With all of it."

A wrinkle formed between his eyebrows. "I know that was

scary, S'more. But the advice worked. We made it. And what about those views? Wasn't it worth it?"

I refused to dwell on the moments before the bear, on the ridge, on the awe and the wind and the peace and the kiss.

I shook my head. "Nope. I can see nice views on travel shows. Or from the window of a train."

His eyebrows knit farther together. "What about whitewater rafting this afternoon?"

"You can go by yourself. I accomplished my goal. Now, I'm going to sit in a lodge with hot chocolate and listen to a podcast where there's Wi-Fi and I'm the top of the food chain. I don't know what I was thinking this week."

"You said you enjoyed almost all of it, were glad you came."

Feeling sick, I pulled my hands free of his and crossed my arms over my stomach. "It worked. That's what matters. I can go back to my safe diet and my paved roads and my science and stop trying to be someone I'm not."

A shadow crossed his face. "What do you mean, *it worked*?"

His tone was dark and my chest clenched, but I forged on.

"Caleb texted yesterday. He said he was wrong and he misses me."

Tanner's jaw twitched. "Why didn't you tell me?"

My stomach squirmed. I swallowed hard and looked away. "Thank you for your help. We succeeded. You coached me, I found your major. Now you can go be an awesome teacher and stop forcing yourself to make sure I'm having fun."

"Oh, I see." Now his voice was hard. His back had stiffened, and his eyes were cold.

"See what?"

"It was a deal, right? What we had on this trip. Help each other, nothing more?" His voice held a challenge.

It had been, to start. Agreeing now after everything we'd shared and done, after realizing my feelings, felt like a lie. Despite that, I said, "Right."

He was still squatting next to me but leaned closer. His expression was stony. "I think you're wrong, about trying to be someone you're not. Didn't you feel alive this week, even if it scared you? You had fun, branched out, challenged yourself, and saw how strong you could be. What life could be like if you stood up to your fears."

Uncertainty stirred inside me. He had a point. But those truths faded, eclipsed by the bear and the paralyzing fear that had gripped me.

"And," Tanner went on, "are you content to be with someone who you have to prove yourself to? Who didn't think you were enough and couldn't see how great you are?"

"I proved myself to you."

"I didn't care if you did any of it, S'more. I mean, I did, because I wanted you to get the most out of your trip, and I had fun spending time with you. But I wasn't the one calling you boring or saying you needed to branch out. I didn't say your worth as a person depended on you trying to be fun or different or anything other than who you are."

I tried to swallow, but my throat was burning.

"The only thing that changed between us is, we got to know each other. I didn't change my opinion of you because you did or didn't do anything. I changed it because I saw who you are and I listened." His eyes gentled. "And it was good, wasn't it?"

My insides were a jagged mess, pieces breaking off my heart like chunks of a glacier crashing into the sea. I couldn't respond, even if I'd known what to say. Not around the ice gripping my throat.

Tanner huffed and rocked on his heels. "You'll take him back, just like that, after he embarrassed you and was a huge jerk? After he was willing to so easily throw away what you had? He only regretted it when he saw you were fine without him."

"You're saying he doesn't really want me?"

"You were with him for nine months and never thought about saying I love you," he said. "Consider why, and whether that's the kind of relationship you want. Just getting by because it's safe and familiar when there could be so much more out there."

Now he sounded like Jordan. "Are you talking about hiking or about a relationship?"

He didn't answer.

"And what else is out there, Tanner?"

He held my gaze, intense, focused. "I think you know."

My heart was a deafening roar in my ears. Our faces were close, and we were probably drawing attention.

My eyes went to his mouth. I swayed toward him, blinked, leaned away.

He shook his head and his lip curled in what was not a smile. He stood to tower above me. "Forget it. If you want to be with Caveman, if he makes you happy and supports you and understands you, if he makes you the best version of yourself, if you enjoy being with him, then do it."

"Fine. I will." I stood, too, angled away from him.

"Fine. I hope your senior year is exactly like your junior one. I hope you're happy going back to your box, like this week meant nothing. But you weren't the only one paying attention this trip. I figured out your career, too."

"I know what I want to do."

"Really? You want to stand in front of a classroom all day and talk to kids who don't want to learn? You loved the tram and the ship and the train bridges. You like building stuff. You love the stars and math and physics. Why aren't you going to study aerospace engineering? It is literally perfect for you."

My mouth opened. Closed. A storm raged in my chest.

"Don't say no just because it might be hard," he said. "Do your research thing. Look at what you'd get to study. Do Mr. Lin's program and see if you like it. Or forget this week, let your fear control you, and live in your safe bubble for next year, for college, forever."

"I like my bubble." My voice sounded defensive.

"Then I'm glad I was able to help, to be a sub until you got your starter back. Enjoy your safe life."

We were standing close now, our chests heaving. His eyes were dark. I was shaking again.

"I will," I said, and marched away.

I was breathing hard as I stomped to the waiting area for the shuttle that would take us to the hotel. Tanner followed in silence. I crossed my arms and waited, several feet away from him, my gut churning. His words echoed and bounced around with Jordan's, making a wreck of my mind.

Caleb was the safe choice. We would lead the Math Bowl team and work at the Science Center. Return to our routines, except I'd have to branch out in where we ate. After all, he had called me boring, and only wanted me back now that he saw I wasn't.

Why was I okay with that?

No. Stop. Tanner was being him, difficult and challenging, that was all.

I peeked at him. He no longer looked fierce and angry, just sad and a little lost.

My chest tightened. I knew he feared real conflict. But we'd been fighting for years, and he'd never been affected like today. Because he hadn't viewed those as real fights? Or because now I was someone he cared about? Because he'd gotten real for once, and I'd run away?

He wasn't my boyfriend. I needed to focus on Caleb and getting my life back on track.

No more adventures, no more bears, and no more Tanner Woods.

chapter Thirty

Post-Cruise Tour: Denali National Park

~

The shuttle was empty enough for Tanner and me to sit alone several rows apart. I was so used to having him at my side this week that the empty spot next to me felt like something was missing. Like the ghost of him was beside me, an accusation.

I tried to organize my jumbled thoughts into neat rows. When that failed, I recalled the feelings chart and attempted to categorize my emotions. But since the one that kept elbowing its way to the forefront was *confusion,* that didn't help.

As soon as the shuttle reached the lodge, I got off without waiting for Tanner. And without glancing back, because seeing his face might've led me to do something rash.

Our parents had stayed at the lodge for brunch with Mr. Ramirez, and when I wandered into the lobby toward the restaurant, my mom spotted me and waved me over.

As I wound through the tables, a sense of normalcy returned.

Tables and people and familiar sounds of conversation were such a contrast to the vast woods and mountains and the wildness of the park.

"How was your hike?" my mom asked. "Did you have fun?"

Mrs. Woods peered past me. "Where's Tanner?"

I couldn't answer, might break down in the middle of a crowded room. My breaths were already coming faster.

My dad stood. "Let's go outside, okay?" He put his arm around my shoulders. "We'll catch up with you later," he said to the others.

I let him steer me outside to a planter and we sat on the edge.

"What happened?" he asked.

"Bear."

"You mean you saw one? Are you okay?"

I was, now. Sitting outside a nice hotel in a paved parking lot with my dad, I could breathe again. "I'm fine." Because Tanner had protected me. From the bear, from myself. "Tanner scared it off."

"I'm sure that was terrifying. Do you want to talk about it?"

I shook my head. I didn't want to *think* about any of it, let alone find words.

"Okay. I'm here if you need to." He put an arm around me and squeezed me to him. "Can I do anything?"

"I'm going to find lunch."

"Want company?"

"No, but thanks. I need to think."

"Meet you later for rafting?"

"I thought I'd skip it."

"You're not getting sick?"

"I've had enough excitement, that's all." Rafting would ramp up the powerlessness to the max.

Plus, Tanner would be there. And I could never face him again.

No, thank you.

"All right," my dad said. "You know where to meet if you change your mind. Sure you're okay?"

I stood and hugged him. "I will be. Thanks, Dad."

Across the road, I found a row of shops and restaurants. The pavement and view of a highway, no matter how scarcely traveled, made me feel closer to civilization and therefore safer.

The gift shops reminded me of shopping with Tanner. It wouldn't be as fun to explore without him.

I was heading to a café when a door opened and Dottie stepped out with her walker.

"Oh, hello, dear." She peered past me. "Where's that adorable boyfriend?"

Tanner's face was the one I thought of, which made sense—he was who she meant, the one I'd been with all week. But still, the idea came too easily.

"At the hotel," I said. "Are you enjoying Denali?"

"I love it here. It gets me every time. Makes one feel small and yet part of something bigger at the same time."

That was how I felt looking at the stars. Why couldn't I capture that here?

Dottie started down the wooden stairs from the shop to the parking lot, and I stayed at her side to help. Tanner would have lifted her up and carried her down if she'd needed it.

When she moved the walker, a clank sounded.

"Oh no." She clutched the rail with one hand, as the walker now stood lopsided.

I bent next to her, and the breeze blew sparkly streamers into my face. "A wheel fell off."

I offered an arm to help Dottie sit.

"Thank you, dear. These old bones aren't as young as they used to be."

"Let me take a look." I sat next to the front poles of the walker. The wheel had slid off the end of the axle. Rather than a bolt, it appeared to have been held in place by a simple cotter pin that extended vertically through the axle.

"I might be able to fix it, enough for you to get back to the hotel. Is your husband around?"

"He's in the room, taking a nap. He's not as social as I am. Needs more alone time, so sometimes we compromise and do things separately."

"Okay, let me think." A search of the area failed to yield the missing pin. If I could find something else that fit in the hole, I could keep the wheel in place.

The streamers continued to flutter in the breeze. They were attached by short plastic sticks jammed beneath the walker's rubber grips, but the sticks were too big for the hole.

I rummaged in my backpack, eyes catching on my LEGO stormtrooper keychain. The ring appeared to be about the right size. I slid the stormtrooper off until I held the empty ring, then slid the wheel on and pried apart the key ring. It just fit. I twisted until it was all the way through, securing the wheel. My worries from the day faded as I worked.

"That should hold for now."

Dottie clomped the walker. The wheel stayed in place. I helped her stand and watched her walk.

"It's good as new," she said. "That's lovely. Very impressive."

"Can I walk with you?"

I kept a hand on her arm as we crossed the parking lot and then the road in case my fix-it job failed. Once she was safely inside the lobby, I jogged back to the café, ordered a sandwich, and took a seat on the patio facing the highway and the endless mountains beyond it.

I was calmer and more logical now that the bear was behind me and I'd had something to focus on, a tangible problem to solve.

Which, of course, reminded me of Tanner and his comments about my future. Making things did bring me joy. When I thought about teaching, I mostly focused on the math part, the pleasure of numbers and concrete laws. And the nice, familiar schedule of a school year. The actual students appealed to me less.

Something stirred inside me, an image I'd never let myself dwell on. Myself, working at a lab or company, designing inventions that made space exploration and research possible. The idea that something I designed or helped build might go off into the cosmos. Or something I researched for outer space making a difference in everyday lives on Earth. Studying not just cruise ship engines, but spaceships.

If I considered this path, it would change my senior year. I'd have to look at new colleges, possibly switch a few classes. Start making connections, though I could bring in speakers from companies or universities for the Astronomy Club. Which would be easier, thanks to Tanner's generosity.

The feeling inside me was like the thrill of the zip line, the curiosity about the tram, the marvel of the engine room, all in one.

It wouldn't hurt to consider the idea more. I'd have to say yes to Mr. Lin.

I opened my email and stared again at the information, the fascinating speakers, tours, projects, that added to the thrill.

Before I could change my mind, I hit reply and told him that as long as my parents agreed, I was in. I didn't have to decide on my entire future right now. I could continue with my old plans if I wanted. But it wouldn't hurt to check this out.

I set my phone next to my plate and waited. For fear or regret or the desire to email Mr. Lin again and say *never mind,* but none of those feelings came. Just anticipation and excitement. I let those linger as I finished eating.

That done, it was time to respond to Caleb. His last two messages had said he wanted to talk and he'd been wrong. If I were him, I'd be nervous about not receiving a reply.

A voice in my head that sounded suspiciously like both Jordan and Tanner said, *Good, make him sweat.*

My lack of response stemmed less from a desire to torture

him and more from the fact that I didn't know what to say. Getting back together by text was as terrible as breaking up in a parking lot.

If that's what I was planning to do. Was it?

One of Jordan's messages mentioned how alive I looked during this trip. Instead of opening my texts, I scrolled through my photos from the last two weeks, but also from the past year. I did look happier than I had in a long time. My smiles larger, my laughter more wild and less contained, my eyes full of joy.

I wanted to cling to that happiness. I'd liked who I was recently, not letting fear stop me, feeling strong and brave.

I lingered on a picture from Math Bowl earlier this year, when our team had won the district competition before going to state finals. Caleb and I held a trophy and smiled at each other, and I remembered being proud, happy our work had paid off, but that expression didn't reveal the same joy compared to what I'd experienced the last two weeks.

Caleb's familiar face failed to stir anything beyond fondness. His hair was shorter here. He was cute. But there was no swoop in my stomach when I saw him. Had he and I ever had that?

I'd thought I wanted someone like me: dependable, stable, studious. But had I been bored with Caleb? Maybe that was why he thought I was boring. Because I'd been going along, doing my thing, and Caleb had joined in, never challenging me.

Unlike Tanner, who stood up to me, forced me to think, stood by my side as he urged me to try new things. And I hadn't minded making changes to accommodate him. Maybe Tanner's and my differences were what made us stronger. If Dottie and her husband had learned to compromise, we could, too.

My feelings for Caleb were safe, inside-the-box feelings. Comfortable, familiar, easy. The only time he had ever surprised me was when he dumped me.

My feelings for Tanner were far more uncertain. They were ATV rides and polar plunges and wilderness hikes, risky and big and scary. I never knew what he might do or say. That made me nervous, but it also meant he was capable of making me laugh unexpectedly or see things in a new way or have experiences I might have missed out on.

Did I want to be with someone who let me settle for less than amazing in my life? Then got tired of me or blamed me when I did? Did I want to go back to the same life? I mean, yes, I enjoyed everything I did. But other than the bear, hadn't this week shown me that it wouldn't kill me to try new things? And that I might actually like them?

I sounded like Tanner.

I'd be fine without either of them. I didn't need a guy. But was it wrong to enjoy spending time with one who made me happy and brought out parts of me I didn't know existed?

It hit me, what Jordan and Tanner had been hinting at, that I hadn't been emotionally devastated by the breakup because I couldn't stand losing Caleb. I had been embarrassed. He'd hurt my pride, and I had been afraid of losing what was known and easy. But I should have missed him. Felt sad about not seeing his face, not talking to him.

The way I already felt about Tanner, and it had only been two hours since I'd seen him.

Caleb deserved more than that. He deserved more than I'd given him this year. And unlike him, I would do it right.

I picked up the phone and made a call.

"Savannah?" he answered. "Are you in Alaska?"

"Yeah. But I needed to talk to you."

"Did you get my messages?" His familiar voice was calming, but calling up his face in my mind failed to make me experience anything but mild regret.

"Why didn't we ever say I love you?" I asked.

"Whaaa . . . I mean, um. What?"

I spun my cup with my free hand. "We were together for nine months. I'm just wondering."

"I didn't—I don't—"

"It's okay. I don't know, either. Shouldn't that tell us something?" When he didn't say anything, I went on. "You're a great guy, Caleb. We're great math partners, and I like that we enjoy the same things. But I think we let ourselves forget that common interests isn't enough for a relationship."

After a long pause, he said, "You might be right. Asking you out seemed logical. We spent lots of time together, and we got along. But maybe romantically, that wasn't enough."

I exhaled. "I realize now that a lot of our relationship was me living the life I wanted and dragging you along. I never asked your opinions or let you make plans. That's on me. I'm sorry."

"And I am sorry for how I ended things. I really didn't mean for it to happen that way."

No hard feelings, as long as *Moore the Bore* didn't stick. "Friends?" I asked. "And future Math Bowl champs?"

"Definitely," he said. "Thank you, Savannah."

I disconnected the call, feeling lighter. We'd be okay. We'd go back to what we had before we dated, when we were science friends. Caleb would find a sweet, nonsarcastic girl who didn't make jokes that went over his head and didn't spend more time complaining about her nemesis than she did listening to his opinions.

I didn't want to be with someone who put me in a box. I was far too skilled at doing that to myself. I wanted someone who showed me I could break out of it then helped me do it and supported me as I did. Someone who wouldn't, as Tanner had pointed out, run away when I tried to climb back into it, but would help me be my best even when I couldn't see what that meant.

I dashed off a text to Jordan telling her I'd call her later and explain a lot. And then I ran to change.

chapter thirty-one

Post-Cruise Tour: Denali National Park

~

I made it to the shuttle bus just in time. Slid into the last seat in the front, a couple rows in front of my parents. My dad raised his eyebrows and smiled.

I fought the urge to twist and look at the other passengers. I assumed Tanner was farther back, that he was going through with the excursion without me. I didn't know if he'd seen me, or if he would wonder what it meant that I was here. My heart was thumping hard, and not from my race to get here.

The bus headed up the highway, and I debated standing, facing the entire vehicle, and shouting to Tanner. Except I didn't know what to say. *I like you? Please forgive me for thinking I wanted Caleb? I know we didn't get along for years, but now we do, so will you go out with me?*

Knowing Tanner, he'd likely appreciate a grand, public statement declaring my affections, in skywriting or on a stadium screen or with a flash mob. But I had no airplane or giant score-board and didn't want our parents doing a flash mob dance to ask out a guy, so I faced forward, my hands twisting in my lap, debating options.

My mom slid into the seat beside me and put an arm around me. "Your dad said you weren't coming. You okay, sweetie?"

"I guess so."

She shifted. "What's up? Are you too cool to talk to me?"

I huffed a laugh. "It's been . . . a big trip."

"All the new things?"

"Partly."

"I'm proud of you for trying. I know a lot of it must have been hard for you."

"Yeah."

She sighed. "I've tried to walk the line over the years. Re-specting that you and I are different, letting you be you, but also trying to make sure you don't miss out."

I leaned my head against hers. "I know, Mom. You did great. It wasn't your fault I was afraid to take risks."

She was silent a moment. "You know, your favorite charac-ters from those movies and shows, the heroic ones? Their ac-complishments, their great discoveries and biggest victories, never came when they played it safe. Living requires some risks. Loving takes risks."

"Like with Dad? Was it hard, to fall in love with him, after, you know?" We didn't talk about my bio dad often, both of us glad to have him behind us. "Did it feel like a risk? Or did it feel safe because he's a good guy?"

Her forehead wrinkled as she considered. "Your dad, your new one. He wasn't safe for me. The opposite, in fact. Your biological father and I got caught up in a whirlwind. The whole relationship was moving, and we never went deep and then it was too late. With your father, it was scarier, because he got to know me, flaws and all, and opening up to someone who truly sees you is far scarier. But it's worth it."

I thought of Tanner. We'd had a whirlwind this trip, but the adventures had been mixed with going deep, with admitting flaws and helping each other through them, and she was right. Those times might have been scarier than riding the ATVs.

Had I played it safe in dating like I had in the rest of my life? Gravitating to Caleb because I wanted something predictable?

"Thanks, Mom. And speaking of taking risks, I need your permission for a science program. Mr. Lin invited me. It would involve more travel." I gave her an overview.

"That sounds incredible," she said. "Do you want to do it?"

"I didn't at first, but now I think I do."

She rubbed my arm. "I'm not ready for you to leave. I'm trying not to think about college yet, but I suppose this program will be good practice for me."

"And for me. Oh. Speaking of new things. Did you hear about the promotion?"

"Mrs. Woods got it," she said easily.

"I'm sorry."

Mom shrugged. "I'm not. She'll be great, and I believe there will be other opportunities for me when the time is right. It's okay to be happy where you are but also look forward. There's a time for each one."

"Still, I would pick you for anything," I said.

She laughed. "Glad to hear it, kid."

The bus dropped us at a large log cabin on a platform over a rushing river. The water curved through mountains, winding into the distance through tree-lined banks. Some areas looked calm, but others rippled with white rapids, wider and faster than I'd anticipated. Why couldn't our final excursion have been a nice, calm covered wagon ride?

I stuck close to my dad as we trooped to a wooden deck. Radar in my brain was alerting me to Tanner's location at all times.

We put on dry suits that covered us neck to toes, to prevent hypothermia in case we fell in. How many people did that? I needed statistics here. Then we received paddles, life vests, and helmets that were marginally more encouraging than the zip line ones.

Our guide took us down a rocky path to the river, where several large rafts were tied. They were basically like flat balloons. We were trusting a balloon to keep us safe on a river full of pointy rocks. Coming here had been a grave miscalculation.

I sneaked a peek at Tanner, walking ahead of me with my mom. His shoulders were relaxed, and he was waving his hands as he talked, nearly hitting someone with his paddle.

It was like family outings before this trip, when we ignored each other. The return to our old pattern hurt worse than I wanted to admit.

Had he written me off after this morning? Decided I was too much work, we were too different? Or would he be open to an apology? To . . . more?

After a briefing on how to sit, how to paddle, and what to do if you were thrown from the raft and set adrift in the raging river, we prepared to board. Our raft held a dozen people plus the guide.

I was near the front with my mom, while Tanner sat farther behind me. I didn't need to be an expert to know I was in the splash zone.

We were off. The river did a lot of the work, sweeping us downstream. It was calm at first, and we practiced paddling. After a few minutes, my death grip on the paddle relaxed. In places, rocky cliffs met the water, and in others, pine trees grew thick on the shore.

"First rapid, coming up," the guide called, and I gripped the paddle again.

The water ahead was churning and white. The ride grew bumpier, and I bounced with each ripple of the water. We paddled hard. Spray shot up, splashing over me. Someone behind me whooped. It sounded like Tanner.

We bumped along, and I focused on digging the paddle into the water and trying not to get launched out of the raft.

It was more terrifying than anything we'd done yet. But thrilling, too.

During a slow stretch, we spotted two bears on the bank. I made myself watch them as we passed. They couldn't swim this fast if they wanted to catch us, not that they noticed us.

When they weren't trying to eat me, they were maybe, sort of, a little cute.

The calmer patches gave me time to think. I was going to take a chance, tell Tanner how I felt. That I wanted to keep spending time with him once the trip was over. That I liked him. Rather a lot.

If he shot me down, that was okay. I didn't know if he would want to try to make anything work beyond this trip. We were very different and had lots of complicated history. This vacation had thrown us together, against our wills.

But the kisses were a good sign.

We went through two more areas of rapids before the guide called out that we were approaching the biggest one.

The bumps were more violent, the spray completely clouded my vision, and my grip was slick on the wet paddle. Cold made my hands stiff. My stomach felt like it might jostle up through my throat.

The same panic threatened as when we'd seen the bear, but I focused on breathing. I wouldn't let fear win this time. I set my jaw and kept paddling. Another wave of chilly water slapped my face. The boat twisted and bumped, turned sideways. We straightened it in time to go over a drop.

The raft tilted. So did my stomach.

And I was airborne.

I plunged into the river, the cold water a shock on my face.

The paddle nearly came out of my hand, but I remembered to hold on. I bobbed on the surface, and the life vest easily kept me afloat.

Next to me, Mom, Mr. Woods, and Tanner had also fallen out. Mom and Mr. Woods were latching onto the rope on the side of the raft. But Tanner was too far away, and the current was carrying the boat out of his reach.

I had half a second to decide.

Rather than reach for the raft or Mom's outstretched hand and safety, I stroked toward Tanner and extended my paddle toward him.

His hand closed around the other end. When I twisted back to the raft, it was floating away.

Remembering the guide's instructions, I rolled to my back and pointed my feet downstream. The water was rocking me, and the roar of it filled my ears. Apparently the dry suit was well named, because only my face was wet.

I felt a tug on the paddle.

"S'more?" Tanner pulled himself to my side and continued holding my paddle so we didn't get separated. Together, we let the current carry us.

"Are you okay?" I asked.

"Fine. But what were you thinking? You could have been rescued."

"I didn't want to leave you alone."

His hand shifted on the oar, and it brushed mine. His skin was as cold as mine, but the contact sent heat through me.

I glanced sideways. His eyes were soft.

"I thought you weren't coming today," he said.

"I changed my mind."

"How come? What happened with Caleb?" Tanner's use of Caleb's real name threw me.

"He's not the one I want. I thought he was. But that was before."

"Before what?"

"You."

Our gazes held and locked, holding as firmly as we clutched

the paddle. My heart felt like it was being swept away, same as my body.

"So you decided to strand yourself in a raging river with me?" Tanner asked.

"Someone recently taught me that I need to take risks for things I really care about. For things I want."

We hit a faster area, water splashing up over our faces, and when we settled again, he asked, "And what is it you want, Savannah?" His voice was low and rough.

I waited until he looked at me again. "Isn't that obvious? I want you. If you want that, too. I mean, us."

The corners of his eyes crinkled as a slow smile enveloped his face. "How can I not want someone willing to face their fears to rescue me? Someone who challenges me and makes me laugh? Someone who helps me be better but accepts me when I'm not?"

He'd said it perfectly. "You are, too, you know," I said. "All of that, for me."

One of his hands reached out and grabbed mine.

Ahead of us, the raft was slowing as the rapids calmed, and the boat started to turn. The current carried us closer to it.

"Almost there," Mom yelled.

Our parents had probably been worried sick, while Tanner and I had a moment, floating freely down an Alaskan river.

"We're fine," I called.

"Better than fine," Tanner said quietly. "Right?"

"Amazing," I agreed, and the water was slow enough now that I faced him and basked in the glow of his brilliant grin.

A rope splashed nearby so the others could pull us in.

"Ladies first," Tanner said with a smirk.

I leaned over to kiss him, chilly and wet and wonderful, before I was tugged aboard.

Once the others had helped us into the raft, we'd continued, with no more man-overboard excitement. When we reached the shore, a bus carried us back to the main cabin. The dry suits had worked, but our parents bundled us up and sat us by the fire.

Tanner and I had shifted to share a blanket, as our parents left to explore the gift shop. I clutched a mug of hot chocolate and huddled next to him on a couch as a cheery fire blazed in a stone hearth.

"So," he said.

"So. First, I need to thank you. For keeping calm when we saw the bear. I would have been that guy's meal without you."

"Nah, it would have moved on. They're big and intimidating, but they're harmless."

"Like you?"

He laughed.

"I'm sorry for saying I was done with it all. I was freaked out, and going back to the past sounded safe, even though I knew it wasn't what I wanted. Even though I wanted to take a chance with you. But then I thought about everything you said, and you were right."

"Don't sound too surprised." A twinkle lit his eyes then faded. "I'm sorry, too. You were scared. It was a terrible time for me to push you."

I bumped his shoulder. "I told Mr. Lin I'll do the program. And I am going to look into engineering majors. Maybe it was bad timing, but I needed to hear it. Thank you."

"That's great. I bet one day you'll build the coolest spaceship ever invented. Hey, since you're making me a plan for researching colleges, now we can do it together. For every idea I come up with, I expect one from you, too."

"Fine. But no sending me eight a day just to mess with me."

"You overestimate the amount of work I'm willing to do. Even to mess with you, S'more. Does this mean I can say my girlfriend is a real-life rocket scientist?"

Girlfriend. I liked the sound of that. I bit my lip. "Are we dreaming? To think this might work between us?"

"I'll happily dream of you." His mouth quirked.

"I'm serious. We're so different. What do we tell our parents? How will it change family events? What happens if we break up and it gets awkward?"

"Whoa, slow down." He set his mug on the table then took mine from me and put it aside, too. "First of all, we don't have to tell them anything, since they saw you kiss me in the river." He was smirking. "And I don't need an exit plan. I'm in."

His words sent sparks soaring through me.

He took my hands. "Yes, we're different, and yes, we'll argue. But it's like that study we did on friction, right? That it can be good sometimes?"

"It's what lets us walk, or light a match, or make car brakes work. Actually, it's partly how airplanes fly, too."

"There you go," he said, smug like he knew he could always

rely on science to make a point with me. "Have I mentioned that you're very smart and I find that incredibly attractive?"

I laughed softly. "Why did you apologize? After kissing me the first time?"

"I'm pretty sure *you* kissed *me*. But the whole agreement this trip was supposed to be about you getting Caveman back. I didn't regret kissing you, but I didn't want to pressure you, if that was still your goal."

"I think it stopped being my goal sometime between almost missing the boat in Juneau and the tour of the engine room."

"It's good to know that the way to your heart is through complicated machinery."

"Or just nice gestures in general."

"I'm great at those."

"Milkshakes help, too," I said.

"Noted."

"I'm going to work on it. The nice gestures."

He squeezed my hands. "You faced a raging river for me. That was A plus."

"Don't get used to gestures that are *that* big. We don't have many rivers in LA."

"Oceans work." He grinned.

"Noted," I said, and he laughed and gave me a quick kiss.

I wanted to get lost in it, but I had more on my mind. "We'll need some compromises. I might go to a party with you, but I'll need warning."

"That's fair. And those milkshakes were good, but I'm not always letting you pick the restaurant."

"Just no seafood," I said.

"You can keep Goldfish in your backpack just in case." He poked my side.

I wrinkled my nose at him. "I like my study schedules, but I won't make you study with me if you don't want to."

"With you, it might not be so bad. I'm a big fan of PDAs. Can you handle that?" He pressed his nose into my neck.

I squawked. "Cold."

He laughed.

"And . . . I will keep trying new things. But not all the time."

"I'll never push you to something that you don't want to do," he said. "See? We can make this work."

"And you'll let me beat you at the 10K?"

"Now you're asking too much."

We smiled at each other, and the same sense of infinite possibility swelled inside me as when I looked at the stars.

"What was your favorite new thing you tried this trip?" he asked.

"You want me to say *you*, don't you?"

His lips quirked up. "Officially being my girlfriend could be the new thing you try today."

"I already went rafting. And swimming. And saw a bear. I do have a veto left—"

He silenced me by covering my lips with his, warm and chocolatey. With one hand, he tugged the blanket around us, drawing us closer, and with the other, he cupped my face.

The fire crackled, and the scent of smoke would forever make me think of kissing Tanner.

Outside the huge windows, the sun was inching toward the mountains. The future stretched out before us, endless as the wilderness. I would face it all and hopefully find, like I had with the boy beside me, unexpected treasures and excitement beyond what I could have imagined.

Our time in Alaska was ending, but for me, I knew life was just beginning.

Acknowledgments

Writing might be a mostly solitary endeavor, but life is not, and I wouldn't be where I am in my writing journey without so many great people.

As always, a huge thank-you to my amazing husband, Russ, for being so supportive, for brainstorming with me, for making me laugh, and for going with me on trips that always inspire story ideas. Thank you to my family for listening, encouraging, and being my biggest fans. I love you all.

Thanks to my agent, Eva Scalzo, for being a partner and cheerleader and for keeping up with all my stories and ambitions.

I wouldn't be writing these acknowledgments if not for my editor, Wendy Loggia. It's hard to believe this is our third book! I've learned so much from you, and it's been a joy to work with you. Thank you to the rest of the Delacorte Press team, as well: Ali Romig, Sarah Pierre, Colleen Fellingham, Tamar Schwartz, and everyone who makes publishing possible. And thanks to Libby VanderPloeg and Ray Shappell for another amazing cover and making this book look so good.

I'm grateful for so many author friends and have been blessed to have some wonderful writers provide endorsements for my books. Thanks to Chelsea Bobulski, Kristy Boyce, Tif Marcelo, Nova McBee, JC Peterson, Annie Rains, and K. L. Walther for your kind words. To the ladies of KidLitNet, thank you for the ongoing support. And, Amanda Stevens, thank you for your friendship through many years.

My critique partner, Jason Joyner, I keep you very busy! Thanks for reading even the books that don't have explosions. I'll try to send you some action scenes soon.

Thanks to the Fellowship. You started out as writing friends, but now you're true family, and I'm eternally grateful for that.

To my in-person friends, your support means so much. Every time you say you're proud, tell me you read my books, ask about the next one, or ask how the writing is going, it feeds my heart.

Thank you to the readers. I'm grateful for every single person who picks up my books. I hope the stories bring you joy and make you smile and encourage you to have adventures of your own.

And saving the best for last, thank you, Jesus, for giving me the gift of writing and for loving me, saving me, and calling me to walk with You.

Two strangers,
one tropical island,
and lots of lies . . .

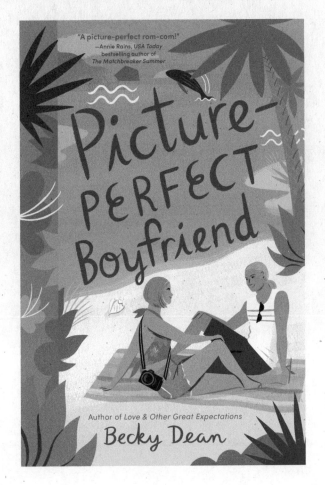

Turn the page for a preview of
another Becky Dean romance!

Picture-Perfect Boyfriend excerpt text copyright © 2023 by Becky Dean. Cover art copyright © 2023 by Libby VanderPloeg. Published by Delacorte Press, an imprint of Random House Children's Books, a division of Penguin Random House LLC, New York.

CHAPTER ONE

Hawaii was totally messing up my plans. To be fair, I rarely made plans, and when I did, they generally went badly. But this one was facing an extra challenge. Why did Maui have to be so insanely beautiful before we'd even reached the ground?

As the island grew larger beneath us, I inched the airplane's window shade up to reveal more details. Vivid turquoise-and-blue water. Brilliant green hills. Bright white line of waves.

My imagination filled with images of sights that awaited, begging me to photograph them. Towering waterfalls wreathed in rainbow mist. Ocean sunsets of tangerine and pink. Turtles and whales and tropical flowers and—

No. That was the old Kenzie. The version of myself I'd left behind eight months ago. The impractical dreamer with impossible wishes.

The new Kenzie had to pretend not to take too much notice. She could enjoy the scenery, objectively. But she didn't obsess about the best camera angle to highlight a waterfall's height, about the time of day to shoot the ocean to show the brightest shade of blue, or about the proper shutter speed to capture a leaping whale. She didn't spend the day getting sunburned while waiting for just the right shot of a turtle coming ashore, or developing prune fingers from hours of snorkeling with her GoPro, filming colorful fish.

And she definitely didn't think about the Nikon DSLR camera tucked into the back of her closet at home in its nice leather bag, alongside the tripod, assortment of lenses, and portfolio full of landscapes and animal photos.

New Kenzie cared about college applications and chemistry club and Future Healthcare Professionals of America meetings, and this week would be full of air-conditioned dinners and sitting quietly under umbrellas on the beach, and possibly days on the golf course, where the waves were a distant backdrop without sound or sea spray.

New Kenzie was utterly boring.

But also safe, family-approved, and free of criticism.

So this was my path, and I would continue on it, even though that had been growing harder lately, taking a steep climb up a rocky hill. Pushing the limits of how long I could try to be someone else. I would not let Hawaii be the thing that sent me tumbling back down.

Our descent grew choppy, wind buffeting the plane from side to side.

Beside me, Mom clutched her book to her chest. Not a romance novel or thriller or other vacation-appropriate fiction, like normal people read. Instead it was a too-long optometry text for her latest continuing education course. Based on how tightly she was squeezing it, she would have been better off holding a barf bag. Although if the book were covered in vomit, that might be an improvement.

A distraction seemed in order.

"How's the book?" I asked. "Can I borrow it when you're done?"

Her eyes got slightly less glassy. "I'm learning about a new method of detecting glaucoma. The idea is fascinating, but the writing style leaves something to be desired. I don't think this editor should be reviewing professional publications."

"Ah. Um. Well, great topic, though."

So not-great. But over the last eight months, I had to admit, my feigned interest in the family career sure had made her a lot less frowny when she looked at me. Plus, the question had achieved the desired goal of distracting her from imminent puking. Finding things to criticize about others often had that effect on her—and for once, the disapproval wasn't directed at me.

"Jacob mentioned he read an article about that," I added.

The glow in her eyes intensified. The only thing she loved more than my made-up, newfound love for optometry was my made-up, future healthcare professional boyfriend. It was good to know my imagination was able to please her, even if I rarely was.

We jostled against each other as the plane dipped lower.

"Close the shade, please. Or put on your sunglasses. The UV rays are terrible for your eyes."

I sighed and shut out the beautiful view. Maybe it was for the best, to keep me from dwelling on out-of-reach dreams.

"I hope your sister and Neal had a smoother ride."

Yes, Alana, my twenty-two-year-old sister, was dating a guy

named Neal. It was like she'd set out to find the most boring guy possible and had ended up with the only college-age guy with that name, just to prove she continued to be the perfect daughter. The one destined to achieve the ideal balance of collegiate-career success and a stable, predictable relationship that my family valued.

"I'm sure they're fine," I said. "If their plane had crashed an hour ago, the runway wouldn't be clear for ours to land."

"Mackenzie! Don't joke about that."

Ah, the We Are Not Amused voice. Hadn't heard that one recently, mainly because I'd been keeping my jokes to myself. I definitely hadn't missed the way it made me feel silly and childish, even though I thought I was funny. Old Kenzie was sneaking through again, as if the wave-swept shores below were pulling her out of the depths.

"I'm sure they're fine," I said quickly. "The odds of a commercial airline crash are, like, one in one point two million." I'd memorized that fact prior to boarding to impress someone—and to calm my always-worried mother. It was extremely gratifying to be able to use it to get myself out of trouble. "They're probably already at the resort with Gran."

Mom's grip on the book loosened. Until the plane shook, and she hugged it to her again. She inhaled slowly before glancing sideways at me. "It was too bad Jacob couldn't join us."

Yeah, well, it was hard for imaginary people to go on real vacations.

My nonexistent boyfriend, Jacob, was attending a nonexistent weeklong biology academy over spring break, fulfilling the lie that

I, too, had found a nice, dull future optometrist to date. We supposedly video chatted about chemistry and college coursework and medical breakthroughs, which would have made me run away screaming if it had been true, since those were also frequent topics at family dinners.

But it made my parents say things like *I'm proud of you* and *We're so glad you've found someone serious like your sister has.* Which were a huge improvement over what I used to hear. *When are you going to grow out of this phase?* Or *Why don't you respect the family legacy like your sister?* And my personal favorite, *Nature photography is a cute hobby but is far too risky and pointless for a real career.*

"He was sorry he couldn't come and wanted to make sure I thanked you for inviting him," I said. "But the program was important to help him get an internship this summer."

"Of course. Career comes first."

I sincerely hoped that was a *my family* thing and not an *all adults* thing, because the idea of career coming first for the rest of my life was almost enough to make me want to stay in high school forever.

My parents found work so important that I still couldn't believe we were here. But the family optometry practice started by my grandfather was doing well, and my dad's blood pressure had been high enough at his last doctor's visit that he and my mom had decided to take a week off.

Hooray, hypertension.

"We look forward to meeting him one day," Mom went on. "And if that internship doesn't work out, we'd love to have him at our office for the summer."

"Right. I've told him that. But he likes to stay close to home. His family is important to him, too."

"As it should be."

Family was the only thing that came close to rivaling work, although for the Reeds, the two were intertwined, like the roots of a tree. Or like an invasive species of vine strangling the tree and slowly sucking the life out of it until the tree withered, died, and toppled to the ground.

No, I wasn't proud that I'd made up a fake boyfriend to impress my family. Yes, it was rather pathetic—but since I *had* been out with real guys before, it at least comforted me to know I wasn't totally incapable of finding an actual human date.

And of course, lying was wrong.

But part of remaking myself had been proving I was serious and capable of *an adult relationship with future potential.* Something my parents had lamented was decidedly not true about those actual human boys. A fictional boyfriend who liked puzzles and science documentaries and was considering a career in optometry like my parents was just the thing.

Naturally, he went to college across the country, so my family wouldn't have a chance to meet him. Ohio State, to be specific, since it was one of the largest schools in the country and my parents had never mentioned knowing anyone from Ohio. The key to lying was making the lie hard to disprove. Like his name— Jacob Miller, handpicked from the most popular baby names list and the database of most common surnames in the US.

Really, my parents would have been impressed at the research that had gone into this lie. Especially coming from me, the child who was *impulsive, disorganized,* and *terrible at planning.* Direct quotes.

The plane bumped its way to a landing. My mom gripped the seat to keep herself from falling forward as we decelerated.

"Well," I heard my dad say from across the aisle, "if it gets worse this week, go ahead and give me a call, and we'll get that figured out."

He handed a business card to the guy in front of him.

It was possible Dad wasn't fully grasping the idea of *vacation.*

He and my brother, Tyler, stood and grabbed our bags from the overhead bins. Dad's perfectly ironed, green-and-orange Hawaiian shirt burned my eyeballs. Was he trying to blind everyone around him in some twisted effort to force them to need his services? It made me extremely glad that I'd locked my Instagram account months ago and no one else in my family used social media, so there was no chance of anyone seeing me in a family photo with such an abomination to the world of fashion.

Mom stood, and I moved to follow.

"Were you planning to leave your headphones?" she asked.

Oh. Right. I grabbed my earbud case from the seat-back pocket. And really, couldn't she have reminded me nicely?

I'd been doing so well lately. I'd only lost one school binder so far this semester, which my parents had never learned about, and forgotten lunch money twice, which, who needed to eat three times a day, anyway?

"Good news, Kenz," Tyler said as he let me into the aisle. "We've landed. You can text Strawberry Jam again."

If Jacob had been real, the nickname might have bothered

me. But that was on me for deciding that my fake boy's middle name was Andrew, giving him the initials JAM.

I ignored the teasing, as always. "He's in class. I don't want to disturb him."

"Are you sure about that?" Tyler asked, raising an eyebrow.

I actually wasn't, since I hadn't seen a clock recently and hadn't calculated the time difference. Why hadn't I thought of that?

We followed the other passengers off the plane. The airport had a casual feel, with skylights letting in bright Hawaiian sun. People in flowered shirts as hideous as Dad's exited planes, while many with lobster-worthy sunburns prepared to board them.

I was definitely not noticing the vivid fuchsia orchids forming beautiful leis, or imagining the flowers in full bloom on actual plants. Or seeing how bright white and silver the clouds were, cleaner and fluffier than back home in Sacramento.

Instead I selected a topic guaranteed to make my parents proud—by pointing to a display in the nearest airport shop.

"Hey, blue-light glasses," I said.

Dad whipped around. "Where? That's a travesty."

"Such a rip-off," Mom clucked. "Poor souls, being tricked into thinking those are needed, and at such high airport prices."

"Regular reading glasses, too." Dad shook his head. "Convincing people they can diagnose themselves instead of getting proper checkups."

"Truly tragic," said Tyler in a dramatic voice that would have sounded mocking if used in relation to an actual tragedy.

Still in the airport, and they'd already resorted to work talk and criticizing others. Two activities my parents would win gold for if they were Olympic sports. But my plan had succeeded—I'd gotten approving looks, distracted myself from thinking about photography, and ensured they didn't suspect I'd been thinking about it, all at once.

My mouth watered as we passed Hawaiian restaurants and food carts offering coconut French toast and SPAM and fresh pineapples. My parents were such unadventurous eaters, I'd be lucky to try the iconic shave ice this week.

"Ooh, SPAM." Tyler craned his neck to see a menu.

"I'm not sure about the safety of meat that lasts that long," Mom said.

"Doesn't tuna last forever?" I asked. "It has those fats that are good for your eyes."

"I don't know if SPAM is the same, but that is a good point."

That tone of voice was a more recent addition to her arsenal—one I called Surprised, Grudging Respect.

This was why I'd made the change. The new me invited so much less drama. If I'd been doing what I wanted, what the old Kenzie would have done—flitting from place to place, running into things because my face was glued to my camera, taking photos of everything in sight—they'd have been telling me to stop dawdling, to pay attention, to quit getting distracted and keep up. To apologize to the poor man with a walker I'd knocked over while watching a pretty cloud. Not that that had ever happened.

"The condo has Wi-Fi, right?" Tyler asked. "I need to keep up with my coding project."

Despite being a sophomore, two years younger than me, he was working on a fancy program for his computer class. He said it would update the optometry office's recordkeeping or book-keeping or something like that. Something I should have understood about running the business side of the practice but didn't, despite working there for months, because—boring.

"Yes, Tyler," Mom said. "I've told you many times. Everyone has Wi-Fi these days."

"Yeah, but they better have good signal strength. Not like the time we went to that conference in Boise and I could barely download the baseball scores."

"I'm sure it will be fine. But remember you're to limit screen time this week. We're supposed to be spending time together as a family."

Good luck getting him to comply with that. Not like Mom and Dad would enforce it, anyway. Not against the brilliant baby of the family, who got good grades without trying and won math awards and who never got criticized for not wanting to join the family practice, because computer programming was a parent-approved career path.

Baggage claim was located in an open-air space, allowing the humid, warm outdoors to seep in. My skin instantly felt sticky. Mom sighed and fanned her shirt, but it made me think of magical tropical nights under the stars and jungles teeming with life and hidden waterfalls.

Which I would not be photographing.

We retrieved our luggage and made our way toward the exit. A cute guy stood alone, leaning against a pillar.

He was watching us.

His light brown hair streaked with blond was pulled into

a stubby ponytail at the base of his head, leaving strands loose around his face. It was so shiny that I wanted to run my fingers through it or ask what conditioner he used. A T-shirt hugged nice arm muscles, and cargo shorts showed off tanned legs. He could have played a young Thor. When he caught me checking him out, his lips lifted.

Oh well. Not like I'd see him again.

As we moved toward him, he pocketed his phone, shoved away from the pillar, and approached. His eyes were locked on me. I slowed. My family paused.

And the cute guy's arms were around me before I could shove him away.

What? I mean, sure, he wasn't bad to look at. And I *had* been staring. But I didn't make a habit of hugging strangers in airports. I stiffened and was ready to plant my knee somewhere that would have made my junior high self-defense teacher proud, when his mouth dipped close to my ear.

"Hey, Kenzie." His voice was low and rough, his breath warm on my neck.

I yanked back. His arms kept me from moving too far, so we were inches apart as I stared into the brightest sky-blue eyes I'd ever seen, framed by long lashes. The mischievous light in them matched the quirk of his lips.

"Surprise!" shouted my family.

My gaze darted from them to the boy, bouncing around, as I tried to figure out what kind of trick this was.

They were all smiling, though the boy's expression resembled more of a smirk.

My family, at least, did not see this as me getting mauled by a random stranger.

The boy released me, stepped away, and moved to my dad with his hand outstretched. "Hello, Dr. Reed. It's nice to finally meet you in person. I'm Jacob."

♥ Escape into another romance!

Delacorte Romance